The People Next Door

ALSO BY KATE BRAITHWAITE

The Scandalous Life Of Nancy Randolph
The Puzzle Of Nelly Bly
The Plot
The People Next Door

THE PEOPLE NEXT DOOR

KATE BRAITHWAITE

LUME BOOKS
A JOFFE BOOKS COMPANY

Lume Books, London
A Joffe Books Company
www.lumebooks.co.uk

Cover art by Cherie Chapman

ISBN: 978-1-83901-599-1

To my favorite ladies of R_____ L_____: Shannon Albert, Carrie Stranz, and Jode Thomas

ONE

Jen
Now
Bayard Square, PA

I'm almost happy.

This, I think, is as good as it gets. The forecast says we're in for one of those sudden July thunderstorms this afternoon, but right now, in my new kitchen with the A/C blowing and windows painted with cloudless blue sky and a line of trees, I forget the humidity and drink in the light and the space. In here, things gleam. Stainless steel appliances were a must-have for Dan. All these cardboard boxes, on the other hand, are a considerable eyesore. My mission for the morning is to get them unpacked. Nina's upstairs organizing her things. I hear the drag of furniture against carpet as she arranges her bed, bookshelf, and dresser into every possible configuration and back again. I'll get started in a minute. Coffee comes first, and honestly, the sheer number of white cupboards available to me is intimidating. My hodgepodge of dishes, old pots and utensils looked just fine when I boxed them up yesterday, but they don't seem quite so desirable today. Impostor syndrome

1

— isn't that what it's called? — when someone feels they don't belong, or unworthy of the position they find themselves in. In my case, it's the simple truth.

I'm two boxes through when the doorbell rings out a shocking, strangled rendition of Beethoven's "Fur Elise". I realize when I viewed the home with the realtor, she used one of those lock boxes. I add "doorbell" to my mental to-do list as I walk to the hall, although I'm not sure if that kind of change is allowed when the house is a rental. I guess I'll find out. My daughter Nina reaches the front door before me and pulls it open. As always, her lack of reserve makes my heart happy.

"Well, hello!"

The voice that greets her is light, female, and super-friendly. Exactly what I'd imagined when we picked out this house in a small neighborhood, about a forty-minute drive outside of Philadelphia.

"Hi," Nina says, as I step up behind her to meet our first new neighbor. The woman is about my height, likely a few years older — although I'm terrible with ages — and holds a white dish under the whitest of dish towels.

"Can you believe that doorbell?" I ask.

"I certainly can! The developer was a classical music fan for sure. Ours was set with Beethoven's 'Fifth' when we moved in. My dogs were terrified." She smiles and offers up the dish. "I'm Vicki Price, from number nine. I just wanted to come by and say welcome to the neighborhood. I made pie."

"That's so thoughtful. Thank you! I'm Jen. Jen Silver. And this is Nina. Please come on inside. It's a disaster, of course, but—"

Vicki follows me into the kitchen, my kitchen, with its long granite island and row of stools tucked under one side.

"I've always loved this house," she says. "So much natural light."

It's strange to think she has been in my house before, perhaps many times. I busy myself finding an empty space to place the pie and take in Vicki's workout clothes, her neat ponytail, her blond highlights, her clear lip gloss. "You know the owners? The Kauffmans? I heard they moved to Florida."

"Yeah. And no, I didn't know them well. They're older. Everyone thought they'd sell." She waves her hands vaguely. "Still. We're all excited to have a younger family in the neighborhood."

"We?"

She pulls out a stool and settles herself at the counter. "The Prestons at number eleven, the Wallaces at number four. The Jones family at eight. They're Australian. You'll meet them soon, I'm sure. Oh, and we have a book club. For the moms, not the dads. Do you read? Honestly, I'm mainly in it for the cheese and wine."

"I do like to read. Although I might like wine more."

We both grin and I feel it, the hint of a friendship. My eyes sting. I didn't move here to make friends.

Thankfully, Vicki turns her attention to Nina. "So how old are you? What grade will you be going into?"

"Fourth. I'm ten."

"Great! And she's going to Fairfax?"

I nod. The schools are one of the great attractions of this area. I've read all the stats. "Do you have kids there?"

"Mine are older. Both at the high school." Vicki rolls her eyes. "Madison — she's fifteen going on twenty. And then my son, Thomas. He'll be a senior in the fall."

There's something in the way she says their names. Vicki's much more at ease talking about Madison than Thomas, but she smiles brightly at Nina and chatters on. Teachers are named. Other children in the street near Nina's age. I don't really follow it all, but my girl laps it up and I feel a little less guilty about bringing her here.

"And your husband? Is he around?"

"Dan? He's at work right now." Vicki's eyebrows lift. She wants to know where, of course. "At the hospital. He's a neurosurgeon."

3

I shouldn't mind being asked. I think I'm going to like Vicki. But I don't really know her and she's squirreling away nuggets of intelligence, bought from me for the price of a pie. I should ask what her husband does, and what she does — although the clothes, the pie, and the fact she hasn't asked what I do for a living, all scream stay-at-home mom. These thoughts tumble through my head as I show her to the door and hope to catch up again soon. But as soon as she's gone, I have a different problem to deal with. Nina stands in the doorway between the hall and the kitchen, her hands on her narrow hips.

"Why did you lie, Mom?"

"I didn't lie. Tell me when I lied."

"You said Dan was your husband. And he's not."

"Not yet." We're mirrored, standing a few feet apart, my hands on my hips too, our feet planted, our eyes locked. "And besides, I didn't lie. She assumed."

Nina puckers her lips. A dimple pops in her cheek as she shakes her head. "Oh, what a tangled web we weave . . ." she says, running off back upstairs. Nina's precocious. I'm not sure what the kids at Fairfax Elementary are going to make of her.

Over the next couple of days, we see more of our new neighbors than we do of Dan. His hours are long and he's as conscientious as you would hope a brain doctor for sick kids would be. Three years ago, on our first date, he was open about it. He was married to his work: it wasn't a cliché, it was real. He wanted a relationship but needed someone self-reliant, with their own life and goals. If he'd known some of my goals, he'd have run a mile. But he didn't bat an eye when I told him about Nina. Or when he met her. Which is more than I can say for our new neighbors at number four.

* * *

"I'm Courtney Wallace. And this is Sasha."

We're in the kitchen — no longer a storage facility for cardboard cartons — and Courtney, a petite woman with

4

shoulder length, expensive-looking auburn hair and the whitest teeth I've ever seen, makes herself right at home, producing a platter and several smaller dishes from the wicker basket her teenage daughter carried in. She banishes my bowl of satsumas from the center of the island and sets out bagels, cream cheese and lox. Paper plates, plastic knives, and napkins follow.

"There. Starting off Saturday the right way," she says. "Is the family home? We'd love to meet everyone."

"Right. Of course. Let me just call them down."

Dan ate breakfast two hours ago and Nina never touches anything until lunchtime. I've tried every cereal, every frozen pancake, every form of eggs, fruit smoothies, you name it. My girl doesn't like to eat in the morning. I'm not sure what they'll make of this spread.

By the time they arrive, Sasha's taken a stool as far away from her mother as possible — or so it seems to me — and she's bent over her phone, scrolling through Instagram. She has hot pink hair, and I wonder what Courtney feels about it, but for now she's busy giving me the lowdown on her preferred grocery story, Wegmans, their favorite take-outs — Red Lotus for sushi, The Bistro for pizza — and the car full of clothes she's taking to the consignment store when she's done here. It's useful information and I'm warming to her, at least until she sees Dan and Nina.

Between the three of us, we call it *the look*. Not everyone does it. When people meet us separately it sometimes gets delayed. Like Vicki Price. She met me and my mixed-race daughter, but not Dan. She might do *the look* when she meets him and I won't judge her for it, at least not right away. We're an unusual family. Two white parents, one dark-skinned girl.

But Courtney Wallace's reaction is on a whole new level. She does a full double-take, shifting on her stool as if the picture we present has thrown her off balance. My face muscles tighten. Nina, though? Nina revels in these moments.

"I'm Nina Silver. Pleased to meet you." She thrusts out her hand toward Courtney. "I love your daughter's hair color."

5

At the mention of her hair, Sasha looks up. She takes the three of us in and simply smiles. I have high hopes for the next generation, I really do.

"Thanks," she says, and turns back to her phone.

Nina grabs a paper plate. "I love bagels. Thank you so much." She proceeds to bombard Courtney with questions about where she works — in the office at Fairfax High School — and whether they do AP classes there which, Courtney says with an awkward laugh, isn't your typical ten-year-old's question, and one she can't really answer as she works in the athletics department.

"Might Sasha know?" Nina's fake sweetness has Dan choking on his coffee.

"I'm sure she does. Sasha? Miss Nina here is asking about high school classes."

If Nina hopes Sasha will a) ignore her mother, or b) answer, but rudely, making Nina seem even more perfect by contrast — yep, that's the way her mind works, believe me, I'm her mother — then she's disappointed. Sasha puts down her phone, pulls out a stool, and beckons Nina over. For the next ten minutes they're in busy conversation and Courtney seems to have gotten over her shock at our unconventional family. She slips right back into her list of recommendations, running through dentists, orthodontists, pediatricians, dermatologists, her preferred OB-GYN, and recommended hair salon, the last of which I actually grab my phone and take the number for.

"But, of course, you'll know who to go to for everything," she says to Dan. "I heard you work at the hospital?"

"I do. And in fact, I'm due there shortly. You'll have to excuse me."

She looks crestfallen as Dan makes a quick exit, and while I resent being trapped here with Courtney and a bagel I'm obliged to eat and rave about, I know why he's gone. Whenever people find out he's a surgeon, they're somehow compelled to relate some story about their own hospital experience. It's rarely to do with his specialty — although if it is, that's sometimes worse — but the stories are usually long and angst-ridden. No one tells him what great treatment Aunt Karen or Uncle Bob, or whoever, received. It's always tales of misdiagnosis, or terrible bills, or long waits for admission, and sometimes graphic details that I, for one, could live without. After another few minutes of cheerful advice, she and Sasha prepare to head out.

"Such a shame Dan has to work today," Courtney says. "Some of us are getting together later. Cocktails on my patio, around six. Pizza for everyone. I hoped you'd all come, but you and Nina would both be welcome."

"I . . ." In truth I'm racking my brains for an excuse not to go. Even though I'm committed to living here, there's a limit to my ability to make small talk with people I barely know. But I also hear Jocelyn's voice in my head, scolding, asking me how I expect to make any progress if I don't jump at this invitation.

"There will be other kids. The Prices will be there. You've met Vicki already, right? And the Prestons. They just got back from a trip this morning. You must meet them. Natalie and Brad. You'll love them."

And there it is. Natalie. The name I've been waiting to hear.

"We'd love to come," I say.

TWO

There are thirteen houses in the neighborhood, arranged, according to Nina, in the shape of a butternut squash. When Dan raised his eyebrows, Nina amended her assessment to "a butternut squash lying on its side" and received a nod of approval. Turns out it's the kind of image that sticks, and so I think of us, at number six, as the first house on the swollen base of the squash and I like it here, because the houses on the turnaround are offset from each other, whereas at number four, where we're heading now, I suspect you can see right across the road into the living room of number ten, and I wouldn't like that at all.

The land was developed around the 2000s: family homes built in colonial style with stucco exteriors, largely now updated to siding in various shades of gray or beige. Our house, like all the others, is set back from the road and as fences aren't allowed there's an appealing openness to the neighborhood with neat grassy yards delineated by driveways and well-kept rhododendrons and hydrangeas. There are lots of trees too, giving the neighborhood a warm, established feel, although the big pine outside Nina's window blocks out a lot of natural light. All in all, it's an attractive suburban neighborhood — think two-car garages, walk-out basements, four or five bedrooms, at least one ensuite. I have my first walk-in closet, at the grand old age of thirty-three, and it's giving me more pleasure than it probably should.

Nina skips ahead as I wonder if the pack of Triscuits and store brand cheese slices I thought to grab at the last minute are going to cut it with Courtney Wallace. I'm also pretty anxious about my outfit — a three-year-old navy dress from Athleta that hopefully says sporty but might be too casual — and I'm trying not to think about the fact that most of the contents of my walk-in have just been walked out of the closet and left strewn around our bedroom. And then there's the prospect of meeting Natalie Preston.

My thoughts drift to Jocelyn and the phone call we had about an hour ago.

"Be friendly. But not too friendly," she said. "You know what to do."

"I do." I tucked my phone under my chin and peeled off the pair of jeans I'd been considering wearing to the Wallaces'.

"Perhaps these cocktails are a regular thing. You could host and I could come over."

"Aren't you staying in the background? Isn't that what we agreed?"

There was a pause. Then — "I was thinking about that."

I dropped the jeans on the floor. Jocelyn is always thinking. I twisted my neck, trying to tease out a knot of anxiety. "Go on."

"It's a family neighborhood. What's more natural than to have your mother visit?"

I fasten on a smile to sweeten my reply. "Sure, Jocelyn. Of course. But let's just see how it goes today first, shall we?"

* * *

I have the same smile on my face as we walk up Courtney's driveway. Nina hangs behind me as I ring the doorbell. "Für Elise". It's fortunate Vicki Price was my first visitor, not Courtney. The man who opens the door looks like he's just stepped off the golf course.

"You must be Jen. Welcome. And this is?"

"Nina. It was so kind of Courtney to invite us over."

"Come on through." He doesn't say his name and I can't think how to ask him, not in his own home, so we follow him, both of us blinking in the layout of the house, which is exactly like ours, but flipped left to right. It's a little disorientating. The kitchen is almost a clone of ours (or perhaps ours is a clone of theirs?) and my eye catches on the large wooden sign above the patio door Courtney's husband is sliding open. "Faith, Family, Friends and Football," it reads.

"Jen! So glad you could make it." Courtney jumps up to relieve me of my cheese and crackers. She drops them inside and when I see the fancy charcuterie and cheese board on the table, I know I need to up my snack game asap. "Sasha, introduce Nina to the other kids while I make Miss Jen a drink. Jen, take a seat there, by Vicki. Margarita? With salt?"

"Wonderful."

Her husband has disappeared back inside. Through the plantation blinds of the window to my left I see a huge TV screen and a largely green image. Looks like the men are watching golf. There are three women at the table and my eyes sweep over them, taking in their clothes and deciding my Athleta dress was an okay choice. They're all smiles as I sit down.

"Jen, do you know everyone?" Courtney leans into the gap between myself and Vicki and places down a napkin and a cocktail glass filled to its perfectly salt-encrusted brim. I'm impressed. "Vicki, Natalie, Daisy. This is Jen."

Natalie is the only one I haven't already met. Daisy Jones is Vicki's neighbor at number eight. She showed up at my door empty-handed but smiling, and I'd liked her, a tall, slim Australian woman at ease in her skin, and quick to laugh at herself. She told Nina she had four kids, a girl, a boy and then a two-headed monster called Colina — really eight-year-old twins, Colin and Lena. I can't make them out in the muddle of kids over by a complex swing set and tree house that looks way too new to have been used by Sasha, and wonder if Courtney is paying her to hang out with so many younger kids.

"Welcome!" Daisy raises her glass to me. "Welcome to the neighborhood."

"We haven't met. I'm Natalie." The woman beside Daisy shifts in her chair and the metal scrapes the stone patio. "My house is number eleven. How are you liking your new home?"

"Oh, I love it!"

It's such a strange experience, meeting in person someone you've seen so often in photographs. She is the same, but also not the same. She's less pretty in real life, or maybe just tired? Her straight blonde hair flows over her shoulders, immaculate in every photo, but up close I can see her roots are showing. She's very fair-skinned and wears little to no makeup. I've always thought of her as particularly feminine, but tonight she seems more feline, with wide green eyes and a face that narrows to a sharp point at her chin. She is thinner than I expected. My eyes are drawn to the bones of her wrists and a sparkling diamond tennis bracelet. I process this and talk at the same time, babbling some nonsense about my closet, and the privacy, and the lack of passing traffic.

"I grew up in a small town," says Natalie. "Quiet, but a riot compared to here. Where are you from, Jen?"

I have a go-to lie for this one. Jocelyn and I gave it a great deal of thought. America's a huge place, but it's surprising how connected people are. Then there's my accent — strictly north-eastern, so there's no point trying to fool anyone that I grew up in Texas or Alabama, for example. We googled small towns, thinking if I said I came from someplace small enough, then any crazy coincidence would be impossible, but it felt too risky. For a while we settled on New York City itself — taking the needle in a haystack approach — but there were too many details I needed to learn to make my story convincing, as well as too many ex-Manhattanites who'd easily catch me out. In the end we went for as near to the truth as possible. Funny, this was also the first lie I told Dan, on our first date. I had asked him how long he'd lived in the city.

"Long enough," he had said. "I've been in Philly since college, but I grew up in upstate New York. Ithaca. Ever been?"

"No." And there it was. First lie of many.

"Rochester," I say, now, to Natalie Preston. "Although I went to college in Burlington, Vermont."

"Really?" Vicki puts her hand on my arm and squeezes. "My husband Jason went to UVM! Although I guess before your time. He's mid-forties. You look a lot younger than that."

It's the perfect diversion. I'm the youngest there and everyone swoons at the idea of being in their early thirties again. The talk moves to fortieth and fiftieth birthday celebration ideas, mutual friends, and other neighbors, allowing me to sip my drink and enjoy the heat from the tequila and triple sec. Courtney knows her way around this cocktail and is a generous host. By the time the pizza arrives I've a light buzzing in my ears. My need to find out everything I can about Natalie Preston fades. For maybe an hour, I think I'm exactly who I've told them I am. I'm their new neighbor, a mom just like them. I'm the wife of a doctor, but I have my own freelance editing career, exciting to Courtney because Sasha writes for the school paper and has been talking about studying journalism at college. I like running and so does Vicki, and I like margaritas — seems we all do — and the tension in my shoulders unlocks. It feels good. For maybe an hour.

The pizza has been eaten, the kids are playing with glowsticks or their phones, and Courtney has lit scented candles to keep the bugs at bay. We've switched to water and light beer. The conversation comes back around to me.

"So, I'm guessing you and Dan were pretty young when you had Nina." Courtney's face is puffy in the candlelight, her eyes small and dark. She's been working up to this for a while, but I'm prepared, and when it comes to Nina, I don't lie.

"He's not her father. I was with someone else for a couple of years. In Burlington. We had Nina. But we broke up."

"Oh, I'm so sorry." Vicki's eyes are wide with genuine sympathy. "That must have been hard."

"It was." I'm surprised to find tears sting my eyes. I tell myself it's the drink, but, of course, it's more than that. This evening, this relaxed feeling . . . Time to focus. "But now we have Dan and we've moved here. Such a great neighborhood. I couldn't be happier."

"Oh yes, Dan," says Courtney, as if she's just remembered something amusing. "I meant to ask you. My husband Geoff looked for him on LinkedIn. Couldn't find him at all."

"That's easily explained. Silver's my last name, not his. It's a professional thing; because I'm freelance. Changing everything would be so complicated."

Courtney smiles, as if I'm a wayward pupil finally answering her question correctly. "Dr. Dan isn't Dr. Silver, then?"

"No." I look around the table, making sure that my eyes fall on Natalie last. I need to read her expression when she hears his name, and she doesn't let me down. In fact, I don't even need to be watching. Because when I say Dan Burrows — the name of the man these women think is my husband — Natalie Preston drops the glass of water she's holding. It smashes into a hundred pieces on Courtney's stone patio floor.

THREE

Jen
Now

The broken glass breaks up the party. Natalie's flustered. She and Courtney fight each other to pick up the pieces and when Courtney's husband switches on all their exterior lighting, the warm intimacy of the evening vanishes. The kids swarm over and are shrieked at to keep back, even though they're all wearing shoes. Vicki leaves first with her daughter, Madison. Then Daisy and her four. Nina and I walk back with them.

"Your husband's out of town?" I ask.

"Back in Sydney, seeing his mom. She's been sick."

"That must be tough. Especially with the distance."

"It is what it is." I can just about see her rueful smile. The children have gone on ahead. Lights pop on in both our houses. I'm not sure how I feel about the darkness out here — the lack of sidewalks, and streetlights. "How about you," Daisy asks. "Do you have family nearby?"

"My mom lives about an hour away. In Maryland. That was one of our reasons for moving out this way. Plus, Dan's work."

"Sounds good." There's a slight slur in her voice but I'm not judging. I probably sound the same myself. I need to be in bed and fast asleep before Dan gets in and starts quizzing me about the neighbors he's yet to meet.

* * *

Sunday mornings in the neighborhood are quiet. Dan's favorite reclining armchair in the window of our living room gives me the perfect view of the empty street. The chair ought to be in the basement — or the trash, for that matter — but we're short on furniture in this big house and, with my back killing me from emptying boxes of books, I appreciate its soft and squishy good points and overlook the worn brown suede and the uncleanable cup holders he loves so much. He's downstairs with his brother, hanging a ridiculously huge TV on the wall while Nina "helps". I hear her giggling and the occasional bump and grunt from the men. I like that there's not much happening. My neighbor at number seven appears and waters the pots at her front door. Maureen. She's much older than us. A little later, Natalie and Vicki walk by with their dogs. Vicki's telling some story and covers her mouth with one hand while Natalie laughs. As they disappear from view, however, Natalie looks back. She surely can't see me, but I shrink in the chair. And then I think how foolish I am. Because it won't be me she's thinking of. It will be Dan.

* * *

Dan and I met three years ago. It's the perfect "meet-cute" story. My car got a flat right outside an out-patient office he shared with a couple of colleagues. I was standing there, anxiously waiting for a tow-truck, when he came out and offered to help. No, he didn't know the whole thing was planned. Didn't know we'd removed the valve core so the tire would go flat. Jocelyn had googled that one. It all worked like a charm.

When I agreed to try and get to know him, I believed I was humoring her. I didn't expect him to stop and help, far less for it to go anywhere. But from the start I liked him a whole lot better than I'd imagined. I liked the tone of his voice, his rueful smile, and the floppy lock of dark hair that fell across his forehead. Things moved fast. He invited me out to dinner. I went back to his apartment that first night. I'd like to say the sex was spontaneous, the result of physical attraction and an immediate feeling of connection, but that could only be true on his side. Jocelyn had picked up Nina for the night, so I'd be free to see "how things played out". We both knew what she meant. When I told her I'd slept with him, she'd clapped her hands like a child receiving a treat. I didn't tell her everything, though. I didn't tell her that the sex was as good as he'd promised, or that I'd felt giddy afterwards, so glad that at least this aspect of what I was doing was honest. In bed, we fit. It wasn't all lies.

Within the week he'd met Nina and I'd installed a lock on my bedroom door so my busy seven-year-old couldn't see something she'd have a hard time unseeing. As it turned out, with Dan's shifts and Nina's school and gymnastic commitments, it was a lot easier to manage than I'd anticipated. When they did meet, they got along. He was tight-lipped about his past, and barely mentioned Ithaca, but I was confident I'd get him talking eventually. Moreover, I was confident that when he did open up, he'd have nothing useful to tell us: nothing, because he was a good guy, the kind of guy who helped out a woman on her own with a flat tire she couldn't deal with. A doctor. Someone who cared. Months passed. We were a couple. I'd forgotten how good that felt. Jocelyn came up to the city and we took her and Nina for dinner at Barclay Prime. I remember we were a little anxious about that. She was confident they had never met back in Ithaca, but if he recognized her, we would be in trouble. But he didn't bat an eye.

"Grandma likes him," Nina said, when I took the Harry Potter book from her hands and turned off her bedside light that evening. "And I like him. He should move in."

I remember how glad I was the light was off. Until that moment I suppose it had felt more like a game than something real. Not that I'm denying responsibility. It was our plan, Jocelyn's and mine, for me to get close to Dan Burrows, to find out what he knew, and it was working. But that was the first moment I felt uncertain, and conflicted. I doubted myself. I wondered if the ends did justify the means. Especially when I considered how I was playing with Nina's feelings. Not to mention Dan's. And my own.

* * *

"Patrick just left. He said to say goodbye."

Dan leans down and his lips brush my forehead. We watch his brother reverse his battered old truck down our driveway and head out.

"We should have given him lunch at least. I feel bad."

"Don't. You know Patrick. He's off to pick up some 'bargain' furniture he bought on Facebook. Always got some deal going on."

"You two really couldn't be more different, could you? Are you sure you're related?"

"Ha. No doubting it."

"I like it about you. The way you look after him."

Dan steps away from the window, putting some distance between us. Compliments always make him uncomfortable — another thing I like about him. "You would do the same," he says, "if you had a sibling. He's my big brother. He always looked out for me. I'm just returning the favor."

If you had a sibling. His words ring in my head for hours. Later, he takes Nina to meet her new piano teacher and I head to the grocery store. The parking lot is busy, full of moms pushing carts with small children clustered to them like barnacles, and I pull in as far away from the store as I can get and reach for my phone. Jocelyn answers on the first ring.

"It's taken you long enough."

17

"Don't be like that. You know it's difficult."

"Hmm."

I picture her. Jocelyn doesn't go out much these days. When I was a teenager, she was full of energy, always on the move. After Ithaca, we lived in an apartment in the center of Rochester and never owned a car. We'd go to the store with a pull-along plastic wagon, the kind little kids ride in, but we used it for groceries. I hated it, but where Jocelyn went, I had to go too. Until I turned eighteen, she made me go with her to work whenever I wasn't at school. She worked shifts at a local convenience store two blocks from our house. The back room stank of vinegar. I'd sit there reading or doing homework until 11.30 p.m. and then we'd walk back home eating chocolate bars or bags of chips she stole and said they'd never miss.

It seemed like nothing would ever change but, with the encouragement of an amazing English teacher, I got myself a full ride to college in Burlington and the six-hour bus trip became my excuse to miss Thanksgiving with her. The first Christmas, I only visited home for four days. In the spring I started waitressing in a bar with incredible live music, found a roommate, and worked through the summers. I met Booker, finished my degree, and thought I'd never go back to Jocelyn. Then Nina came along.

She was six months old when I carried her off the bus back in Rochester. Tiny but strong. Bright-eyed. Always hungry. The driver was kind. He set up her stroller and pulled out my bags while I settled her. Jocelyn didn't bother to meet us. I pushed Nina the whole way home with one bag on my back and the other strung across the stroller's handlebars. Even now, I don't know what I was expecting when I walked in the house. Jocelyn didn't look at us, didn't stop what she was doing, didn't even stand up.

"You know where everything is," she said, over one shoulder, and she was right, I did. I remember the crashing feeling that I'd made a terrible mistake. I felt it in my chest, as if there was a chain in there and Jocelyn only had to pull on it to turn me back into that damaged teenager, rarely allowed out of her sight. But things had changed, Jocelyn had changed, which, after that first swell of panic, I registered even as I pulled Nina from her stroller.

Jocelyn was sitting on a substantial-looking office chair (new) staring at a computer screen (also new). It was so quiet in the house I could hear her mouse click. What could be so absorbing that she didn't turn, didn't want to see Nina, didn't want to meet the girl who, even if it was bending the truth, would grow up calling her grandma? I crossed the room and stared at the screen. It was the first time I saw her photograph, but far from the last. Natalie Preston.

* * *

"How was she?"

There's a wheezy urgency in Jocelyn's voice. She's in a different house now, a fancy, full-service bayside apartment in Havre de Grace, Maryland, that she "looks after" for a friend, but she's sitting on that same chair and staring at a computer screen, I'm certain of it.

"Pleasant. A little older than she looks in the photographs. Slightly less put-together. More real."

"And what happened? Anything?"

I tell her about the broken glass and Jocelyn loves it.

"It's beginning," she squeaks. "When will Dan meet her? You need to be there to see it. You need to make sure they don't bump into each other on the street or something."

"I saw her walking her dog this morning."

"What kind of dog?"

"What kind of dog? What difference does that make?"

"It's a Pomeranian. Which you would know if you'd done more research. Might be useful. If you would let me visit . . ."

My teeth clench. "Are you going to go on like this every time I call?"

"Alright, alright. Have it your way. But make sure Dan doesn't wander out and meet her without you there to observe them."

"He's not some dementia patient, Jocelyn. He doesn't wander. He goes to work and comes home. He gets in and out of his car in the garage. I don't think his feet have touched anywhere beyond our driveway yet. I can handle this."

"Nina would love a dog. Have you thought of that?"

Jocelyn's conversation is always like this. Scattergun. Mild crazy mixed with passive-aggressive. "You already know she wants one. What kid doesn't? But how can I bring a dog into this mix? It's bad enough involving my own daughter—"

"I'm not suggesting actually *getting* a dog. But it might be something to talk to Natalie about. It could be your next move. You met her last night. Did she like you? You need to befriend her."

"I know—"

"So she has a dog. Go ask her where she got it."

Before I can respond, she cuts off the call.

I sit for a little. One of the more exasperating things about Jocelyn is that as annoying as she is, she's also not wrong. I do need to find a connection with Natalie Preston. I do need to get Dan and her in a room together and get them talking about growing up in Ithaca. I need to show Jocelyn, what I've felt from the first: Dan Burrows had nothing to do with what happened to our family. I just really need to do it soon. It's early July and this has to be over before the end of August. I can't — won't — put Nina into a new school only to pull her out again if the shit hits the fan. She still has a place at her school in the city. Of course, she told everyone she was leaving but I called the district office and retained her place for fourth grade. Our old apartment hasn't been released yet and the rent's paid until the end of September. I've promised Joe at the agency to give them a month's notice or move back in — with or without Dan.

FOUR

Jocelyn
Then
Ithaca, NY

The phone call woke me up so, of course, I was annoyed. I knew it would be Sal. It always was. *Another drunken crisis*, I thought. An argument in a bar. Some guy buying her too many drinks, thinking he was on a sure thing, only to find she was already buzzed when he'd met her. A month before, she'd puked on some creep's shoes, and he'd punched her in the face. She'd called me, screaming about calling the cops and suing the motherfucker, before falling asleep while I was still on the line. Lord knows I loved my little sister. But Sal was a mess.

All I had to do to hear her latest calamity was to stretch out an arm and press a button. My phone was in the living room, and I liked sleeping in there with the TV on, the volume low. The rumble helped me sleep. Living alone sucked, but at least there was no one judging me.

Sal's sobbing was intensely familiar and wearisome. I must have lain there for a full minute just listening, imagining the tears streaming, the spit pooling, the rawness of her throat, the hunched rocking mess she so often became.

"What's happened now?" I said at last. "Calm down and just tell me."

"She's . . ."

Her breath hitched as she tried to stop sobbing. "She's what? And who's *she*?"

"Lynny."

Her daughter, Lynette. "What has she done? Is she okay?" My mind went to all the usual places. A car accident. A teen-age tantrum. God forbid, a rape.

"She's missing."

I sat up and gripped the phone. Spoke through my teeth. "She's not missing, Sal. She's out. She's what, seventeen? Do you remember the shit you did when you were seventeen?"

"No." The word came out heavy. Sober. I glanced at the clock on my DVD player. It was after 2 a.m.

"Maybe she fell asleep at someone's house. What's her friend called? Nicole?"

"Natalie. And no. I'm telling you she's disappeared. The police won't even look." Her voice cracked and the crying started again. I resigned myself to the inevitable.

"I'm coming over."

* * *

Sal's house was on one of those steep Ithaca side streets built for mountain goats, not people, and I knew every crack on the sidewalk. We had lived there as children, and as adults for a while, even though Sal's drinking and the luggage carousel of ill-assorted men she hooked up with drove me crazy. A few years ago, after a final argument over Lynette's sassiness, with my sister siding with her monster-teen over me, I had taken myself and my car to Candor, a half-hour drive out of Ithaca, and rented a mobile home with two bedrooms I hated sleeping in. Now I thought of our mom and dad as I stuck my key in the door of Sal's house, just as I always did. They'd be shaking their heads at me. Whispering. Saying I should never have done it. Leaving Sal like I did. With two girls to deal with. Selfish. I heard it in Mom's voice, never mind she'd been dead for years.

"It's me."

Sal was in the living room, alone thankfully. My sister was enough of a handful, without her younger daughter Genevieve sitting there, chewing her nails.

"I'm putting the lights on."

"No."

I ignored her, needing to see her face. Sal's voice only ever told me so much. Dim light washed across the familiar brown room. She was huddled on Mom and Dad's sagging couch. The purple throw she'd covered it with had slipped, revealing the faded florals so familiar from our childhood. Nothing Sal ever did — not the candles, the incense, the gaudy "Mediterranean" tableware, not even the hi-fi and shelves of CDs — really changed the underlying sadness that washed over me whenever I came back.

"Is Genevieve asleep?" A nod. "Does she know what's happened?" The smallest shake for no. "Tell me everything." I sat in Dad's chair and leaned forward with my elbows on my knees. "Start talking."

"Lynny said she'd be home by 10.30 p.m. She promised."

I waited.

"She was going to a party. With Natalie and some boy she was seeing — Connor, maybe? — but they're just friends now. He's from school. He had gotten them fake IDs. They'd get some liquor, she said. But then she was going to come home and tell me all about it. She was excited. She looked so pretty."

"What about you?"

"Me?" Her gaze dropped. No story with Sal ever came out straight. I always had to follow the path, take the right turns.

I tried another tack. "When did she leave the house?"

"Seven."

"And what did you do then?"

"Made Genevieve dinner. Cleaned up." Her lips formed a line and she glared at me. "What do you think I did? Read a book?"

"There are worse ways to spend the evening."

"I guess so." There is fire in her eyes now. Just a spark. "Or I could have sat on the sofa eating grilled cheese. You know, spilling the grease down my sweater. Watching game shows."

I said nothing, but it was hard to keep my eyes on her face. I probably did look a mess. There probably were stains on my sweater. I probably was addicted to *Jeopardy*. She could be such a bitch.

"Okay. Yes. I went out. Just to the Chanticleer. Only had a couple. I was home and sober by ten thirty."

"I'm not an idiot, Sal. Or the police."

Mention of the police crushed her. Her face folded in on itself.

"Alright, I was back by twelve. I thought she was home and in bed. I don't know why I checked. Maybe her door was ajar? I don't know. I was feeling something. Motherly." The word came out reluctantly, heavy with sarcasm and maybe even self-recrimination.

"You love your girls, Sal. I know you do." Jealous, she had said I was. Jealous of her bond with her kids. Angry I couldn't have her all to myself. I'd pack my bags the next day.

Sal twisted the tissue in her hands. "She wasn't in there, Jocelyn. She's not in her room. And I knew at once that something was wrong. I called her. Texted. No reply. Something is *really* wrong. Lynny's a good girl, you know that. She wouldn't do this to me. Worry me like this. She always, always comes home."

"I know." And I did know. Lynette and Sal were close. I wouldn't call her older girl good, but she loved her mom. They were buddies in a way I almost found laughable, given

24

how our mother had brought us up. For her, Sal and me were a disaster waiting to happen that became a self-fulfilling prophecy of unruly behavior and waywardness. Lynette and Sal? They were best friends.

"Tell me what the police said."

"That she'll be home in the morning. That she's with a boy."

"They might be right. She could've met someone . . ."

"No."

She was small, my sister, Sal. Fine-boned, with small ankles and wrists, slim hips, and slightly turned-in, narrow shoulders. Men wanted to protect her. They mistook size for fragility, seeing finespun glass where they should have seen hard wire. But even metal can snap.

"What about Natalie? Have you called her mom?"

She looked uncomfortable again. Hooked her long brown hair back behind her ears and twisted it into a bun. "She refused to wake Natalie up. Told me to sleep it off. Said Natalie hadn't even been with Lynny, and I know that's not true."

"Did you tell her they'd gone out partying?"

Sal's eyes dropped to her lap. No, then. And perhaps not surprising. Sal was Lynette's friend, imagining herself a sister more than a parent. I could see her being reluctant to spill their secrets to one of the "real" grown-ups.

"You think she'll be back." I didn't expect an answer, but it made sense. Sal hoped Lynette would be back and didn't want to burn any bridges, panicked though she was. That was good. My sister knew her daughter. She'd always had this kind of spooky sense about her kids, knowing when one of them was upset, sensing their fears. She showed up early once to pick Lynette up from a birthday party, arriving just as her daughter crashed off the bouncy castle and broke her right arm. "And she will be," I said, slapping my palms on my sweatpants. "She'll come rolling in that door with some crazy story and a bagful of 'I'm sorries' and you'll be cooking her breakfast and forgiving her while I roll my eyes in the background."

Sal threw me the ghost of a smile. "I hope you're right, Jocelyn. I can't bear the thoughts I'm thinking."

"Then stop thinking. Come on." I struggled to my feet, feeling my knees complain. Sal took the hand I offered her, and I pulled her up into a hug. While I scooped up the throw from the sofa, she flicked off the light and after one piercing look at the front door, walked up the stairs and into her room. I used the bathroom and then followed her. Sal was already under the covers, small and curled, her back like a shell. I lay down next to her and pulled the throw over me. The pillows smelled of Tide soap and nicotine although she hadn't smoked in two years. It had been our parents' room, then Sal's. For a moment or two I listened to Sal breathing, matching mine to hers, as I'd done many times in the past. She was asleep in seconds.

FIVE

Natalie Preston's dog is this white Pomeranian cottonball. It looks like it's smiling, right up until it wriggles its pufferfish body and takes a chunk out of your ankle. There is no way I'm getting one of those. But I've researched breeders (none nearby), sucked in my cheeks at the price of a puppy (exorbitant) and thought up a bullshit reason for why I want a dog exactly like her one. It's Tuesday, early afternoon. Nina's practicing piano and Dan, no surprise, is at work. I'm ready. I stroll down the driveway to our mailbox, giving me the perfect view of Natalie's house. Her car is there, with the trunk open, and both garage doors are up.

"Natalie — hi!" She appears at her car just as my feet hit her driveway. Perfect.

"Oh, hi, Jen. How're you doing? Settled in?"

"Getting there." There's no awkwardness about her, which I thought there might be, given her reaction to hearing Dan's name. But I guess she's regrouped since Saturday because she's smiling and seems relaxed. "There is something you might help me with, though."

Her brows lift and she folds her arms across her chest. "Sure. What do you need?"

"Dog advice."

Her arms drop to her sides. "Of course! Do you want to meet Wookie? Why don't you come inside?"

Wookie? I follow Natalie, asking myself what name I'd give to this dog I have no intention of getting. Definitely not Wookie. Maybe Jaws.

Her home surprises me. The garage is a clusterfuck of boxes, tools and gardening equipment. Along one wall there's enough bottled water, paper towels and canned goods to stack an aisle in Costco. For all I know, Natalie and her husband are survivalists or preppers, stocking up just in case of Armageddon. Inside, everything is very brown and old-fashioned. This must be the original kitchen with dark cherry cabinets, and chintzy curtains at the windows. There's a heavy mahogany dresser full of family photographs and a group of old, worn-out teddy bears sit kind of creepily on an accent chair by the French doors to her garden. It's an old person's house. With a dog that's growling at me.

"Wookie!" Natalie scoops up the snarling beast. "So, you're thinking about getting a dog?"

"Yes. Nina, my daughter, has been begging for one for months, years even, and now we've moved out of the city finally . . ."

"It's a big change, right? How long were you there?"

"Three years."

A tall, super-skinny girl walks into the kitchen. She's wearing shorts and a vest, and her long hair is knotted on the top of her head like a pineapple.

"Grandad wants more water," she says, waving an empty tumbler in the air.

"Erin, this is our new neighbor at number six. Mrs—"

Confusion ripples across Natalie's face as she turns to me. "Call me Miss Jen," I say.

"Hi." She gives me a timid wave and smiles through a tangle of braces. "I think I met your daughter Nina at Miss Courtney's house? She's a sweet girl. Funny."

"She can be. But not right now when she's tormenting me into getting her a dog. What do you think, Erin? I came over to ask your mom where she got Wookie."

"Ugh, do not get a Pom!"

"Erin!"

"That dog only loves you, Mom. You know it. He hates Dad."

"Right so that's exactly what I wanted to ask you about," I say. "I was thinking about a Pomeranian because when I was growing up my grandma had one that looked just like yours — seriously exactly like Wookie — but I remembered it hated my Pops and really if I'm going to give into this dog demand, I need Dan to like it too, or at least for it to not hate Dan, if you see what I mean."

"Is he a dog person?"

Erin has floated out of the room with water in one hand and a bag of Goldfish in the other. Natalie's question catches me off guard.

"Dan?" I realize I have no idea how Dan feels about dogs.

"Brad — my husband — never had a dog until now, and I always think Wookie can tell he's just not a dog person."

I find myself shaking my head. "I don't really know. I don't even know if he had a dog as a kid or not. Is that terrible of me?"

"Of course not. You've been together what — a few years? I'm sure you haven't talked through every moment of your life history." She puts down the furball and it jumps on the chair at the window, curling up with all the glassy-eyed bears.

"Definitely not. He doesn't talk much about his childhood."

This is a risk. The plan is to be as normal and natural as possible but with all that I know about Natalie Preston, and all *she* knows about Dan Burrows, I can't resist.

"Doesn't he? Some people don't. Not everyone's childhood is happy. Not everyone grows up in a safe neighborhood like this one."

"Did you?" I ask. "Grow up in a place like this?"

"No."

There's a heaviness in her voice. Her mouth forms a flat, sad line. I'm tempted to cut through the subterfuge. Natalie doesn't feel like a bad person to me. But that's not the plan. I'm here to see how she and Dan interact. To get them to tell me what really happened twenty years ago in Ithaca. I'm as sure as can be that Dan knows nothing, but Natalie? She's our last hope for finding answers. Only then can I decide if I'm marrying Dan, if we're staying in the neighborhood, and if Nina really is going to Fairfax Elementary in the fall. I've got two months, and a plan to execute.

"So, I was thinking of having people over on the weekend," I say. "Drinks on the patio, like Courtney did. On Saturday. Do you think anyone would be up for it?"

"Oh, I'm not sure." Natalie goes to her sink and starts rinsing things. It feels like a brush-off.

"It would just be ladies. Dan so often works on Saturday nights. I'd love the company."

Her shoulders drop and she stops with the dishes. "I do know Vicki's free. But you'd need to check with Courtney. I'm sure Daisy will be around."

"And you? Will you come?"

"Sure," she says. "Why not?"

* * *

I leave Natalie's house with her breeder's name and number on a Post-it that goes straight in the trash when I get home. Saturday is four days away, but I need to manage everything. When Natalie meets Dan, I must not miss a thing. Will he recognize her right away? Say anything? This needs careful handling. I quickly text the other neighborhood women to see

30

if they are free. And then I shoot another text to Courtney, asking if she thinks Sasha would be available to babysit Nina for a few hours on Friday. I've promised Dan a date night at a local restaurant. I'm not expecting fireworks by putting Dan and Natalie in the same room, but she did drop that glass when she heard his name. If I'm wrong, and Jocelyn is right, this might be the last happy night out Dan and I ever have.

* * *

Sasha arrives promptly at 6 p.m. on Friday night with a bundle of brochures in her arms. For colleges, she tells me. Nina's helping her work out where she wants to apply. I swear no ten-year-old in the world knows as much about higher education in the US than Nina does. If Sasha hasn't already seen the Tina Fey movie *Admission*, I'd bet money she'll be watching it tonight. Even if she *has* seen it, I'd still make the bet. I know my Nina.

The restaurant's noisy. There's a hum of conversation and the clickety-clack of silverware, glasses and plates, and the scent of sage and thyme wafting out from the kitchen has me salivating. It's a tiny place, crammed with tables for two and four and it's hot — so hot, condensation fogs the windows.

"Kind of rustic," says Dan, raising his eyebrows at shelves of metal watering cans sprouting succulents, and a pile of milk crates stacked with wine glasses at one edge of a tiny bar.

"I love it. It's what we moved here for."

"It might be what *you* moved here for . . . Wait, no. I'm only teasing. It's very . . . cute."

"I'll admit, it's no sports bar. But for a dinner to celebrate our move from the city—"

"It's perfect." He raises his wine glass to mine. "I do love my shorter commute to work. You were one hundred percent right about that."

We talk about his work for a while, and then a golf trip he might take late August. We have no vacation plans together

31

but that was my choice. I've got no time to waste on beach vacations this summer, but I can't help thinking about the trip we took with Nina to Canada last year. I've framed so many of the photos: Dan and Nina on the Maid of the Mist. Me and Nina having dinner at the top of CN Tower with Toronto lighting up the night behind us. Nina writing on a slate in the schoolhouse at the Black Creek Pioneer Village. It's the life I wanted for her and now I'm putting it all at risk.

Our entrées arrive, and our talk moves to my work. I'm a freelance editor specializing in the hospitality industry, combining, in Nina's description, my two great loves — pasta and punctuation. Even without her here, we play our customary alliteration game. Dan starts.

"Are your pan-seared scallops scorched sufficiently?" he asks.

"Points for scorched. And yes, they're perfectly done." I take a good look at his plate. "Would your halibut have more heft with a hint of horseradish?"

He chokes back a snort of laughter. "Heft? Heft? What kind of word is that? Where's Nina when I need her?" He reaches for his phone and while some people might not think it romantic, I love that he's texting my daughter and including her. We both jump when his phone buzzes with her reply.

Never mind "heft", she has written. *HORSERADISH?? WITH HALIBUT?? EWWWWW!*

"Points deducted," Dan says to me, mock stern.

"I deserve it." Right then my phone also buzzes. I look, laugh, and hold it up to Dan. Nina has texted. *POINTS DEDUCTED!!!*

Smug doesn't do justice to the expression on his face.

* * *

When I'm eating dessert and Dan's on his third glass of wine, the conversation takes a turn. He reaches across the table and runs his fingers over the back of my left hand. Over the rings I wear.

32

"We really should get married, you know."

I smile through a mouthful of tiramisu but say nothing.

"We could set a date. Now. Right now."

Part of me, a surprisingly large part of me, wants to say yes. "I thought we'd agreed to talk about this at Christmas?" I flip my hand over and grab his fingers so he can't pull away. "I want to marry you. You know I do. I just need to—"

"To what? To be sure?" He leans back and empties his wine glass. "Those rings are ridiculous. And telling these nosy new neighbors we're married when we're not? I should never have agreed to it."

"They're not nosy. They're perfectly normal. But we're not a conventional family. And the realtor hinted some of the neighbors weren't too happy that the house was rented, not sold. It's easier to handle it this way. We fit in. One less thing to answer questions about." I smile, trying to recapture the earlier, easy atmosphere between us. "I'm nearly ready, Dan. You know I love you. Let's not worry about it. Not now. Not when we're having such a nice time together."

The tension goes out of his shoulders, and he reaches for the wine bottle. "Christmas," he says. "And when I do finally talk you into it, we're buying new rings — *I'm* buying new rings, and those ones can go back to whatever flea market you found them in."

Thankfully, this pronouncement settles him. My hands drop to my lap, and twist at the small stone in my pretend engagement ring. The wedding band cost me $8.99 on Amazon, but the other ring? It's a good thing Dan has no idea where that came from.

We talk about new furniture we need to buy and whether to have someone in to replace the light fixture in the dining room. He's taken a major dislike to it. I don't think we'll use the room enough for me to care what it looks like. The conversation is light, we're teasing each other, flirting, and on the way home, although Dan closes his eyes, his hand slides up and down my leg as I drive. Nina will be in bed, I think; Sasha keen to take her money and run home. This is the normal life I've wanted for myself. For Nina. I let myself enjoy the moment and forget about Natalie Preston and my plans for tomorrow night.

The neighborhood's dark as we drive in. No lights on in Natalie's house, but it looks like someone's still up at Courtney's and several of Daisy's front windows upstairs are lit although all the blinds are down. Everything is as it should be. Except at the top of our driveway there's a car.

"God," I say. "I'm sorry, Dan."

He squints and leans forward, my headlights showing him what I've already realized. "Fuck. Your mother's here."

SIX

Jen
Now

Jocelyn and Sasha are in the kitchen, heads together — one gray, one pink — looking at a laptop. They're an unlikely couple. Sasha's been out in the sun and wears a crop top and shorts, her skin glowing pinkish brown. Jocelyn is alabaster pale in comparison. Her arm, next to Sasha's, looks large and unwieldy and the elastic on her sleeve cuts her skin just below the elbow like a tourniquet. Their expressions are similar, though, they both frown as if we're intruding, and Jocelyn snaps the laptop shut before I get near.

"Mom," I say. "This is quite the surprise."

She doesn't reply. Instead, she hovers around as Sasha collects her things and Dan pays her. At the door, Jocelyn folds the girl in a hug, and instructs her to text her when she's back in her own home. Two houses away.

"You've exchanged contacts?"

She just looks at me and smiles.

"So, Jocelyn," says Dan. "Are you staying over?"

"Oh, dear me, no. I'll drive home tonight. Thank you for offering, though."

He didn't offer, we all know that, but Jocelyn is playing some game here . . . and we all know that too.

"Hot chocolate? Before you go?" I ask. She's a sucker for chocolate in any form. Dan makes his excuses and heads upstairs.

* * *

We go sit in her car with our drinks. It's the only place I can be sure Dan won't hear us. Our breath fogs the windows, and her car smells of cigarettes.

"Where have you been, anyway? The girl called it a 'date night'. I almost spat my drink."

"I thought you gave up smoking?" I wave my hand at the pile of stubs and ash spilling out of a gnarly pottery dish she's wedged between the cup holders and the shifter.

Jocelyn ignores me. "You need to be careful. Don't think I don't see what's going on."

"There's nothing going on. Or at least nothing you don't know about. Natalie Preston is coming over tomorrow. I've said Dan will be out, but he'll be back at eight thirty. He's going to walk right in."

"I should be here. An extra pair of eyes."

"No. We've gone over this."

"She won't recognize me."

"She might."

Jocelyn breathes out heavily and her chin drops to her chest. She knows I'm right. It was a long time ago — more than twenty years — but we're both thinking about it.

"I liked the girl, Sasha," she says. Good. Changing the subject is Jocelyn's way of conceding. She knows she can't meet Natalie Preston. I was a child back then. I look entirely different now, but Jocelyn has only grown older and fatter. If Natalie recognized her, we'd be lost before we've even begun.

"Is that why you came? To check on who I'd left Nina with?"

"Maybe."

There's no "maybe" about it, but I let it go. Having my own child has softened me, and changed my understanding of Jocelyn. She has her demons, we both do, and Nina is precious to her. How can I fault her for that?

"Sasha seems like a great kid," I say. "Nina loved her at once. Told me they're nerdy soulmates."

"She reminds me of you at that age."

I doubt it, I really do. Jocelyn paid no attention to me, and I mean none, until Lynette went missing. She'd deny it, but it's a fact. I take another mouthful of hot chocolate, feeling the hot liquid warm my throat. I want this conversation to be over. I want to be back in that restaurant laughing with Dan and texting with Nina. I'm afraid of what Jocelyn and I have set in motion here. Of what's going to happen.

"She might be useful." Jocelyn sounds wistful, playful even. I read it as a danger sign.

"She won't be. This isn't about the people here. It mustn't be. It's about making Natalie talk. Nothing more."

"If you say so." She knocks her now empty mug against mine. "You can get out now. I'm tired and I've got a long drive."

Am I supposed to feel bad for her? We both know what happened. She called Nina and learned I was out. She had a panic attack — part real, part self-induced — and drove up to make sure Nina was safe. Her choice. I'd bet a kidney that as soon as her mind was at rest, she'd gone right back to her normal scheming self and spent the rest of the night weaseling information about everyone in the neighborhood out of Sasha. I shift in the car seat, open the door, and swing my legs out.

"Don't expect me to call you tomorrow night. I may not be able to."

"Don't worry about me." She sounds bitter — nothing new there — but for once I don't bite my tongue.

"Worry about you? You? We're here, Jocelyn. Me and Nina. Living here. Doing this. Doing what *you* wanted. So why don't you go home and stay home. I'll call you when I can."

* * *

Saturday is a flurry of activity. Nina has gymnastics so I drop her at the door. It looks more like a warehouse or an airplane hangar from the outside, but inside there's some state-of-the-art equipment including a forty-foot tumble track, two balance beams, bars, vaults, no less than three trampolines, and a sea of shiny blue floor matting. Normally I sit in the waiting room and watch her practice. I try to read, but instead spend the time wincing, worrying, and imagining horrible injuries occurring. The wall of awards, the hygiene records, the clear safety regs and the sheer volume of staff they always have on duty? Okay, they're reassuring, but I'm always happy when her classes are over. Nina's good, and more than that she loves it, so I've suppressed my desire to push her away from the sport and just made sure Jocelyn never sees her in action. It's bad enough trying to reassure Dan who can't understand why my palms are sweating every time Nina turns a cartwheel or does a handstand on the beam. He laughs at me, but I can tell from his side-eye glances he thinks I'm a little crazy. Jocelyn's batshit cringing and nervous tapping would seal the diagnosis. Dan likes to tell me nothing bad is going to happen to Nina, and I love to hear it. I crave hearing it. But I know bad things can happen. I really know.

For today, I shelve all such thoughts. Nina will practice while I shop. I'll go back and pick her up and she'll be right as rain. I'm eighty percent confident. The twenty percent of doubt is about my usual anxiety level. I'll take it. I head off to Trader Joe's and Whole Foods, Courtney's face in my mind, my focus on giving my neighbors the right impression.

An hour later, I'm back outside and Nina bursts out through the doors with a grin on her face as wide as Christmas. She's met two girls who go to her new school, in her grade no less, and they have given her the full rundown on all the teachers.

"I do *not* want to get Mr. Todd," she declares from the backseat. "He never gives extra recess and knows nothing about science. Kitty said every plant in his classroom died last year. Also, he has hairy nostrils and she said it's really off-putting when he leans over people to correct their work. At least that's what her sister told her. Kitty and Julia both *long* for Ms. Chesland. She's strict but fun. She has a marble jar and puts marbles in when kids do extra math. When the jar's full? Party!"

"She sounds awesome! But even if you do get Mr. Todd, I'm sure he won't be as bad as they say. It's supposed to be a great school."

We take a little detour to drive past the elementary building on the way home. I've a queasy feeling in my stomach. Will we even be here for her to run through those double doors in the fall? Maybe after tonight I'll know.

"*Mom!*"

Nina's cry jolts me to attention and I slam the brakes. I see a blur of brown fur as a deer leaps across the road and disappears. I missed it by a whisker.

"Are you okay?" I wrench around to look at her. She's pale, but nodding, and I drive on while my heart thuds in my chest and my ears.

* * *

The near miss with the deer stays with me. It was so, so close. Since the age of twelve I've been consumed with this desperate sense of life's uncertainty. Every day that ends without total disaster is simply a day of near misses. A day where I've been lucky. A day spent holding my breath. It was obvious my anxiety would spiral when I had Nina. *So* obvious. But it's taken me years to understand it and to be able to control my reactions, for her, if not for myself.

Outwardly I'm fine. I spend the afternoon prepping for my guests, forcing myself to go through the motions. There won't be kids, but I still bake a batch of brownies from scratch. I can already hear Courtney asking where I bought them, or what packet mix I used, just so she can recommend a different, better, product. Inwardly, I replay the moment with the deer but instead of missing us, it smacks the center of the windshield. The airbag explodes into my chest and neck. Glass flies everywhere. I twist round to Nina. All I see is blood.

I've bought a shrimp platter and a carne asada with sides — both from Whole Foods — that I carefully rearrange on my own dishes, so it looks like I made them. It's cringeworthy, and perhaps in another life, I'd be embarrassed to act like this, who knows? After all, in a different life — and this is another thing I think about often — I'd feel differently, I'd *be* different. People talk a lot about how life is a journey but what they mean is, it's all about what track you are on. It starts with your family. And yes, there are stations, or stopping points, where you can change direction, and make your own choices. It's just *my* choices weren't choices at all. You could say my life was derailed when I was twelve. Yes. You could definitely use that term.

As the blur of deer hurtling toward my windshield starts up again, I blink and force my focus on my white, white kitchen. Sugar syrup is next on my to-do list, for the mojitos I'm serving. I allow a moment of indulgence, remembering my first taste of this mintiest, freshest of cocktails. Turks and Caicos. My first trip on a plane. In a time before Nina. Before I went back to Jocelyn and let her suck me down with her into our disastrous shared past. It was our first trip together. Me and Booker's.

* * *

The bottomless pina coladas on our snorkeling boat trip (amazing!) had just enough rum in them to warm my already warm toes, but not so much that I couldn't manage the bike trip Booker suggested that night, to the "real" bar the locals running the snorkel trip had given him directions for as they dropped us back at our resort. This was Booker all over, and one of the things I loved about him. He could talk to anyone. He *did* talk to anyone. And people talked back, responding to his wide, warm grin, his quick laughter, his ability to talk about everything, whether he knew much about it or not, although he usually did. He is a human sponge. I can hear his voice telling me so, and that's another thing about Booker I found so marvelous: his ability to talk about himself without showing off, or being awkward. He was just being who he was, a man comfortable in his own skin. That drew me in. It drew a lot of people in. I see it in Nina. I *love* to see it in her.

The local bar he found was lively. Some soccer competition was showing on three screens above the bar and plenty of men and women in soccer shirts were watching raptly, rising to their feet, or putting their heads in their hands in waves, as they followed the action. Booker chose us a table overlooking the road. Outside the bar everything seemed dark and peaceful. There were no streetlights, and few cars. The air was warm but fresh – nothing like the humidity we'd left behind in Burlington. We held hands. We talked about the fish we'd seen. About the book I was reading and couldn't wait to finish on the beach the next day. And we drank mojitos, thick with rum, sweet with sugar and mint, cold and delicious. He wore a crisp white shirt, the one his mother said made him look like Idris Elba, only more handsome. She wasn't wrong. It was the perfect evening. We were perfectly happy that day and for months afterwards. Booker and I made each other happy. Until I ruined it.

* * *

The buzz of a text message jerks me back to the kitchen.

I know you said 6.30, but I could really use a beer and a break from these crazy kids right now!!!

I look at the clock and sweep my eyes over the island. I'm ready. The distraction is welcome.

Sure. Come on over whenever yr ready.

Within minutes, Daisy strolls in through the garage. "My kids are eating," she says, sliding a can of lite beer over to me and cracking open one of her own. "It's like watching feasting turkey vultures. I can't stand it."

41

"Four kids. I don't know how you do it."

"Badly." We clink our cans, and she grins. "Cheers mate. I love them, of course. But they are one hundred percent driving me to drink."

"I could have fed them. Given you a break."

"Oh no. No chance of that. Not when Courtney had said no kids."

"Right. So she did." I'd found it odd at the time. I consider Daisy for a moment and then take the plunge. "Why was that, do you think? I mean, the kids all ate at her house last weekend. I kind of imagined I should offer the same."

In fact, I had offered. After seeing Natalie, I'd fired off a bright invitation to the same group of moms that had been at Courtney's house, explaining Dan would be at work, but I'd love to see my neighbor ladies and kids were welcome. Courtney had replied within seconds:

> *Oh, you are so sweet! Let's just do us girls, though. I'm sure the kids can fend for themselves. Who knows, maybe even our men can feed them for once! See you Saturday ☺ I'll bring a salad!*

Everyone else had swung in behind her and it had bothered me, at least on Nina's behalf, because now she'd be in her room all night doing who knew what. I catch myself there. If there was one thing I don't have to be anxious about, it's what ten-year-old Nina will be spending her evening doing. She is on book two of the *Hunger Games* trilogy. Up to her eyebrows in Katniss and Peeta's victory tour. She'll be just fine.

Now, Daisy won't look me in the eye. Instead, she shrugs and changes the subject. Is it me, or are these neighborhood women not quite as friendly as they like to make out?

SEVEN

Jocelyn
Then

I woke up before Sal. I slid out of bed, trying not to disturb her — not an easy thing for a woman of my size. She'd gone out like a light the moment we lay down, but I couldn't have said the same for myself. What sleep I had was fitful, filled with unhappy dreams that evaporated the moment I opened my eyes. Sal's drapes, hung there by our mother decades earlier, were thin, and I could tell the sky was lightening outside, although daybreak was a way off yet.

6 a.m. I used the bathroom but didn't flush. Sal needed this sleep. I padded past Genevieve's room and down the stairs but paused at Lynette's still open door. How long had it been since I'd crossed that threshold? A while, for sure. It had been years since it was mine, the prized larger downstairs room for the elder sister, the cause of a hundred squabbles with Sal when we were young and the eighteen months between us were a chasm in my mind and a crack in the pavement in hers.

Lynette's room looked exactly as I expected. There was a heap of makeup on her dressing table, Mom's old one, I noted, thinking how distracted I must have been in the night not to have seen it was missing from Sal's room upstairs. I saw shiny tubes, brushes, stacks of square boxes of glittering eyeshadow, crumpled tissues and blackened balls of cotton wool. The wastebasket under the table was full to overflowing. Her bed wasn't made, and she'd left a half glass of cola leaning against one pillow. There were clothes everywhere, piled high on an old armchair I'd found left outside a house at the bottom of the hill several years ago.

Lynette had been furious as I'd "embarrassed everyone" by dragging it up our sidewalk on a big square of cardboard, huffing and puffing the whole way and "making a show" of us all. The girl had sulked for about half an hour before Sal said it could go in her room because now Lynette was older and she might have friends over, her room should be more of a hangout space. *Then* she couldn't get the chair in the house fast enough.

And Sal was right. Lynette was growing up. She barely gave anyone but her mother the time of day from sixth grade onwards. Lynette ignored Genevieve and amassed a succession of best friends who she hustled into her room with barely an introduction. The door would close, and the music would start. Some days we barely saw her. Her impact on the house became the stink of incense burning, and the thump of her music through the wall. When I challenged Sal to do something about it, she sided with her daughter and I moved the hell out. Things hadn't been the same between us since.

I set about breakfast, filling the coffee pot, finding an open box of waffles that just needed a bit of a scrape to get the ice off, and checking the date on a carton of eggs before whisking them up to scramble. Sal wasn't much of a housekeeper, but then neither was I. We'd grown up on Hot Pockets and Eggo waffles and what was good enough then was good enough now, as far as I could see. But all the while I was busy, my mind was on Lynette, trying to remember the last time I'd seen her. The situation was exasperating. The damn girl needed to walk her heinie back through the door, preferably before her poor mother woke up. Sal would be all over her for sure, but I rehearsed a few sharp comments I'd be making to the girl when her mother was out of earshot.

I heard a noise in the hallway and braced myself for Sal's crushed face when she saw her daughter wasn't back yet, but it wasn't Sal, it was Genevieve. Shit. I'd have to tell her.

"Oh."

She stopped up short when she saw me at the stove. No smile. No hello. Nice welcome.

"Your mother called me last night. Your sister hasn't come home." Genevieve was a small girl, thin and wiry like her mother and sister. Nothing like me. They all made me feel cumbersome and clumsy. Right now, Genevieve was wearing *Toy Story* pajamas that were too small. Lynette had developed early, getting her period near the start of middle school, requiring bras earlier than either me or Sal could remember needing them, but Genevieve still looked like an elementary kid. She was always pale, her long, dark hair sucking what color there was from her cheeks. My news didn't seem to bother her.

"She's probably crashed somewhere."

"Well, that's what I said, but your mother thinks otherwise. Make yourself useful and find me a paper and pen. We need to make a list of her friends."

Genevieve shuffled off into the living room and came back with a used envelope and a pen. I poured a coffee for myself and sat down across the table from her. There were four names on her list.

Natalie Eason
Mel Parks
Sherri Knowles
Connor Goodman

"That's it?"

"She fell out with Katie King over the summer. Or Katie fell out with her. It's hard to know."

"Right." Katie, I remembered. She and Lynette had been at elementary together. She was half-Asian, Chinese maybe, and Sal and I had joked about how our parents would have spun in their graves to see a kid like that in their house. I was pretty sure Sal had encouraged the friendship simply for that reason. Even after they were dead the impulse to give Mom and Dad the middle finger never left either of us. But Katie was no longer a feature and since I'd moved away, these four names didn't mean much to me. I'd heard of Natalie Eason, but never met her. "What about this Connor?"

"She was dating him, but she told me they broke up a while ago."

"I thought she never spoke to you."

"She doesn't really. But she comes in my room sometimes and starts talking. I'm not allowed in her room, but if she wants to come and talk to me, I don't mind."

Genevieve was passive. I'd never liked this about her. As much as Lynette's constant attitude was annoying, Genevieve's quietness was even worse. Unnerving sometimes. I sucked down some nasty comments and pressed on. "So, what does she talk about, then? Boys?"

"Not really. Nothing since she told me about Connor."

"What did she say?"

"Not much. He has a lot of parties. He wouldn't invite her friends one time and she got mad with him. But they're friends again now. At least I think so."

"And these three?" I tilted my neck to read upside down. "Natalie, Mel and Sherri. What are they like?"

"Nice, I guess."

I bit down a wave of irritation. "She's probably staying over at one of their houses. Do you know where they live?" She didn't answer, but pushed her chair away, scraping it across the linoleum with a nasty squeak. In a moment she was back with a spiral-bound book.

"This is an old school directory. They should be in here."

I took it from her and flipped through, reading out four addresses for Genevieve to write down.

"You could call them," she said, when we were done.

"No. Your mom called Natalie Eason last night and her mother was a total bitch. I'm going over there."

"Are you worried, then?"

She said it lightly, but I could hear the tension in her voice, and she was looking right at me, a rare thing for Genevieve.

"No," I said, not because I wanted to reassure her, but because I wasn't. "But your mom is. So, we're going to find Lynette asap and then I can get back to my day off work in my own home. I hate this house."

I didn't wait to see her reaction. I took Sal up a cup of coffee and told her we needed to get on with finding her annoying daughter.

EIGHT

Natalie
Now

I'm hesitant to accept Jen's invitation, but a mix of curiosity and a sense of the inevitable wins out. Dan Burrows has moved into my neighborhood. Avoiding him in the short term might be possible, but long-term? Not a chance. And so I say yes, and fill the days up to Saturday with memories and just maybe a hint of excitement. I don't dwell on the reason we split up. Years of practice keeps the doors closed on that story. It's amazing how you can just *not* think about something if you put your mind to it. Instead, I remember how I once thought him the hottest thing in a pair of jeans to walk the planet and wonder how he's aged. And how he'll think *I've* aged? No, he's not going to be home when Jen has us over on Saturday, but I fit in a hair appointment just in case. The night before I lie awake in bed staring at the ceiling while Brad snores softly beside me. Brad's a decent man. Good-humored enough to let out a crack of laughter when I told him who'd moved into the neighborhood.

"The real, one and only Dan Burrows?" he'd laughed. "Wow, do I need to worry? Maybe work out a bit harder?"

Brad, the same age as me, is a fitness fanatic who has run seven marathons. He's a handsome man, and he knows it. We're happy together and I don't see Dan Burrows upsetting him. He knows Dan was my "first", but he also knows — without knowing why — that I walked away from the relationship without a backward glance. By Saturday night, I'm ready to get this meeting over with and only sorry Dan's going to be at work.

Still, it's strange being in Dan's house. I focus on Jen. She's younger than the rest of us and clearly nervous. I see Courtney intimidates her: every time Jen speaks her eyes slide toward Courtney as if she's checking she hasn't made a gaffe. It's ridiculous, really, but then Courtney intimidates everyone, at least at first. It's been a while since Vicki and she have hung out on such friendly terms, but Jen doesn't need to know any of that old news and anyway, things have been better in the neighborhood in the last year or so. No need to rake up old gossip.

"Jen," I say, stretching across the island for a celery stick and hummus. "This all looks amazing."

"Thanks! I'm just so disappointed we can't sit outside. I guess we could use the rain, though."

"Did you call the lawn service I recommended?" Courtney sits in the middle of the island next to Daisy, who is gulping down the wine as usual.

I perch next to Vicki at one end, while Jen flits around, moving things that don't need to be moved and speaking too quickly and too enthusiastically. I imagine the conversation Vicki and I will have tomorrow when we walk the dogs and force myself not to catch her eye.

"Yes, yes. Thank you for that. We're on the list."

"And how are the twins enjoying camp, Daisy?"

Now I do look at Vicki. Courtney is so much the lady of the manor tonight and it's got to be annoying her, but no, Vicki just smiles and looks like she's interested in Daisy's story about Colin winning a medal for climbing a rock wall, only for the medal to go missing and then turn up underneath Lina's pillow.

"She denies having anything to do with it, though. Even suggested Colin might have planted it there to make her look bad. I mean, come off it. She's not quite nine years old and already a little Machiavelli."

"Where does she get that from, I wonder?" Jen's smiling, but I feel Vicki tense up beside me.

"Is everything our kids do our fault?" she asks, her voice tight.

Courtney reaches for her wine glass, but instead of drinking, she lightly taps the base with her perfectly manicured nails.

"I sure hope not!" declares Daisy. "Because if so, I'm in a world of trouble. Although I can always blame their father."

"When is he getting back?" I'm keen to move the conversation in a different direction. "He's been gone a while now."

"Tell me about it. The minute he's back I'm out the door. I'm thinking facial, mani-pedi . . . hell, maybe I should book myself a night in a hotel. A night alone. Just imagine." Daisy pours herself another generous glass of wine. I can't help noticing she hasn't answered the question.

The conversation meanders on. Courtney is talking about Sasha's college applications and Jen and Vicki discuss good local places to go for a long run. That frees me up to look around and try to get some sense of Dan. Did he eat breakfast this morning on this stool I'm sitting on now? I saw some men's shoes and a North Face raincoat in the closet when I hung up my jacket earlier. Clearly his, and yet there's no sign of him in this kitchen. It has that just-moved-in feel. No photos or notes flapping from the fridge door, no family photographs. There must be some somewhere, I'm sure of it. Before I even know I've made the decision to look, I'm on my feet.

"No need to tell me where the powder room is," I say, and step out of the room. *Let the kid be upstairs*, I think, passing the bathroom door and tiptoeing into Jen and Dan's family room. The lighting is low-key, and the furniture doesn't look like it belongs here, but there's a sideboard with three framed photographs. I snatch up the first one and hold it under a standing lamp in the corner. My eyes flick to the window. Anyone outside could probably see me here, but since everyone is in the kitchen and it's pouring rain, I think I'm good for at least a minute or two. This is Nina as a baby. Not what I'm looking for, so I put that back and grab the other two. Bingo.

Dan is in both these photographs, one with just Jen, another with both Jen and Nina. He looks the same. I've an urge to laugh. Of course, he looks older, it has been years, but his haircut's the same, his grin is the same, he retains that good-looking, clean-cut appearance that I swooned over as a teen. It's reassuring and alarming at the same time. I have good memories of Dan, but bad ones too, and seeing him brings a wave of sadness and even tears to my eyes. I've got to get a grip. I put the frames back just so, and head for the bathroom. My hand is on the doorknob when I hear her voice.

"Sorry, Natalie. I was just bringing extra paper. I suddenly remembered I meant to do that earlier." Jen is there, a roll in each hand.

"Oh, there was some," I say, "By the way, your soap smells great. You must tell me where you got it."

Her nose wrinkles a little. "Just from the grocery store. It's nothing fancy."

"Right." She's still standing there so I swerve around her to make my way back to the kitchen. It feels awkward, and not just because she almost caught me snooping around her house. Again, I tell myself to get a grip. After all, when she finds out about me and Dan, things are going to go to a whole new level of awkward. This is basically the calm before the storm.

Back in the kitchen, the moms have moved around a little. Vicki's looking at her phone, and Courtney and Daisy are discussing some high school sports team. Since Erin is playing high school field hockey in the fall, although softball is really her game, I lean in and listen to Courtney. When

Jen returns, she stands at the other end of the island next to Vicki and I'm able to keep one eye on her while making the minimum required expression of interest in the conversation I'm supposed to be part of.

To be honest, Jen kind of fascinates me. She has long and very straight black hair — natural I think, not dyed. Her face is more interesting than conventionally pretty — she has a kind of a long chin when you consider it — but I know it's her eyes that Dan will have fallen for. She has blue eyes, wide and almond shaped, with long — again natural, I'm sure — soot-black lashes. She's skinny, even skinnier than I am, and there's an energy about her, a restlessness, that Brad would hate, but Dan, who was always serious and surely is no less so now — he's a brain surgeon, for heaven's sake — doubtless admires. Oh, and she's young. I'm sure that won't hurt.

Overall, I feel more relaxed now I've seen his photograph. It makes it real. I guess there was always the chance that he could have been a whole other Dan Burrows. Facebook had given me nothing and the hospital had him listed but no photograph on their website. In fact, it was the lack of a Dan Burrows neurosurgeon on Facebook that had me convinced it was him. Dan was never the kind of guy for social media. He was always way too busy with sports or studying and he never had the kind of ego that needed shoring up by likes. There was only one time I saw him struggle emotionally, and who could blame him for that?

"Did you hear that, Nat?" Daisy's face is pink, and her accent has gotten stronger as she knocks back the wine.

"What? Sorry. No. Hear what?"

"Courtney says . . ."

"Keep your voice down, Daisy!" Courtney speaks in a loud whisper and clutches both our forearms.

"Sure, sure. Natalie, Courtney says Coach Smith might get fired next week."

"What? No? Erin will be miserable if that happens. What's the story?"

Vicki's looking over. I try making a face that conveys there's nothing for her to worry about. Just the usual Courtney gossip factory.

Courtney keeps her voice low. "Three complaints made over the playing time given to certain team members in the play-offs last year."

"But they won, didn't they? Erin says the girls love Coach Smith." I can already hear Brad bitching and moaning just at the possibility the school might offload the most successful softball coach they've had in decades.

"What's the big story?" Vicki's voice is sharp. Clearly my facial telepathy was a miss, but I needn't have worried. Courtney is only too happy to repeat her whole story, with a huge backstory for lucky Jen, who, given her daughter is still in elementary school, can have no interest in the high school athletics department. I watch her hand snake across the countertop. She makes a show of clearing up some plates and turning to the sink, but in the window I can see her texting. Dan, most likely. I think of what I'll say when we do finally meet. There will be no repeat of my glass-smashing performance at Courtney's house, that's for sure.

NINE

Jen
Now

She was sneaking around. I'm certain of it. That story about the hand soap? Um, no. While they're all busy talking about some school thing, I text Jocelyn and tell her. Her reply is typically snarky.

Of course she did. She's a bitch, just like her mother was

I know nothing about Natalie's mother and I'm wondering whether I can take the conversation in that direction — maybe start up something that will lead Natalie to reminisce about the past — when Courtney, de facto pack leader, brings up mothers. Or to be precise, Jocelyn.

"Sasha said she met your mom last night, Jen. When she was babysitting. She loved her!"

"The feeling was mutual," I say.

"Your mom was here?" asks Vicki. "Does she live nearby?"

"Havre de Grace. It was one of the reasons we moved here. Closer to her, but not too close, if you know what I mean."

"I'd love my mom to be nearby," Vicki says. "The kids miss her so much. I miss her. You must miss your mom, Daisy."

"Mmm. Not so much. My mother's a woman of strong opinions, particularly on parenting. There's a way of doing things. And it's her way. My way? No such thing."

Like Booker's mom. Or at least I thought so at the time.

"My mom was a bit like that." Natalie nods.

"Was?" I ask. Everyone else looks away.

Vicki beckons me over to the wine fridge, purportedly to help her find the bottle she brought, but really to whisper in my ear.

"She passed last year. Heart attack. Very sudden," Vicki murmurs. "The wound's a bit fresh. I'm surprised Courtney brought up mothers — or I would be, if it were anyone else." The bitterness in her voice is unmistakable.

"You don't like Courtney?"

"What? Oh, no. I don't mean anything by it. I shouldn't have said that. I just feel bad for Natalie, that's all. Now she has her father to worry about. Her brother lives on the west coast. It's all fallen on her to take care of him."

"Is he sick?"

"ALS."

While Vicki opens the wine, I move back nearer to Natalie. Courtney's hand is on her back, gently circling. "I'm so sorry to hear about your mom," I say. "My dad died in a car crash. It was a long time ago, but such a shock."

They both look at me, surprise writ large on their faces. I'm surprised too. I don't know what made me want to share that, right now, with these women I barely know.

"I'm so sorry." And Courtney does look sorry. I guess we all recognize tragedy. On some level we all know that life is a high-wire walk, and how it feels to look down. "How old were you?"

"Six. I don't remember the details too clearly. It must have been tough for my mom to have to tell me. She says I didn't understand it for the longest time and would ask when he was coming home, but I do remember the day it happened quite clearly. There had been a lot of snow. The roads were a mess. You could barely see out the windows it was snowing so hard."

Natalie's nodding sympathetically. Heck. I'm afraid she'll say something about Ithaca, which ought to prompt me to say something about Dan being from there also, so I keep sharing. "My mom was a mess. My aunt — my aunt Sal — had to help look after us. We missed a lot of school. I almost had to repeat. It was tough."

"We?" asks Natalie. "Do you have siblings?"

"What? No." Ugh. I can't believe I said "we". "I meant just me. But we were close-knit after my dad died, you know. Me, my mom and my aunt. I grew up with 'we' this and 'we' that. It helped, I guess."

"And where's your aunt now?" asks Courtney. "Is she in Havre de Grace with your mom?"

"No." Their eyes are all on me and I know that the best way to get out of this whole conversation is just to tell them the truth, at least in part. "No. I'm afraid she passed away too. She died when I was fourteen."

I watch their shoulders slump with the weight of my sharing. My oversharing, even. Thank goodness for Daisy Jones.

"Well, that's a damn shame, Jen Silver. And I think it calls for another glass of wine. Or two." She slaps her hands on the island and shakes me into action.

"How about some music?" Vicki says, and while more drinks are poured, we fuss over connecting Vicki's iPhone to my speaker. We are like rocks in a jar, shaken up, but resettling into a more comfortable pattern. Courtney starts telling Natalie about a new collagen-rich moisturizer she says is a must-have, and Vicki and Daisy talk me through the best local restaurants. Turns out they all love the place Dan and I checked out last night. This is better. I'm back on firm ground. But I've one eye on the clock on the microwave.

I'm kind of proud of this bit of my plan. At six o'clock I texted Dan saying I was having the neighborhood wives over and said they'd be sorry to miss him. It wasn't the first time I'd gotten his shifts "muddled up" so no surprise he replied with the face-palm emoji and said he'd be back at 8.30 as expected. It's 8.28 now and there's no time for Natalie to get herself out of my house without seeming extremely rude/weird. All I need is for there to have been no traffic . . . and as if on cue, I hear the rumble of his garage door rolling open.

* * *

I can tell he's in a good mood just by the way he walks in the door. Dan's body language is so readable. When he's happy he stands tall and moves fast. But let's face it, when you're a brain surgeon at a children's hospital there are going to be some rough days, no matter how good you are. When he's down, he literally shrinks. It's like the space between his vertebrae disappears. His shoulders collapse. The muscles in his face let go. Everything in him sinks. He bends with the weight of whatever just went awry. But not today. Today he has been successful. Positive energy bursts through the door with him. He knows he will have an audience and he's a handsome, successful man, ready to charm his new neighbors. If this whole evening wasn't a set-up, I know I'd feel . . . what? Proud? Happy? In love? I do feel those things, I really do. But I step back. I crush the impulse to rush over and tuck my arm in his. I don't kiss his cheek and bring him forward to introduce to these women who might be my new best friends. I step back and lean against the range. I wave at him and smile. And I watch.

Courtney rushes over first, kissing Dan on each cheek as though they've known each other forever. Vicki stands and offers a little wave. Daisy is effusive, maybe the Australian way — or more likely the wine — and Natalie stands back and waits. There's an energy about her. She has the advantage over Dan, in that she knew who he was, if not that she was going to meet him tonight, and what I read in her face the most is excitement. She's nervous, twisting her wedding ring, moving back and forth on her heels as he smiles at Daisy, but I don't think she's anxious or unwilling for this meeting to take place. Finally, his eyes meet hers.

"Wow." Dan's head goes back, and his eyebrows shoot up. "Wow. *Natalie*? Is that you? Really you?"

"I guess so! Wow. And it really is you! I heard the name, but I couldn't be sure—" She steps forward, and they embrace. Dan seems reluctant to let her go. He leans back but doesn't let go of her shoulders. I find myself swallowing saliva.

"Would you believe it, ladies?" Dan turns to the rest of us. "Natalie and I went to school together. We didn't know each other well, but all the boys knew who Natalie Eason was!"

I see it. The merest wrinkle of confusion in Natalie's face. It's nothing more than a narrowing of her eyes, but it's there.

Dan's still talking. "Jen! Can you believe it? Natalie and I were both at Senior High. In Ithaca."

"Go, Little Reds!" Natalie beams at everyone. "Dan was on the lacrosse team. Man, they never lost a game."

"And Natalie here was only probably the most popular girl in the school." Dan steps back and shakes his head. "Well, I think this calls for a celebratory beer!"

He busies himself in the fridge and then comes over and puts his arm round me. His lips brush the hair on the top of my head. "Wow," he repeats softly. "What a small world."

The ladies stay for another hour or so. Dan drinks three more beers. He smiles over at Natalie but stays pretty much glued to my side, something I find as gratifying as it is interesting. The conversation stays general. Dan deflects Courtney's attempts to draw him out on hospital politics but shows interest in her thoughts on country club membership, golfing and pickleball — a new game that we *simply must get into* — her words. I nod and keep smiling and refilling glasses and chip bowls but it's almost an out-of-body experience. If I hadn't stuck to seltzer (faux vodka tonics so as not to come off as a killjoy) all night, I'd think I was mildly drunk. I don't know if it's adrenaline, or anticlimax, or just the shock of finally engineering this meeting between Dan and Natalie and finding that I've no idea what's supposed to happen next, but I feel so out of it I have a hard time following anyone's conversation. When they all head home my relief is almost overwhelming. We go upstairs and while I check on Nina, Dan puts his PJ shorts on and sits in bed flossing his teeth with one of those pick things — his regular signal that he's tired and sex is a no for him.

I'm thankful to avoid faking it and have the chance to just lie there and compose my thoughts. Tears prick my eyes.

* * *

I let a good hour pass before I'm convinced he's sleeping. Generally, Dan hits the sack hard but seeing Natalie Preston out of the blue like that? Surely that's playing on his mind? I lie and slow my breath to a steady rhythm. I imagine he's doing the same and feel a little crazy. Jocelyn has probably worn a hole in her carpet, pacing around, waiting for me to send an update. But I'm not moving until I'm certain he's really sleeping. And yes, I do torture myself wondering what he's thinking about.

Jocelyn will see this as a sign they are hiding something, but my fears go in a different direction. Natalie Preston is a good-looking woman. And I *know* they dated in high school, a fact he clearly signaled to her not to mention. Perhaps I'd feel better if the moment they'd gone he'd pulled me upstairs and into his arms.

His phone buzzes occasionally and soft light breaks the darkness. Texts from the hospital come in every night, but it only rings in a true emergency. When we first got together, I thought he was being stalked by some other woman. I'd find him up in the night in the bathroom, looking at his phone. He'd reassured me and I'd gotten kind of used to the rhythm of it all, understanding that a doctor like Dan is always, to some degree, on call. Now I imagine other texts arriving, though. Texts from Natalie Preston. No, I hadn't seen her pass him her number. But if anything, she'd been *too* distant with him. After the initial "wows", they'd both acted like they barely knew each other.

When I'm finally satisfied Dan is asleep, I fold back the comforter and unplug my phone. Downstairs, I settle myself in the old lounger by the living room window. Rain still splashes down. I select a folder called "Travel", open WhatsApp, and continued the text chain between me and Jocelyn that no one, *no one*, can ever be allowed to see. Her message greets me, blinking green into the darkness.

Well?

I start typing.

TEN

Jocelyn
Then

Natalie Eason lived in one of the better parts of town. Bigger lot. More yard. A driveway. Frilly shit at the windows. Treatments, fancy folks called them. There were weeds in the path to the door, though, which made me feel a whole lot better, and gave me something to focus on after I rang the bell. I couldn't look at Sal. I didn't need to look. She was a mess, a jangling mess. We both knew it would be me doing the talking.

"Can I help you?"

For sure, she thought we were selling something. Magazines? Encyclopedias? God? Her eyes darted over us, and she filled the doorway with her body so I couldn't see inside.

"You're Natalie Eason's mother?" I asked. "We're Lynette Knox's family. This is her mom. I'm Lynette's aunt."

"You'd better come in." She held open the door and pointed us through an archway into a formal sitting room with leather chairs — actual real leather — set around a fancy gas fireplace. It was like something from a magazine. I could picture it at Christmas, all swagged up with bows and

61

nutcracker soldiers. Nothing out of place, except for right now, with me and Sal.

We shuffled uncertainly until she followed us in and sat down in an armchair. No coffee offered. No sympathy. I nudged Sal and we perched on a sofa that looked twice as deep and twice as wide as any couch we'd ever owned.

"She hasn't come home, then?" Mrs. Eason asked.

"She has not. And so, we'd like to talk to Natalie."

Her eyes flicked to Sal while I was speaking. She was measuring us up and not liking what she saw — Sal's sweat-pants and clogs, my Jets hoodie that had seen better days, not a flake of makeup between us. No, we did not belong in this woman's sitting room. Well, I didn't like what I saw either. Herringbone ankle-length pants. A cream-colored blouse. Earrings. Some fancy-looking watch. It was Saturday morning, for Christ's sake. She looked like she was ready for coffee and cake at Nordstrom. A walking definition of uptight.

"My daughter has no idea where your niece is."

"Is she worried?"

A crease appeared between her eyebrows, like the thought had never even occurred to her. I leaned forward. "Because my sister is. Very worried. Lynette is a young girl, nearly a woman, but not really, you know. And while she may well 'turn up', as the cops so unhelpfully put it, there is a chance that something bad has happened to her. Which is why we want to talk to her friends. As soon as possible."

She said nothing.

"I'm sorry, am I boring you?" I asked. "Or are you hard of hearing?" I watched her face flush, with deep satisfaction. She must have been *burning* to tell me where to go, but she wasn't that kind of woman. She was more of a mean-silence-and-looks-that-kill kind of a gal. Well, she was welcome to stare at me all day. I lifted an eyebrow. She got to her feet.

"I'm here, Mom."

Natalie Eason must have been hanging in the hallway. She slid in and folded herself into the armchair next to her

62

mother who slowly sat back down. Natalie was all arms and legs, wearing pale blue trackpants with a matching three-quarter zip, her long blonde hair pulled back in a ponytail. She looked younger than I'd expected somehow, and I felt a stab of anxiety, realizing just how young Lynette really was.

"Natalie," I said. "When did you last see Lynette?"

"Yesterday. Here. She left about six."

"And you don't know where she is now?"

"No. I wish I did."

"I'm sorry we can't be more helpful." A man's voice floated in from the hallway. He, presumably Natalie's father, moved to stand in the archway, but didn't come all the way in. He was tall, athletic-looking, more casually dressed than his wife, and yet no more welcoming. I don't know. A kid goes missing. I expected her friends' parents to be a bit more concerned.

"It'd be helpful if your daughter can tell us what Lynette's plans were last night. Where was she going when she left here? What kind of a mood was she in? Has she texted you? Anyone else?"

The girl's eyes flicked to her father, then to Sal, then back to me. I didn't like it but forced something like a smile on my face and tried to look unthreatening. "Natalie?"

She licked her lips. "We had a fight. About nothing." Her eyes went to the father again. "About grades. Homework, really. She wanted to borrow mine and I said no. We were supposed to go for pizza at the Nines and hang around the Commons. There was a party. At Connor Goodman's house." This time she glanced at her mom. "His parents are out of town."

"And you didn't hear from her later? See her at the party?"

"No. I met up with my boyfriend. We hung out on his porch talking. We were going to head to the party but never did. Look," she fished in her pocket, "here's Connor's address and the names and numbers of a couple of girls from my class who were bound to have been there. I've called the first two, but they said they didn't see Lynny. I don't have Connor's cell number. But I'm sure he can tell you way more than I can."

* * *

Afterwards, we sat in the car while I called the girls on the list. Natalie Eason's parents made me think we would find Lynette faster if we talked to the kids direct. But none of them had seen or heard from her. Sal called Lynette for the thousandth time but still no answer. She called Genevieve just in case Lynette had shown up back at home, but no, no sign. I drove to the address Natalie had given us for Connor Goodman. She had to be there. If she wasn't, I was actually going to get worried.

ELEVEN

Dan
Now

Natalie Eason.

Natalie fucking Eason.

Not someone I ever wanted to see again. Does it worry me? Finding out she lives right across the street? No. But it is annoying. As soon as Jen and Nina clear off to gymnastics or wherever the next morning, I grab my phone and call my brother. He can't be coming round here again.

He knows why.

TWELVE

Jen
Now

The next two weeks are screamingly frustrating. I watch Dan like a crazy person but see no sign of him trying to connect with Natalie. This ought to be a good thing. It's what I want — for Dan and Natalie to have nothing to do with what happened in Ithaca, and for me and Nina to settle into living here in a *real* way, the way Nina and Dan believe we are. But whenever I let myself believe in a normal future, other thoughts tangle me up. My life has been marked by abrupt endings. My dad. Lynette. Sal. Booker. This crazy pretense might all have been Jocelyn's idea, but I bought into it. Because I do, I truly do, want to know what happened to my sister, Lynette. I've been so certain Dan knows nothing, but then why was his first impulse to lie? He said he barely knew Natalie at Ithaca Senior High, and she went right along with him. Why? Why? Why? It's all I think about, all the time: when I run with Vicki, or play board games with Nina, or stock the fridge, cook dinner, fold laundry, or even, no small thing, as I edit a microhistory about baking. All the time. Why?

Since I do still work for a living, I'm very thankful Sasha has taken Nina under her wing. I'm paying her to drive Nina to piano and gymnastics and this past week they've gone swimming. We arrived too late in the season for Nina to join the local pool, but Courtney has "pulled some strings" (bullying may have been involved) and gotten her enough day passes to last three visits a week through August. I owe Courtney one for sure.

Even so, when my phone rings and lights up with her name I'm tempted to send Courtney to voicemail. I look at the computer screen in front of me — I have pages and pages to get through by Friday — and my finger hovers over that red decline button. Curiosity wins, though. What could she need to call me about? Courtney is a texter. I pick up.

"Is Sasha at your house?"

I blink in surprise. "No."

"Shit."

"What's happening, Courtney?"

"I don't know where she is. Can you ask Nina?"

"Of course. I'll ask her right now. Hang on. Nina? *Nina?*"

She appears in her doorway as I reach the landing. *Oh, thank God.* "Nina, have you heard from Sasha today?" I'm forcing myself to act normal, although I probably sound completely crazy, blundering up the stairs and shrieking. "Her mom is looking for her."

"No. She said she was busy today, with a friend or something. She said we'd go to the pool tomorrow, though."

"Okay." I put the phone back to my ear. "Did you hear that, Courtney?"

"Yes. Can you ask her which friend? I'm trying not to panic here but . . ."

"Did she say who, Nina?" I ask, but my girl just shrugs. "Sorry, Courtney, she doesn't know." I walk back down the stairs with the phone gripped tightly. Although my first panic about Nina has gone, I'm experiencing waves of nausea. "Have you tried Find My iPhone?"

"Her phone is off. The car is here. I have no idea where she is. She went to bed at 10 p.m. last night. I haven't seen her since."

"Has she ever done anything like this before? Could there be a boy she's seeing? Someone she hasn't told you about?"

"I don't know! Oh. Look, I have another call."

She cuts the line.

* * *

I will get no more work done today. Even though I'm sure Sasha will turn up soon, the turmoil that I *know* Courtney is going through is all I can think about. I put on some coffee. I empty the dishwasher. I keep on my feet, circulating around the first floor, walking past every window and looking out as if I can somehow conjure Sasha walking through the neighborhood, heading in to explain that her phone ran out of charge, and she's just been to the mall or out for a bagel with some new friend she hadn't quite gotten around to telling Courtney about yet.

Memories flood my mind. If I close my eyes, I'm right back there in the doorway to Lynny's room with questions exploding in my brain. How long until I can text Courtney? Will she even tell me that Sasha's okay when she finds her? I start shaking and lean over the kitchen island, pushing my cheek into the cold granite. Nina can't see me like this. *Sugar*, I think. There's a bag of fun-size Twix Dan loves in the pantry cupboard. I eat four. Then I circle the windows three more times. The street is empty. I could have dreamed the whole conversation. Except I haven't.

It's 11.20 a.m. Nina will need lunch soon. I was planning on going to the store this afternoon once I got my editing done. The thought of the work sitting open on my computer makes me nauseous all over again. I will get it done later. Later, when I know Sasha is back. I walk past all the windows again. Still nothing. It's 11.22 a.m. I try to write a grocery list but holding the pen requires more concentration than I can muster. I walk past the windows again. Vicki and Natalie are standing at Natalie's mailbox. I throw on a pair of sneakers and head outside.

"Have you heard anything?"

"What about?"

"No?"

It's clear from their faces that neither woman has any idea what I'm talking about, so I fill them in on Courtney's phone call. Vicki is unfazed.

"She's probably just snuck out to hang with some friends. Courtney thinks she knows everything about her kid, but what teenager tells their mom everything they're doing?" Her skeptical expression and dismissal of it all makes me feel so much better.

But then I look at Natalie. Her face is white.

"Oh my God." Natalie's hand goes to her mouth and her knees buckle. "Oh my God," she says again. I follow her gaze and see a police car has turned into the neighborhood. It moves slowly but relentlessly and turns up Courtney's driveway. "Come inside," says Natalie. She clutches at our arms. Vicki shoots me a surprised look, and we all move quickly up the driveway and into Natalie's home. She leads us into the dining room, and we gather at the window, watching Courtney's front door open and swallow up two men in police uniforms. *This is really happening*, I think. Happening again.

"Are you okay, Natalie?" asks Vicki.

She shakes her head and then gestures to the dining table, and we all sit down. I think I know what's coming. Jocelyn's face swims into my mind and under the table I open up a recording app on my phone and set it running.

"I had a friend once," Natalie says, "who went missing. As a teenager. This just . . . wow. This just brings it all back."

"Oh my God." Vicki stretches her hand out and rubs Natalie's arm.

I don't move. I can't move. I can't move at all.

"What happened?" Vicki asks.

"It was a girl I was at school with. One Saturday night. She was supposed to go to a party, but she never showed up. The police weren't too interested. Said she had run away."

"And had she?" Again, it's Vicki talking. I feel like my lips have been stitched shut.

"I . . . Do you know, I can't even talk about it."

"That's okay. You don't need to say anything. How traumatic, though."

Natalie is nodding. "I don't think I've ever really gotten over it."

It's the oddest thing. Anger fires in my chest when she says that, but it flares and then it's gone, like a burst of gas in flames, disappearing almost the moment it arrives. Warm feelings follow. Fellow feelings. Losing my sister hurt Natalie, it really did. I hear it in her voice.

"What happened to her?"

"Jen!" Vicki is shocked, annoyed at me, even. So be it.

"She hadn't run away. She died." Natalie moves abruptly back in her chair and goes to the window.

"What did the police say?" I press. "What was her name?"

"Lynette." Natalie turns back and sits down again. She runs both hands through her hair. "She was so funny. That's what I remember the most. She had a wicked sense of humor. She sassed our history teacher every day for a year. That poor woman had no answer for Lynette." Natalie has a distant look in her eyes but Vicki glares at me. She thinks I need to shut the heck up.

"I'm so sorry for your loss," I say.

"Thanks." She sniffs and Vicki darts into the kitchen, retrieving a box of tissues. "Wow. I try not to think about it, to be honest," Natalie continues. "Especially now Erin is a teenager."

"How old were you?" I ask.

"Seventeen. We were juniors."

"That's terrible."

She nods. "Yup. I can't even talk about the details. Let's just say there's a lot of water in Ithaca. Steep ravines. Rocks. Deep rivers."

"She drowned? My God, that's awful." Vicki reaches out and hands Natalie a fistful of tissues. She is crying now in a large silent stream and the drops are falling on the table and spreading across the dark wood.

"Such a horrible accident," Natalie whispers.

We are all silent while she regroups.

"That is a terrible story," I manage to say.

And it is. It really is.

But it's not what the police told my mother.

THIRTEEN

Natalie
Now

After Vicki and Jen leave, I walk back into the dining room and just sit there. Sasha disappearing makes me sick to my stomach. It brings it all back, much more than just seeing Dan Burrows again did. When he wasn't up for explaining to everyone just how friendly we had been back in Ithaca I'd been mildly surprised and a little offended, but it was probably for the best. I realize I lost it a little just now, when I heard about Sasha. I mean, I never talk about Lynette. Never. Now I imagine Jen asking Dan if he knew about the girl I was friendly with, the girl who drowned. Hopefully he'll say he knew her even less than he knew me. And that will be just fine. I suck in a deep breath and send up a prayer that Sasha reappears soon and this whole thing blows over. I don't want to think about what happened in Ithaca. But for a while, that's exactly what I do.

* * *

An alarm on my phone jerks me back to the present. Dad.

His medication is all in the cupboard over the fridge. Everything's counted out. Prescriptions organized and automated. Home visits on the calendar. My work hours reduced to make it possible. It was Brad's idea, and he got the kids on board. What kind of person would I have been if I'd refused? Now our downstairs is full of extra furniture I promised Mom I'd never part with, and we've allowed my widowed, sick father to take up residence. There have been many adjustments, including accepting we can only go out of town if a paid nurse stays in one of the kids' bedrooms, since the spare room is fully occupied by my father. It was the right thing to do. It's still the right thing to do. But today, thinking about Lynette, the old anger is back. I pour out his 2.30 p.m. laxative drink, lay out his pills and water, and trudge upstairs with his tray.

It is *his* tray. He used to have a decanter and whiskey glasses on it. When I used to wish illness on him — and I've done so many times — cirrhosis of the liver was a favorite, along with embolisms and debilitating strokes. Sometimes I've thought I'd enjoy seeing him in court for a DUI and even imagined placing an anonymous call to his local paper to make sure his disgrace was as widely known as possible. I didn't see ALS coming. But here we are, a year on from Mom's death and he's going downhill quickly.

I don't bother knocking. It's not like he can tell me it's okay to enter.

I'm pleased his room is at the end of the hallway. We don't walk past it to get anywhere else. Walking past it would be worse, like we were ignoring the struggle going on behind the door, but the end of the hallway makes him a destination, albeit not one of my choosing. It's shadowy inside. I need to get Brad to fix these plantation shutters. They look good and cost a lot, but they're old and loose, gradually sliding closed by themselves like some bad metaphor. I don't immediately look at my dad. Even though I've hated him for most of my adult life, I can't help feeling emotional about what's happened to him. This illness is horrifying.

He's sixty-eight years old. Until a few years ago he was still a healthy-looking man. His face was a little weathered with years of alcohol consumption and not enough water, but he was an active tennis player, and an avid golfer, still tall, slim, proud of having kept his hair when his brothers had both gone thin on top in their forties. Now he's rail-thin. Skin hangs from his arms and legs where his muscle mass has been destroyed by disease. His face is pale, but not as altered as his body. His hands are stiff and useless, his spine's twisted, his legs immobile. His eyes flick to the door as I enter. Most of his face is hidden by the ventilator mask. It puffs his cheeks out and the strap across his forehead pushes down his brow, so he's almost unrecognizable. His hair sticks up in gray tufts and needs washed. That can wait until the evening nurse visits at 5 p.m.

I set down the tray and start talking about the weather. It's sunny out and I turn the slats of the window blind so he can see the blue sky, but a bright shaft of sunlight hits him square in the eyes. I don't shut it. In fact, I find myself smiling. There's a tyranny in nursing him, I've discovered. It's not pretty, but there it is.

FOURTEEN

Jen
Now

"Did Miss Courtney find Sasha yet?" Nina wanders into the kitchen with a book in her hand. She's in denim shorts and a tee from her old elementary school. One foot bare, one in a sock, something she often does, and I find super weird. Quirky, Dan calls it, putting it kindly.

"Probably. I'm sure she was just over at a friend's house. I'll check in with her mom later. What are you reading?"

She waves her book at me, grabs an apple, and meanders off again. I realize I've another reason for urgently not wanting anything terrible to have happened to Sasha. Nina. What would it do to her if her new friend never returned? There's a Pandora's box of adult horror just waiting to suck my girl in. The instinct to protect her is so strong, and yet my own mom didn't protect me at all. Having Nina changed a lot of things for me. Especially about how I felt about my own mom. And Jocelyn.

I haven't messaged her yet about Sasha going missing, or what Natalie said this morning. It feels wrong to be thinking about all that when there's a crisis unfolding just a few doors away. It's three o'clock now. I fill a tall glass with water and go out on the deck. The heat slams into my face. Pennsylvania summers are thick and humid. We don't have any fancy furniture out here yet, only two wooden Adirondack chairs Dan's brother brought over. I didn't ask where they came from, just gave them a good scrub.

I look at my phone as if it's going to give me answers. Probably I should tell Jocelyn about Sasha. Probably. How will she react, though? Look how it made me feel. How it made Natalie feel. I think I should wait until I hear something from Courtney. I don't want Jocelyn upset. I certainly don't want her driving up here. She will panic about Nina if I tell her Sasha's missing. But I *want* to tell her. A trouble shared is a trouble halved. I open up my phone as far as the WhatsApp icon, still in two minds about whether I'm telling her or not, and I see I've missed a message from her.

If you hear anything strange today, don't panic. Everything is under control. Everyone's fine.

Sent at 6.30 a.m. What the fuck?

Jocelyn — what the actual fuck? WTF!

She types right back.

LOL

I think about throwing my phone off the deck. Instead, I type.

Do you know where Sasha Wallace is???

76

She replies with a photograph. A selfie. I can't believe what I'm seeing. Jocelyn and Sasha, heads together. On a train.

That girl's mother is going out of her mind! The police have been at her house!

Excellent. Does Natalie Preston know?

Natalie Preston? I feel like my head might explode.

Yes, she knows! She totally freaked out.

Good.

I don't respond. I can't think of anything to say that isn't a barrel of f-bombs. The implications of Jocelyn's message blow my mind.

Another message arrives.

Sasha just texted her mom. Crisis over. Meet you this evening outside Nina's piano lesson.

She ends with a heart emoji.

It's hard to be angry and relieved all at the same time, but I remain that way for several hours. Nina and I eat dinner, and she chatters on about the Jacqueline Woodson novel she's reading and how she'll need at least one more trip to the library for books to take with her when she goes to stay with her dad the weekend after next.

"So soon? That's come around quickly."

She reaches out and squeezes my hand. "It will go by in a flash. You'll hardly have time to miss me."

"Hey, kiddo. Who's the parent here? I'll miss you more than you know, nugget. But you'll have a great time, and I'll get *lots* of editing done. I fell way behind today."

"I told you not to worry about her," Nina says. "Sasha can look after herself."

"I told you sos" from a ten-year-old can be annoying, but in this case, I give Nina a pass. Sasha had texted her not long after I finished messaging with Jocelyn and the part of me that's relieved the girl is okay feels thankful. The part of me that's *furious* sits on a low burner waiting until I see Jocelyn alone.

* * *

As I clean up after dinner and drive Nina over to her piano teacher, I take a break from my issues with Jocelyn and think about seeing Booker soon. We will do what we always do if the weather is good. He drives down from Vermont as we head north. We meet up in Poughkeepsie and take a walk across the Hudson bridges. It works for us all, breaking up the drive, and stretching our legs. If the conversation stays light, we have something to eat together. We behave like a normal family — like the family we might have been. Sometimes it feels so easy, other times, not so much. I'm always nervous. Every time, I think, this will be it. The time he brings someone with him. I dread it happening and I'd never admit it because it's pathetic. I hate how much I'm looking forward to seeing Booker.

We draw up outside the piano teacher's house and I see Jocelyn's car is already there, a few houses along. There are no streetlights, so Nina doesn't notice, she just hops right out of the car and runs up the path to ring the doorbell. In a moment she's gone, swallowed up for forty-five minutes of scales and recital practice while I'm believed to be running errands or catching up on email. I back out of the driveway and pull up further down the street, right behind Jocelyn. She clambers out and comes to sit in my passenger seat.

"I can't believe you pulled a stunt like that."

"I know, I know." She's wheezing a little, but I can't be distracted by worrying about her health.

"I thought we were in this together?"

"That's what's bothering you? And there was me thinking you were worried about poor Courtney, who you don't even like."

"Who says I don't like her? Anyway, that's not the point. Just tell me what the hell you were doing with Sasha."

"Did you get anything from Natalie? That's the important thing."

"We'll get to that." I fold my arms across my chest and stare out into the darkness. "Start talking, Jocelyn."

And so she does. Sasha, she tells me, is not getting along with Courtney. They've been arguing for months about where Sasha should go to college, with Courtney pushing her toward Penn State or Pitt and Sasha wanting to be anywhere but Pennsylvania. Her dream college is New York University, but Courtney won't even visit. Jocelyn sounds quite indignant on Sasha's behalf, which, given how reluctant she was to let me go to college, is pretty rich. But I don't say any of that.

"Sasha's mother needed to be taught a lesson. Sasha's not a child and doesn't need protecting every minute of the day."

"Is that what you told her? As you persuaded her to sneak out of the house this morning and run away to New York City for the day?"

"Calm down, Jen. It was all her idea, not mine. We talked it through at your house after Nina was in bed. Sasha asked me for a ride to Wilmington so she could take the train. It was too early for any of her friends to drive her and she was desperate. I picked her up at the end of the street at 6 a.m. I even took the train up there with her to make sure she was okay. Sasha went and toured NYU. She loved it."

"And what did you do?" I can't see Jocelyn in the city. Sasha, yes. Jocelyn, not so much.

"Took a walk. Read a book."

She's very smug at this point and I think about the recording on my phone. I'm tempted to lie to her. This was a lousy stunt. Jocelyn, of all people, should not have thought this was okay to do to Courtney, however annoying Sasha claims she is. But then I remember Jocelyn's only doing this because she needs answers about Lynette, and so do I.

I play the recording.

When we get to the bit where Natalie said it was an accident, Jocelyn nods, long and slow, but says nothing. I wonder if she's gone back there, in her mind, to those awful months before they found my sister's body? Or to the two years afterward, before we sold up and moved to Rochester? It's a mistake I've made before, imagining she thinks like I do when I know she doesn't. Sometimes I wonder if she even has feelings — normal human feelings — about it all? For years she's been like a dog with a bone about what happened. After today's adventure with Sasha, I wonder what lengths she'll go to, to find the answers she needs.

We're sitting in semi-darkness, but I see a different light to her eyes when she turns to me. Her hand, when she clutches mine, is warm and doughy. I think I'm not going to like what comes next, and I don't.

"You need to talk to Dan," she says. "It's time we asked him a few pointed questions about this *accident*."

FIFTEEN

Jocelyn
Then

It was a ten-minute drive from the Eason house to Connor Goodman's. Normally Sal was a terrible passenger, wincing as I drove down the narrow streets like she expected me to knock the side mirror off every parked car. But there was no normal anymore. We drove in silence to Connor's home, up near Cornell. It was set back from the road and the kid was outside when we pulled up. He was barefoot, despite the cold, carrying a black trash bag and picking cans out of a hydrangea bush.

"It must have been some party," Sal said, a flicker of optimism in her voice. She was thinking Lynette might be here. Inside somewhere. Maybe fast asleep. I hoped to God she was.

"Hey." We left the car at the bottom of his driveway and wandered toward him. "Got a minute?"

Connor was tall and lanky. He had straggly brown hair in need of a wash and his face was paler than milk, making his teenage stubble and pimples stand out. Hungover, clearly. Wary, certainly.

"What do you want?" He glanced back at the house and then moved down the driveway toward us, trash bag still in hand. "Who are you?"

I put up my hands. "We're looking for a girl from your school. She didn't come home last night. Lynette Knox. You know her?"

"Yeah." He glanced back at the house again. The door was open. I couldn't decide if he was trying to avoid eye contact, worried about something in the house, or just worried it was going to blow shut and lock him out.

"Did you see her last night?"

"No."

"She wasn't here? At the party."

"What party?"

There was a bullishness about the way he said this that made me want to punch him in the face. I bet his parents hated him. He probably ran party central there because his parents couldn't stand to be at home with him, the smug little shit.

"Is she here?" Sal stepped forward and I wasn't sorry to see Connor take a step back.

"Hey, what the fuck?" He looked back toward the house again, another anxious glance, and that was enough for Sal. She charged past him, heading for the door.

His bag hit the ground, cans exploding noisily across the asphalt. Connor was fast. Faster than Sal but still he needed to shove her to make it through the door first. I wasn't far behind, but happy to be running in second spot as Sal stuck her foot in the door and howled when he tried to ram it shut. In a moment I was there too, throwing my full weight on the almost closed door. Connor, little shit, was no match for us both. A grunt. A thrust. We were in.

"Jesus, what's wrong with you?" Connor backed away while Sal ran up the stairs. "What's she doing? What do you want?"

I put my hands up again. He was a skinny kid, but if he charged me, I'd be sorry. "Listen we're not here for trouble.

82

Just looking for Lynette." I tipped my head toward the stairs. "That's her mom. She's going out of her mind."

"You can't just barge in. And I already told you. She wasn't here."

"Yeah, well, you also said there was no party." I didn't need to take my eyes from his face. The house stank of booze. The door stood open to a room on his left. Red solo cups everywhere. Behind him the kitchen was visible. Bottles and more cups.

"She won't find Lynette up there." His shoulders dropped and he walked into the kitchen. From the doorway I watched him pull another trash bag from under the sink and start dropping bottles inside. Glass on glass. Maybe his hangover wasn't as bad as I'd assumed.

"But you do know her," I said.

He shrugged. "Everyone knows everyone. But I don't know where she is or why she didn't show last night." He pulled a crooked, unpleasant smile. "It's not like I take a register. People come. People go."

"And leave you to do all the cleaning up."

Connor had no real friends. I read him easily and almost felt sorry for him. Almost. The clatter of Sal coming back downstairs reached me. She hadn't called out. No Lynette.

But she didn't come into the kitchen like I thought she would. More doors opened and closed. Then a banging.

"What the fuck!" Connor shoved past me, back into the hallway and into a sitting room, bizarrely devoid of furniture. There was a set of double doors, obviously leading into another room, and equally obviously locked as Sal stood there, hammering the wood with her fists.

"Open this! Open it now!"

"I can't."

She stopped and turned. "I want my daughter."

"She's not in there! There's nothing but furniture. Look, lady, quit banging. I don't have the key. My brother took off with it. Yesterday afternoon. He said at least no one would trash the furniture."

I didn't think he was lying. What he said made sense. I watched as Sal's fury subsided, slowly seeping out of her.

"Where's my baby, Jocelyn?"

There was heartbreak in her voice. And nothing I could do but put my arm around her.

"Let's go home and check on Genevieve," I said.

She let me lead her to the car. What Connor Goodman did next, or thought of us, I didn't care.

But later, I wished I had.

SIXTEEN

Jen
Now

I wait until Friday to talk to Dan. Jocelyn's messages mount up, but I ignore her. This conversation will take place on my terms, not hers, and it'll happen when I think he's relaxed — something he's not for quite a lot of the time. I won't be recording it either. That would be a step too far, even for me.

Nina is at the pool with Sasha watching her. Dan's brother was supposed to be coming over to do something in the garage — I wasn't really listening to the detail — but he's canceled — or Dan's canceled him, I'm not sure which. It's hot again. The kind of heat that clings to your skin the minute you take a step outside. The deck is so hot I can't step on it barefoot. You could fry an egg on it, I swear.

We are in the kitchen when I decide it's time. Some sport is on in the background. I see bikes and a splash of yellow, maybe the Tour de France? Dan is sipping coffee and scrolling through his phone.

"I forgot to tell you," I say, "there was quite the drama in the neighborhood the other day."

He looks up, brows raised, expression skeptical. "Surprise me."

"Sasha Wallace went missing."

"Jesus. But they found her?"

"She called her mom in the afternoon. She'd taken off to New York City for the day."

"Wow. Ballsy."

"Apparently, she wants to go there for college. She was proving to Courtney she could be independent. What she didn't figure — as I suppose only a self-absorbed teen might not — was that her mother might totally panic, involve the police, and imagine a thousand terrible things had happened."

"That's nuts. Good to hear she is okay. I hope you told Nina never to pull a stunt like that."

"Believe it. Anyway, it caused quite a stir. Courtney called me to see if Nina knew anything — she didn't — and then I was out talking to Vicki and Natalie about it."

He stiffens. Just a little. "Yes?"

"Yeah, so did you know this girl who drowned when you and Natalie were at high school? Natalie was pretty freaked out about Sasha and told me and Vicki all about it. I had no idea."

I watch him pinch the bridge of his nose between forefinger and thumb.

"She was called Lynette," he says, his voice slow and somber. "Lynette Knox. I didn't know her well, but yeah, I knew her."

"Natalie said she was supposed to go to a party one night, but she never showed up?" My tone is light, I phrase it as a question, but he doesn't bite.

"That was a long time ago. High school. Another life, really."

"But it must have been shocking. Someone you knew disappearing. Dying."

"Yup."

There's a moment of silence. "That's it? 'Yup'?"

He leans back on his stool. "What do you want me to say? I assume Natalie told you about it. She was the one that was friends with her, not me."

"Natalie said she was funny. The girl. Lynette. Said she gave some of her teachers a really hard time. It must have been so shocking. For everyone who knew her. Even if they didn't know her well. I mean, she was what—? Only seventeen. Imagine something like that happening to Nina."

"Nothing's going to happen to Nina, Jen." He surprises me by walking round the island and putting an arm around me. "She's a good kid. A great kid. Far too smart to let something like that happen to her. And she has us. Looking out for her. Keeping her on the right path. Not everyone has that."

The implication is clear, but I find the words, just to be sure. "So, this girl you knew? She wasn't smart? She didn't come from a good family?"

"No." He walks back to his stool and his phone, shaking his head, looking smug. "No. That girl was a disaster waiting to happen."

SEVENTEEN

Dan
Now

After Jen heads to her office, I hit the garage. Patrick was supposed to be helping me hang a bunch of tool boards this morning but with Natalie around, that's not going to happen. Now, not only am I stuck doing this shit without help, I also have Ithaca to think about.

* * *

I was eight years old when I decided I was going to be a doctor. Our older brother was sick — again — and we were in the hospital waiting room while they ran some tests and discovered a heart defect. We had been in that place so often I felt like the toys belonged to me. My favorite was Operation, kind of a surprising choice given our location, and even though the game had no batteries I would lie on the floor for hours, perfecting my ability to remove the bread from the fat guy's breadbasket for a thousand imaginary bucks a pop. Surgery meant money, I learned that early, and it also brought respect. The way my parents deferred to Christopher's doctors was nothing short of marvelous to me. Everyone straightened when one of those men came by — nurses, family, patients. And what power. I'd seen doctors make and break my parents with just a few words. In the end they couldn't save Christopher, but by then the ambition was fixed in my mind. And our trips to the hospital were far from over. Although Patrick and I were fine, my parents had lost one child and weren't planning on losing another. We were tested, checked, and tested again and again. Patrick, especially, always worried them.

I wanted nothing in life but to do well in school and become a doctor, but at thirteen I developed a new ambition — quite separate to my main life goal. That was the age I decided I wanted to sleep with Natalie Eason. We were in the eighth grade.

It was her smell that decided me. It wasn't her long, blonde hair, or her cute freckles, the hint of curves under her outsized hoodie, or her long legs and her short shorts, although these were all things I spent a great number of hours thinking about for the next few years. It was her smell. Something half-way between a ripe pear and candy. Fifteen years later, with Ithaca and Natalie miles in my rearview mirror, I smelled it again in a Victoria's Secret, buying underwear for a gift for an on-again-off-again girlfriend. I ended up walking out of the store empty-handed. Too many memories.

Wanting to sleep with Natalie Eason felt like a simple ambition in eighth grade, but by eleventh grade, I was getting nowhere. Natalie never seemed to see me. I passed her in the halls every day; we had been in the same social studies class in ninth grade, the same Spanish class in tenth, but in eleventh grade my class choices — heavy on science, no time for study halls — didn't match with any of hers and I had the strong sense my time was running out. I needed a way for her to notice me and started looking at her friends.

She ran in a gang of four girls. Whether they knew it or not, those high school girls were pack animals and maybe they felt they had to be. Natalie Eason was never not with at least one of Mel Parks, Sherri Knowles and Lynette Knox.

Mel was a non-starter. She had been in my physics class sophomore year and hated the fact that I beat her on every test. She wasn't the kind of girl that wanted to make friends with the smart kids. She wanted to be better than us, and in many ways she was. She dated the tight end on the football team and was a flyer for the cheer squad. Mel was petite, pretty, and very, very book smart. She had it all already. No reason for her to waste her time on Dan Burrows. Sherri was more approachable. I liked her. She lived three doors along the street from me and I often saw her walking up and down from town with her grandma. She was a nice girl. A nice person. Which was why I had to choose Lynette. I couldn't pretend to be interested in Sherri just to get near Natalie. It would be like pulling the stuffing from a cute little teddy bear. Lynette, on the other hand? Cute didn't know Lynette Knox.

It was difficult to imagine what made that girl so hard, but she was the kind whose tough exterior ran all the way through. She was sharp and funny, but also deeply, deeply unkind. Later — but before Lynette went missing — Natalie joked that long ago she and Mel had agreed if anyone had the potential to make their school lives miserable it was Lynette Knox. And so they'd agreed to befriend her, to "keep her close", where they couldn't become targets because they had her back.

I decided to speak to Lynette after I heard Connor Goodman had dumped her. She'd be on the rebound, I figured, happy to have a bit of attention. I watched her around school, noting where her locker was, following her at the end of lunch for a few days, even though that made me late for chem. I waited for a Friday — there was a home football game and afterwards there was always a party. I'd even gone to a couple, although I'd mainly sidled around, talking to a few guys on the team I knew before heading out again. I wasn't much of a drinker, or a stoner, but I had a few friends who were, and if there was a chance of Natalie Eason showing up, I wanted to be there. So far, she never had, and now I was going to make that work in my favor.

It didn't take much to tempt Lynette to the party after the football game. A couple of spliffs, a few compliments, and she was all over me. I played it interested, but aloof . . . and she lapped it right up. The next Monday at school when I walked past her and Natalie, Lynette couldn't wait to catch my eye and say hi. I was polite but offhand. Didn't even glance at Natalie Eason. Lynette caught up with me on the way to the bus after school wanting to hang out. I had her over to my house a couple of times. My parents were at work and Patrick was always oblivious to anything I was doing. Lynette and I messed around, we bitched about people at school, she brought some vodka she'd stolen from her mom — who sounded like a total head-case — so we drank it and fooled about some more. It wasn't serious. Not on my part because I was playing a long game, not on hers, because she just wasn't that kind of girl.

"So, what do you think of my friends, then?" she asked me one afternoon, when we were done trash-talking pretty much all the rest of the grade.

"Like who?"

"Mel."

I shrugged. "She's smart. If you like that kind of thing."

"Do you?"

"There are different kinds of smart."

"She's pretty, though."

"I guess. Not my type."

That pleased her. We were lying on my bed. She draped a bit more of herself over me.

"What about Natalie, then? She has great hair."

"Do you think?" I tried to sound incredulous.

"Everyone says so."

"Then I guess she has great hair. I can't say I'd noticed. You sound a bit jealous."

"No." She slapped me across the arm.

"No? Are you sure?"

"Of course, I'm sure." She didn't look it, though, and I knew a sore point when I saw it.

"So, you don't think I'd like her if we all hung out?"

"Why would I think that?" She curled her lip and her eyes narrowed.

"Oh, you know. Some girls are insecure. Keep their boy and girl friends separate. It's a confidence thing."

"Or a trust thing." Now she sounded surly.

"If you say so." I shrugged, as if the conversation was not a big deal, but inside I was laughing. Lynette Knox was an easy mark. She'd have to introduce us now.

Three weeks later and it was Natalie Eason who was over at my house after school, lying with her blonde hair on my pillow and blowing smoke rings in the air. Lynette was furious. She watched me and Natalie hook up at a party and pretended not to care — at least when her friend was looking. But when Nat was off in the bathroom, Lynette was in my ear in a moment.

"I wish you luck with her," she said in a low voice, "because you're going to need it."

"Oh yeah? And why is that?"

"Have you met her family?"

"No."

"You might want to keep it that way."

"And why is that?"

"Because they're very fucking weird."

Of course, I ignored her. Typical bitchy girl spitefulness. I kept my eyes on the prize, and if it crossed my mind that Lynette was, in fact, more fun than her avowed best friend, I crushed the thought.

* * *

A car door slamming brings me back to the present. Nina. She bowls right into the garage, stops up short when she sees me.

"Nice work."

Her head is slightly tilted, her lips pursed in appreciation, her hands on her hips. She is a miniature Jen and I register a flicker of regret. There will never be a miniature Dan for me to find myself in. But I've made my peace with it.

"Thanks. How was the pool?"

"Good. I'm just gonna change and go over to play at the twins' house. Miss Daisy invited me."

"Okay, well tell your mom. She's in her office."

"Yup."

She dashes up the steps and disappears into the kitchen. I find myself smiling. Ithaca, and everything that happened, settles back into the past where it belongs. I like the present. And Natalie Eason's fat mouth will not be a problem. I won't let it be.

EIGHTEEN

Jen
Now

Jocelyn isn't impressed with my conversation with Dan and doesn't spare me her commentary. She regards her little escapade with Sasha as a triumph and blames me for not making more of the opportunity she'd delivered. But while she's right that I haven't gotten far with Dan, Natalie Preston is proving to be a different story. On Sunday night, my phone buzzes.

> *Sorry about the other day. Felt like I made a bit of a fool of myself. Glad Sasha is okay, tho.*

> *Yes!! Very happy for Sasha and Courtney. And don't worry about a thing. It must have been a terrible time. No wonder S disappearing brought it all back.*

> *Thanks*

I stare at my phone, in urgent need of inspiration.

Hey, so Vicki and I are going running tomorrow. Any interest in meeting up for coffee afterwards? Creek Farm?

I wait. Watch for those three dots.

Sure, why not? What time?

* * *

Vicki introduced me to Creek Farm Marketplace. It's some kind of repurposed farm building, painted traditional Venetian red, and attached to a dairy farm and apple orchard swollen with the kind of bucolic charm I didn't know I was missing in my pre-Pennsylvania-outer-suburb life. It smells of baked goods and hot fat — one of its main attractions is freshly made apple cider donuts — and boasts a range of fresh local fruits and vegetables, home-made pies, and made-on-the-premises ice cream in three flavors. There's also a café, very informal in style, with mismatched little tables and mismatched wooden chairs, perfect for hikers, cyclists and, in our case, runners, who can trail in wearing muddy boots or sneakers, wet or dry, sweaty or not, and enjoy a beverage after the pleasure of free parking in the farm's spacious lot.

Vicki and I finish a four-mile circuit at a steady pace and cool down for a few minutes before joining Natalie inside.

"You two put me to shame!"

I can't tell if she's being disingenuous. Natalie's dressed head to toe in Lululemon and looks like a yoga instructor. A hot yoga instructor, although I'm not sure there is any other kind. "I wish I could run," she says, "but my Achilles. Ugh."

Natalie launches into a detailed explanation of all the exercises she's currently undertaking in an effort to avoid having surgery. This leads Vicki into a story about her husband's slow recovery from a shoulder operation. From there we quickly turn to kid talk and while I'm anxious to somehow get back to Natalie's past and what she knows about Lynette, I know to bide my time. And I am a mother. It's not hard to talk kids, so long as no one gets competitive. Happily, it looks like our kids are all so different and we can share without comparing. Vicki's and Natalie's children are all older than Nina. Erin, who I met on my faux dog research visit to number eleven, is fourteen, a year younger than Vicki's daughter, Madison. Erin is sporty, playing softball in the spring — well, year-round really — and field hockey in the fall, whereas Madison is "definitely her father's daughter" and does high school swimming "very reluctantly" but is a real star on the school debate team. They both have boys, but where Vicki's son is a rising senior, Natalie's has only just finished sixth grade. Neither rate much of a mention. Both women are lovely about Nina and enthusiastic about how she will do in the elementary school.

After a while it starts bothering me that neither of them mentions Sasha's New York adventure. I mean, it seems like a fairly significant event. There were cops on the street. Courtney is someone they both socialize with. I feel like Sasha taking off without telling Courtney would rate a mention, quite separately from my intention to shake Natalie into talking more about Lynette. When the conversation switches to husbands, I'm afraid I've missed my moment. But Natalie's husband Brad has annoyed her by playing golf with Courtney's husband Geoff for the millionth time this summer, and I jump right in.

"Did he say if Geoff was upset? About Sasha disappearing like that?"

Vicki makes a noise, somewhere between a snort and a laugh. "Does anything *not* upset Geoff?"

I'm not sure what to make of that, so I look at Natalie and lift my eyebrows.

"If he was, Brad didn't mention it," she says. "You know, Sasha is a great kid, and Courtney — well, Courtney is Courtney — but she and Geoff can be a bit . . ." she hesitates, and her eyes flick to Vicki and back, "odd at times. I don't want to talk out of turn, though. I mean, I don't want to say anything negative."

"But?"

She shrugs. "Oh, I don't know. They're a blended family. They do things differently than we do. Vicki?"

If Natalie is looking to Vicki for help, she's quickly disappointed. Her friend holds up both hands and gets to her feet. "If you don't want to be negative about Courtney and Geoff, I'm not the person you need. I'm going to pee."

Wow. I try to school my features and hide behind a sip of coffee. "A blended family?" I ask.

Natalie leans in. "I'll tell you quickly. We need to be talking about something else by the time Vicki gets back. Sasha is Courtney's daughter, not Geoff's. He has his own daughter, Paige, from a previous marriage, about the same age as your Nina. There was some trouble between Paige and other kids in our development. It's complicated. Anyway, Paige used to stay with Courtney and Geoff on the weekend but since that all blew up, she hasn't been back to the neighborhood. Vicki didn't appreciate what Courtney had to say when it all kicked off. There's some bad blood." She looks toward the bathrooms and her face changes. "Think of something. Change the subject. Quick."

It's an opportunity I can't miss.

"So . . . tell me everything you remember about Dan from high school?" My voice is bright. "I'm hoping for some juicy gossip. He doesn't talk a lot about his life before med school, really. I bet he was super cute as a teenager."

Vicki is back in her seat and clearly approves of my questions. "Yes. I love it. Come on, Nat," she says. "Spill."

"I guess he was," Natalie says. "He was a little on the nerdy side of things. But I remember he went to a few parties. Smoked some weed."

"Seriously?" I've seen him drunk but never stoned. "Well, I guess you know what they say. It's always the quiet ones."

"Did he know that girl?" Vicki asks me. My God. I could kiss her. "The one Nat was friends with?"

"Yes. Yes, he did." I let that hang in the air.

There are a few moments of silence, then Natalie bites. "What did he say about her?"

I make a face, like I'm kind of embarrassed to say. "To be honest, I got the impression he didn't like her much. Didn't think much of her family."

"Seems a bit harsh," says Vicki. "What do you think, Nat?"

Nat stretches her back. "I guess he's not wrong."

"You don't have to talk about it if you don't want to." Vicki squeezes her hand.

Oh, but she does. "Did she come from a bad background?" I ask.

She nods. "I don't think she ever knew her dad. Then she had a stepdad, but he ran off when she was young. Her mom was an alcoholic. Her aunt was weird. Even her grandparents were weird. Super religious or something."

"Wow. That's a lot. You know there was a girl I was friends with at school with a similar story." Vicki launches into her own history as my mind spins.

Her stepdad ran off? *Ran off?* The rest of it doesn't shock me, but the thing about my dad? I can remember the day Mom told me he'd died in an accident so clearly. I remember the cold, the snow. But Natalie is speaking again, and I force myself to focus.

"Yeah. She sounds similar. Lynette was obviously affected by her family, like I guess we all are. Back then she seemed so cool to me. Kind of untouchable. Now I think about it, all that hardness was probably a front. She acted like she cared about nothing. I thought she really did care about nothing. Except her sister. She had some fancy name, I can't remember what. But Lynette would do anything for her. She made her meals, bought her school supplies. I remember her saying her mom was always too busy. Lynette made a big deal sometimes about how my mom was a stay-at-home mom and how spoiled I was. But then she would come over and stuff herself with cookies or whatever, like she hadn't had a meal in a week. And my mom would give her leftovers to take back to her sister. Nothing was ever said. We just all knew Lynette's mom was a problem."

"What happened when she disappeared? It must have been terrifying."

"It was. But it built up slow. I mean, I was one of the last people to see her before she disappeared."

"You were?" Vicki's voice pops with excitement. She's totally here for the drama.

"We were always together on Saturdays. Normally there would be four of us, but the other two girls were out with one of their families for dinner. Lynette and I hung out for a while and then she went off to a party."

"You didn't go with her?" I ask.

Natalie colors just a little. "No. There was a boy I was seeing." She sucks in her cheeks and Vicki laughs. "Anyway, the first thing I heard was the next morning. Lynette never went home. Her mom had called my house but my parents — well, they thought she was drunk and didn't even wake me up. Not that I knew anything anyway, but I guess I always felt bad about that. I was just sleeping in my bed like normal, while my friend was . . ."

"That's not your fault," Vicki says.

"I know, I know." Natalie shakes her head and carries on. "Anyway, Lynette's crazy aunt showed up with her mom the next morning. I told her about the party and she and the mom went off to try and find out if she was there. News spread quickly after that. There were searches. 'Missing' posters. School felt super weird. But after a week or so the word went round that she had run away. Everyone was talking about her family. We wanted to believe she'd run away although I think all the time, we knew she hadn't. I mean, she'd have told one of us, right? And she'd said nothing."

"She didn't have a boyfriend?"

"No one serious. Lynette didn't do boyfriends."

"Was she gay?" Vicki asks, and Natalie laughs.

"No. One hundred percent not gay. But she was very anti-men. I mean, she'd hook up with boys and fool around like we all did. Maybe what I mean is she was anti-relationship. She said boyfriends were for suckers. Christ, she was only just seventeen. We thought we were so grown-up."

I'm struck again by the genuine sadness in Natalie's voice when she's talking about my sister.

"I wonder what happened between you leaving her and her drowning," I say. "I mean, I don't know Ithaca, but Dan said there are a ton of creeks and waterfalls. Was she found near your house?"

"No. Nowhere near."

"So, what did they think happened? How did she get there?"

"No clue." Natalie looks about ready to be done with the conversation. Which makes me press on.

"I mean, did someone drive her? Did she hook up with someone and have an argument? Did she even have a cell phone? I guess they were still new back then."

Natalie puts her hands to her face. "Hey, I'm sorry, ladies, but can we change the subject? It kind of brings it all back, you know."

"Of course!" Vicki is hand-squeezing again. "We won't mention it again. Will we, Jen?"

I've no choice but to agree.

* * *

I call Jocelyn on the drive back home from Creek Farm.

"So, I just had coffee with Natalie Preston."

"About time." She sounds like she's in a bad mood. I couldn't care less. Her bad mood can have nothing on mine.

"Yup. Super-interesting talk about Lynette. Particularly about her family."

I'm driving past a field of corn. The sky is cloudless. Thank God for hands-free phone calls. I'm strangling the steering wheel.

"Pff. Don't pay any attention to her."

"No? *No*? I don't know, Jocelyn. She seemed pretty well informed."

"What did she say about us?" Her tone is bored. I wish I could see her face. But this can't wait.

"She said, Jocelyn, that Lynette's stepfather left. *Left* as in ran off. As in, abandoned them. Not, as in — died in a fucking car crash."

"Ah."

"Ah?" Anger tears through me. "Jesus Christ, Jocelyn. Jesus Christ." I hit the button and end the call. I'm driving too fast and have to slam on the brakes. This is not good. Not good. My phone starts ringing, and I decline the call. It rings again. I decline again. By now I'm only a minute from home. By the time I pull into the garage she has sent multiple texts.

We need to talk.

I can explain.

Anyway, did she say anything useful?

I put my head in my hands and let out a howl of frustration. Not for the first time, I think Jocelyn Silver might be a sociopath.

NINETEEN

Jocelyn
Then

Sal was exhausted after our visit to Connor Goodman. I drove us back home in silence, while she slumped with her cheek against the passenger window. When we got to the house, she walked straight past Genevieve and up the stairs. The way she closed her bedroom door? I felt it in my guts. If something bad had really happened to Lynette, I wasn't sure my sister would be able to handle it.

In the meantime, I was left with Genevieve.

"Well?" she said.

"No one's seen her." I sat down on the couch, feeling heavy with what was to come.

"So what now?"

The answer was there, but I was reluctant to say it. For a minute, I had a sense of hovering on the brink, about to set things in motion that I couldn't control. But who was I kidding? Lynette was missing. We'd been past the point of no return for hours. I picked up the phone and called the police. And then we waited.

* * *

My feelings toward the Ithaca Police Department weren't too friendly. They knew us, or they believed they did, and I knew before they showed up what they'd think of this situation with Lynette. I had to try and get them onside, though, and while we waited, I thought about how to talk to them about Sal's daughter in a way that would make them take us seriously. I rehearsed what I'd say about her and began digging around Sal's drawers for school photos — something to make Lynette look soft and vulnerable, not the hard-assed teen I knew.

If I was being completely honest, I was never fond of Lynette, not even when she was little. The house wasn't large, our parents weren't happy with Sal getting pregnant, and that baby was noisy. Her "stuff" spread like duckweed. Some days when I got in from work there was nowhere to sit down. Baby clothes, toys, boxes of diapers, bottles, just baby crap wherever I looked. Everything stank too. Sal took to motherhood, though, even our mother admitted that. The physical work that a baby demanded — feeding, hugging, changing, rocking, lifting and carrying — Sal did it all without a murmur of complaint. She crooned; she sang. She was a natural. We had always been so close, Sal and me. A team. The baby changed all that.

In between Lynette and Genevieve being born, our parents died. That was the first time the police came to the house, but it wasn't the last. Afterwards, I hoped it would just be the three of us. Sal moved into our parents' room, and we didn't miss them. But within months Sal took up with John Knox and he moved into their room with Sal. Mother would never have let her be so stupid. I couldn't see what she saw in him. Yes, he talked nice to her and brought her booze. And he didn't seem to mind her having Lynette already. Before I knew it, my sister thought she was in love for the first time. He didn't love her back. That was obvious from the get-go. He loved the free roof over his head, though. And call me cynical, but I swear he only got her pregnant with Genevieve to establish his position and muscle me out.

What he didn't bargain for was post-natal depression. It hit Sal hard, and he couldn't understand it, seeing how she'd been with Lynette and how she changed after Genevieve was born. They both drank too much. There were arguments. In public. Police involved. More house visits. Warnings. Promises made and broken. The drinking got worse. When you see a man putting empty bottles in the trunk of his car because he's too ashamed to put them out on the sidewalk for the trashman, you're seeing a man with a problem. And when drinking at home with a miserable, sick partner, two kids, and with your partner's sister who you can't stand the sight of gets too much, what do you do? You go looking for a better life. It took him a while. But when Genevieve was six years old, John Knox took off with all his things and our mother's wedding ring. He was a piece of shit. Genevieve was better off thinking he was dead. The car crash story was my idea, but Sal had been right on board.

From then on things were better again. Just me, Sal and the girls. We were a team and should have stayed that way. Except Lynette turned thirteen. I thought she was turning wild and said so. Sal and I fell out. Lynette was her business. Hers alone. If I didn't approve of her kid or her parenting, I could move the hell out. And so I did. But I should have stayed.

* * *

The cops finally showed up about three in the afternoon. The phone hadn't rung. Lynette hadn't appeared. Sal was still upstairs, and Genevieve hadn't moved from the sofa, she'd just sat there, staring at the front door. I'd roused myself enough to make some coffee and shove some stuff in drawers and cupboards to make things look a little less chaotic, but I don't think it did any good. There were two of them, a man and a woman. Him, I knew. I watched their eyes swivel, taking everything in. All I could think was if this was Natalie Eason's house, everything would go differently. Natalie Eason's parents didn't have throws covering up old furniture, or dusty racks of CDs and DVDs on display. They had fancy curtains and matching pillows, expensive-looking ornaments, and shiny mirrors. The police would take a family like them seriously. Us? Not so much.

"Will Lynette's mother be joining us?"

This was the younger one, Officer Prentice; a woman in her thirties, wearing a lot of makeup and perching on the edge of the sofa beside Genevieve as if she was afraid of catching something.

Officer Markham, the one who'd been here too many times, who thought he knew us, waved his partner's question away. He was a big guy, in his fifties, with thick hair and a mustache. He looked like a kind grandpa, but Markham was as judgmental as they come. "No need to disturb her," he said. "I'm sure she's feeling very *emotional*." The way he said it? He'd decided she was drunk. I wanted to stand up for her, but when I'd argued with him in the past, it hadn't ended well.

"I can tell you the facts for right now," I said, instead. "She was last seen by her friends around 6 p.m. last night. I have a list of their names." I waved it and Markham nodded toward the woman. I handed it over and watched her eyes scan the list. "We've asked them all, but they're not helping. They'll tell you this is out of character, though. Lynette's a good girl. A good student. A good daughter and sister. She hasn't run away. My sister's sure she hasn't."

"What time did your sister call you?"

"2 a.m. I drove straight over."

"And you're living where now?"

I gave them my address. It wasn't a good address. A trailer park. I imagined this female officer's thoughts. She'd see me as trash. As all of us as trash. Lynette included.

"Lynette and her mother are close. Good friends. There's no family drama. No issues. She has no reason to run off. None. Something's happened."

"Whoa, slow down." Markham had an easy smile. Too easy for my taste. "One step at a time," he said. "One question at a time. There's no rush here. Just the collection of facts. Go ahead, Prentice."

The woman had her notebook out and turned toward me, her knees pressed together and her pencil at the ready. "When did your sister expect Lynette home?"

"10.30 p.m. Like I say, she's a good girl."

"And do you usually hear her come home?" Markham lifted his glasses and looked over at Genevieve. I'd practically forgotten she was there. Shit.

"Sometimes. If I'm awake. I go to bed earlier than Lynette does."

"I'm sure you do." He smiled at her, all reassuring and calm voiced. I knew he was an evil bastard, but Genevieve had no idea. "But what about your mom? Does she stay up waiting for Lynette to come home?"

I needed to stop this. "I just said she called me at 2 a.m., worrying about her daughter."

"If you could let her answer the question, Miss Silver?"

"Yeah," said Genevieve. "Yeah, she does."

"Including last night?" The woman leaned forward. I'd felt the question coming before she said it. The whole thing was a slow-motion train wreck.

"Last night?" I watched Genevieve's throat move, willing her to lie, just for Sal's sake, for Lynette's.

"Was your mom home at 10.30 p.m. last night? When your sister didn't come home?"

"No, but—"

"Listen," I burst out, "she was home late, but not very late. And she saw her daughter was missing. And she got

106

worried, and she called me. Whether Sal was here or not isn't the point. The point is her girl is missing!"

But Markham was already on his feet. "The point is, Miss Silver, that you can try and paint a pretty picture, but your sister is known to us. This is a small town. Your family is known to us. And yes," he turned to Genevieve then, a small concession that I knew was totally meaningless, "we will do all we can to find her. We'll talk to the school. To her friends. But most likely your sister is a runaway. The sooner you all start accepting that, the better off you'll all be."

I watched them gather their things. The woman took the photograph I'd gotten out and the slip of paper with the names of Lynette's three friends and the boy, Connor Goodman. But I saw what would happen. The list would be tucked in some folder, slid into some file cabinet somewhere. The police didn't give a damn about Lynette. And they were never going to.

After they left, I sat back on the sofa and put my hands on my cheeks. My skin felt hot. Lack of sleep made my eyes itch. I closed them, pressing cool fingertips against the heat of my eyelids, while Genevieve moved around the room, hovering, like some dumb bug.

I needed her to stop hovering.

"Don't fucking speak, Genevieve," I said. "I'm going to open my eyes soon. And I don't want to have to look at your whiny bitch face when I do it. Do you hear me? Take your stupid ass to your room and don't come out till I tell you."

TWENTY

Jen
Now

I don't speak to Jocelyn for four days straight. I've wanted Nina to have a family. But maybe Jocelyn is not the kind of family we need. On the odd occasion my mind drifts toward the father who abandoned me, I shut myself down. The last thing I need is another crazy relative. If he'd wanted to find me, he could have. He's as dead to me as if he really had died in a car crash. End of story. Being outwardly normal is my superpower, and so I complete my work on the microhistory and run laundry for Nina's visit with Booker in Vermont. He is in my thoughts, and I let him in, because it's better than thinking about my dad, or Jocelyn, or Natalie and Dan, and this whole farce of a situation I've brought us into. For four days I choose to be who Dan Burrows believes me to be. I don't mention Natalie, or his past, or our future, for that matter. We just live in this house like normal people. I let myself be nervous about taking Nina up and meeting Booker, like anyone would be nervous about meeting their ex and the father of their child, when their history is like ours. Which is not particularly complex. And entirely my fault.

My ability to acknowledge this is a recent development. Back nine years ago, when I took Nina and left him, everything was his fault, or if not his, then his mother's. I will ask how she is, Charmain, when I see him. And he'll tell me she can't wait to be with Nina, and I will know that to be true.

But before I can see Booker, I have a fire to light, and I need Jocelyn to watch it burn. I call her, and, of course, she acts as if our last conversation never happened.

"You have some news?"

"More of a plan. Are you busy tomorrow?"

"No."

"Good."

"Where are you? You sound out of breath."

"I just finished a run. I'm walking the neighborhood. To cool down."

"What if someone hears you?"

"I'm not an idiot, Jocelyn. Dan's on the Peloton. You're the one who told me Natalie's routines. I watched her drive out earlier."

"Hmm." I can hear some rustling from her end of the call. The unwrapping of a chocolate bar, I have no doubt.

"That stuff will kill you."

"Then I'll die happy. Come on, then. Tell me the big plan."

"I'm going to have a fight with Dan."

* * *

It's not hard to start the argument. I catch Dan at the worst time possible — when he's just in the door after an overnight shift. He wants to shower and then sleep. If Nina's out, he'll often suggest I take the shower with him and so far, I've never said no. Today, Nina is over at Daisy's house with the twins, and Dan is about to be disappointed.

The skin around his eyes is puffy and he walks in looking deflated. That's my cue to ask him how he is, to smile (very important to smile) and make him feel like his tough job is worth it because he gets to come home here, to me. How do I know that's my cue? Because he literally told me so. Dan is a person who likes things the way he likes them. And he gets what he wants because he asks for it. Another thing he literally told me about himself. I liked his honesty. I admired that about him. But his honesty is in question right now.

"Hey," he says, laying his suit jacket on the island and loosening his tie.

"Hey." I don't smile. Or make eye contact.

"Everything okay? Where's Nina? Is she home?"

"She's at Daisy's. And yes. Everything's fine. I suppose."

His eyebrows shoot up, but he doesn't press me. Instead, he sticks his face in the fridge and rummages.

"Coming upstairs?"

"I don't think so."

He stops in the kitchen doorway and frowns. "What's going on, Jen?"

"Natalie Preston."

His lips compress. "Come on, Jen. Natalie?"

"How well did you know her?"

"Are you being serious?"

"She knows more about you than I do!"

"What? No. Of course she doesn't. You're being ridiculous."

"Am I? She told me you were on the lacrosse team — first I've heard of it." My eyes are on him, glaring, asking for a fight. But also watching. And his relief is palpable.

"So what?" He comes toward me and grips my shoulders. "Jen. High school sucked. Ithaca sucked. It's in the past. Not interesting."

I twist away from him. "Easy for you to say. But how do you think I feel, listening to Natalie Preston talk about you at school, and about that Lynette girl? You know she asked me the other day if you were a dog person, if you had a dog growing up, and I had no clue. She probably knows. She was probably just asking me to show up how little I know you. Whereas you and she went to school together. Went through a trauma together . . ."

"Whoa, whoa, whoa. Jen. What trauma?" He runs his hand through his hair. Part of me feels sorry for him. He really does look tired. I tell that part of myself to button it.

"Look, you clearly didn't want to talk to me about it. But Natalie Preston made the disappearance of that girl sound like it was a major deal. You were all kids. And someone you knew had died. And so horribly. I googled it. There are a ton of articles. She was so young. You all were."

My tone is accusatory. I'm hoping for one of two reactions. What I think will happen is that he'll shut me down. He'll stomp off upstairs and decide he needs to have a talk with Natalie Preston. That's what I've prepped Jocelyn for. I'd prefer it if he reacted differently. I'm hoping that he'll open up. Sure, he's tired, but there's a chance he'll see that by talking, we can both feel better. I'm hoping he can tell me something I can believe about how well he knew Natalie and Lynette, something that will allow me to tell Jocelyn there are no answers here and I can get on with being Jen Silver and becoming Jen Burrows.

He does neither of these things.

"What is this really about, Jen?"

I have no idea what he means and say so.

He shakes his head. "No. This isn't about me, or about Natalie Preston or that girl." He looks angry, but also smug. Like he really thinks he has things figured out. "I know what you're doing."

"What I'm doing?" I sound lame, repeating him, and I'm not prepared for what comes next.

"Trying to create something. Start an argument. Tonight, of *all* nights." He raises his eyebrows. I see the beginning of a sneer. "I mean — this isn't about me at all, Jen, is it? This is about what you're doing tomorrow. This is about Booker."

I almost laugh. Honestly, if his face were not quite so serious, I probably would laugh. After all I *am* trying to create this drama, and I am doing it because I'm seeing Booker tomorrow. But only because I'll be out of the way and Dan will have his first real opportunity to try and talk to Natalie Preston.

That's what I've been aiming for. That's why I have Jocelyn lined up and available all day, basically spying on them both.

"What does you not sharing anything have to do with Booker?"

"You tell me."

"There's nothing to tell."

"Have you told him we're getting married?" Dan pulls at his tie, while staring at me.

"I . . ."

"You haven't. And why is that?"

"You know why."

"No." He shakes his head and comes to stand opposite me, across the island. His tie is stretched between his fists on the granite. His shoulders narrow and he leans in. "No. I know your *stated* reason — that there's 'no point rocking the boat' until a date is set. But you see, when you've been apart from a guy for nine years, and you're living in a big old house with a different guy who you've been with for three, it seems to me that there is no boat with the first guy left to rock. You shouldn't care a damn about Booker. And yet you clearly do."

I'm shaking my head. And yet he's not wrong, not entirely. He's also not finished.

"You know what I think? I think we're having this made-up little fight because you're seeing him tomorrow. I think you're pushing me, trying to wind me up, because your panties are in a knot about seeing your ex. I don't know if you still think you're making up your mind between the two of us. Right now, I'm not sure I even care if you are. But I do know you're being a bitch, and I'm way too tired to play into it. So, have a great evening. I'm going to bed."

* * *

I sit there for a while after he's gone upstairs, just looking at this kitchen and thinking.

I'm shaken up. Being called a bitch is not my favorite thing. It stirs up bad memories, particularly around those years in Rochester. A few deep breaths are required. I've never believed Dan had anything to do with Lynette's death and tell myself I still don't. We — Jocelyn and I — have always thought Connor Goodman and Natalie were most likely the ones with the secrets, the ones we believed had the answers or at least some clues for the answers we need. In the face of how much Natalie clearly cared about my sister, I've started doubting there are any answers to find. Perhaps she's right, and Lynette's death really was an accident. If it was, there's no need for me to prod and poke at Dan in the hopes he and Natalie will show us the truth. This whole argument might never have happened. The way he just belittled me, the fact he called me a bitch — none of that need ever have been said.

Except it was.

And I don't like it. I don't like it one bit.

* * *

Dan and I spend the night in the same bed but with our backs to each other. My alarm goes off at six and he doesn't stir. I suspect he's awake, but if he is, he's not in the mood for reconciliation. Fine. I shower and wake up Nina. Her bag is all packed and she doesn't want breakfast. Hopefully she'll sleep for a few more hours in the car. We're on the road by seven. Dan doesn't get up. Fair enough, he's angry with me, but not saying goodbye to Nina is churlish. I tell her he's tired after work the day before.

It's about a four-hour drive to Poughkeepsie. While Nina sleeps, I think again about Booker. We do this trip maybe four times a year, and I'm always nervous about how I'll feel when I see him again. Dan's accusation from the night before rattles around my head this time, though, jostling among the memories. He's way off base on one thing, that's for sure. There is no "making my mind up" option, no choosing between Dan and Booker for me. I don't think Booker would have me back if I begged him.

* * *

113

We met in the bar I worked at in Burlington, when I was nineteen years old. He played violin in a band everyone loved. The staff, the regulars, we all treated Booker's band like they were our own favorite celebrities. Which, in a way, they were. There was always a lot of flirting, mainly coming from the lead singer and the drummer, who would chat up the three of us girls who worked most weekends. They'd buy us drinks and invite us to parties, but Greg, the bar manager, would always send them packing, saying we were too young for them. With Booker it was different. He was nearer us in age, a college student who'd joined the band for some extra cash. When he started hanging around the bar when the band wasn't playing, Greg nudged me in the ribs and told me the good kid looked like he had his eye on me. The good kid. He was right. Booker graduated *summa cum laude* in journalism from the University of Vermont.

I was never sure what he saw in me. Self-confidence wasn't my strong suit. When I met his cousins for the first time one Fourth of July, his cousin Ed told me how happy he was to meet Booker's "hilarious" girlfriend.

"Hilarious?" I queried. "Not drop-dead gorgeous?" And he'd gone off laughing. Problem was, I was only half kidding. Booker, in my eyes, could have gotten with any girl who took his fancy. Why me? Me, with my straggly black hair and cheap, thrifted clothes? With my nerdy love of books and a fascination for Dorothy Parker? I wasn't that funny, or pretty, or cool. Whenever I was with Booker I felt important, though. I felt like Jen Silver might be someone worth knowing. Whereas Genevieve Knox? I told him nothing about her at all.

* * *

Once Nina and I navigate the spaghetti twists and turns of the Pennsylvania Turnpike and head north on the I-95, my mind circles around to what might be happening back at home. Have I managed to push Dan into talking to Natalie? And will the technology really let Jocelyn spy on them from the comfort of her condo over fifty miles away?

I guess we're about to find out.

TWENTY-ONE

Jocelyn
Now

I can see it pains Jen to show me how to log in to their Ring and Blink systems. I'm sure as soon as she's back from meeting Nina's father she'll be itching to change every password. I'll never mention it, but I'll know. I've already watched Jen and Nina get ready to leave on their trip. It would give me such comfort to be able to keep an eye on them. You would think she'd understand, but she doesn't. No, she'll be cutting off my access as fast as she can when she's back. For now, I'm just watching the Ring feed, staring at their gray front door, the huge pine tree in their front yard, and the other view of their closed double garage. I could look inside, but Dan Burrows eating his breakfast and either watching TV or doing a work-out sounds like a whole new level of boring to me. I position myself on the couch with my three monitors in my eyeline. If anything changes, I'm sure to see it, and the joys of Words with Friends and Candy Crush keep me company for now.

I've been lucky with this condo. Up here on the eighth floor I've a view of the Bay and watch the sea and the sky change color all day long. It's not the kind of place I ever imagined being able to afford. Marcie left me all her furniture and only charges me a pittance for the sublet. Who would have thought a cat-sitting job in Rochester, New York, would lead to an easy life in a condo in Maryland? I'd been skeptical when Marcie moved down here and hooked up with Bob, but happy enough to cat-sit for weeks at a time whenever they went on vacation. She knew I liked being nearer Philadelphia and Nina, so when she moved in with Bob, and he said his allergies meant Seinfeld the cat had to go, it was as good as my lottery numbers coming up. Would I move down and look after Seinfeld full time? You bet I would. Like I told Marcie's daughter, it's also an insurance policy. Marcie can leave Bob whenever she wants to. When she finds him too annoying, she comes down here for a night or two. There's some upheaval, I'll admit. I have to shift my monitors and notebooks off the dining room table, and sleep in the actual bedroom instead of on the couch with Seinfeld. But it's a small price to pay. And right now, Marcie and Bob are on a nice long cruise. There is nothing to come between me and my surveillance of Dan Burrows.

* * *

It's the garage camera that kicks into action first. The door is opening, and I wait to see if Dan is heading out somewhere. Let's hope not. For a while nothing else happens. I stand up. I sit down. I think about needing to pee. Seinfeld brushes against my leg and I pick him up for a hug. He's not a fan of such attentions, but I'm working on him. Just when I'm ready to go back to Words with Friends, I see Dan. He comes and stands in the garage doorway, looking down into the neighborhood. He's dressed in casual weekend clothes — shorts, polo shirt, loafers with no socks — but he looks tense. His arms are folded across his chest, one foot taps the ground.

"Oh, Seinfeld," I whisper. "I think we might be in business."

I slide into my office chair and grab my pen. I've a new yellow legal pad and I make a note. *Garage door. 9.42 a.m. Dan waiting. Anxious.*

Now he's stepping back. I can't read his facial expression anymore, but I watch Natalie Preston quickly cross the screen and enter the garage. It's hard, in the shades of gray the camera offers, to be sure, but I think I see his hand on her arm, they may even have embraced. Heat floods my face as I grab my phone. I connect to the Blink system in the kitchen hoping that's where they are headed. It has the best camera angle, my best chance of seeing everything.

The audio kicks in first. Sounds of a door closing and footsteps. Then Dan's voice.

"Why the fuck have you been talking to Jen about Lynette Knox? About me?" He walks into the kitchen in front of her, not even bothering to see her reaction. I see her, though. She pulls up short like she's been smacked in the face.

"Don't speak to me that way."

He turns and leans against the sink, arms folded. She's just in view, at the corner of the screen and her hands are on her hips.

"Alright." He draws in a deep breath. "Alright, let's start again. "Tell me everything you've told her."

"I've told the story we agreed on. The same story we've told for years. What do you take me for? I don't see what's got you so wound up about it."

Dan rubs a hand across his forehead. "*She*'s wound up about it. Or more about you. It's hard to say which. You must have said something that implied we used to be together."

"Absolutely not. Listen. I've spoken to her a grand total of five times. You've barely been mentioned."

But there must be something in her face that surprises him because he steps toward her. "What?" he says.

Now her arms go across her chest. "Okay, so when she first said your name, it was a shock. We were on Courtney's patio. I dropped a glass."

"For fuck's sake, Natalie."

"It was fine. Totally fine. It seemed like an accident. It was an accident. The next time I saw her she was completely normal. She was over asking about Wookie and . . ."

"Wookie?"

"Our dog."

Even fifty miles away and through a screen I can sense Dan Burrows' disdain.

"After that I saw her here . . ."

"Hang on. Back up. She said something about a dog last night, before I texted you."

I write that down in all caps. *THEY'RE TEXTING.*

"It sounds like she was a little cray-cray last night. I know she's your wife and all, but—"

"Are you saying she came over to your house to talk about a dog?"

"Yes. She said Nina was desperate for one and said she wasn't sure if you would like one or not. I guess it was a bit odd. She said she didn't know if you'd had a dog growing up. But I didn't say anything to suggest I knew you hadn't. Nothing. I had no idea at that point if you'd want to admit our connection, so I was super careful."

"Hmm. I don't like it. I've never heard Nina say she wants a dog."

"Trust me, Dan. All ten-year-old kids want a dog."

"I don't know. I don't like it."

"What?"

I watch her move closer. And Dan step away.

"This." He waves his hands at the space between them. "What's in the past should stay there."

"And that includes me?"

"You. What happened. All of it. I'd have thought you felt the same." I watch as he rubs the bridge of his nose. "After all, how is your dad these days?"

My scalp prickles. His tone has shifted. I should be writing this down. I lean into the screen.

"He's sick, actually."

"Right." Dan is nodding slowly, his chin pushing forward. "How bad?"

"Bad enough." Her voice turns icy. "And how about your family? How's Patrick? Still driving around in some banged-up truck?"

I manage to scribble *Her dad. Sick. Patrick?? Truck??*

"He's good, thanks."

Dan's voice sounds tight. They fall into silence. I'm trying to think if I've ever met Dan's brother but come up blank.

"Look, Natalie, it's not personal. But surely you can see this is far from ideal."

"Well, it's not every day your ex moves into your neighborhood."

He shakes his head. "You're not kidding. At least Jen has no idea about that."

"Ah."

"What?"

"You may want to tell her."

"Tell her what?" His voice comes through louder. I see Natalie Preston tense up again.

"Tell her we dated in high school."

"And why would I do that?"

"Because it's true, for one thing."

"The truth is not exactly what we're going for here."

"I know that. But didn't we always agree to stick to as close to the truth as we could? And anyway. Brad knows."

"Who the fuck's Brad? Oh God. He's your husband." Dan plants his elbows on the island and props his face in his hands.

"Listen. At first, I thought you were right to keep the past in the past. But Brad thinks it's funny. There's no way he's not going to mention 'us' to one of the other husbands." She moves to stand opposite him. "And so, I was thinking. What's the big deal? Really. I mean, why haven't you told her already? If anything, *not* telling her is much more weird and suspicious. How long have you been together? You must have had an old-boyfriends-old-girlfriends conversation. For Christ's sake, she's had a child with someone else. You must have talked about that."

"I don't talk about Ithaca. Ever. To anyone. We agreed."

"No, Dan. We agreed not to talk about that night. And I haven't. But you're going to have to tell your wife something

119

about me now, and you need to do it soon. Brad knows you were my first. And you can stop looking like that. It's the kind of thing couples tell each other."

I can hear her implication through the screen, even though I can't see her face at all now. I wonder what she really thinks of Dan Burrows.

"You've always been way too closed off," she says.

"Can you blame me?"

"Yes, Dan. You know I can."

* * *

She leaves without another word, but I sit for some time watching Dan at the kitchen island. I feel waves of emotion. Most of all, I feel vindicated. It jolts through me, a defibrillated pleasure, long-awaited and needing to be savored. For years I've told Jen that Natalie Preston knew more than she was saying. For *years*. And I was right. Phrases jump out at me, and I write them down, afraid the conversation will slip away like a dream.

> *We agreed not to talk about that night.*
> *Didn't we agree to stick as close to the truth as we could?*
> *How's Patrick? Still driving a banged-up old truck?*
> *How is your dad these days?*

Words with Friends and Candy Crush hold no interest for me now. I need the hours to pass and Jen to call. I need to speak to her before she goes home to that man.

120

TWENTY-TWO

Jen
Now

Booker is waiting in the parking lot when we arrive. Nina flings herself from the car and into his arms. It has been six weeks since she saw him last, although he Facetimes with her almost every day. He's a good dad and I'm glad she has him.

"Hi." He has his arm around her, and her head is tucked up against his chest. He lifts his free hand in a greeting. His smile is a little tentative. His eyes are as warm as ever.

"Hi." No hugging. No touching. The pleasure I feel every time we meet turns bittersweet so quickly. "Shall we hit the welcome center before we go?"

"Sure."

We use the facilities and buy some water. Booker has brought a cooler with hoagies which he slings over one shoulder. We take the elevator up to the bridge and start our walk. Nina is the center of attention, chattering on about Daisy's twins who had never even heard of the Hudson River until Nina told them all about it the day before.

"You don't know what you don't know, baby," her father says. He's admonishing her a little but I'm okay with that.

We've talked about how smart she is, how it's important she learns to be proud of herself without belittling others.

"True. And they know now, anyways," Nina agrees, dashing off ahead. We both smile. She is getting older, but the long, straight walkway across the river is so inviting. Every time we come here there are children running and skipping their way across with the wind blowing their hair and their eyes wide, drinking in the expanse of air above and sea below. It's a precious place.

"How's the new neighborhood?" he asks.

"Good. Very grown-up."

"Middle-class?"

"Totally. I have my own walk-in."

"No?" He clutches at his chest. "Be still my beating heart. It sounds so exciting."

I shake my head but I'm smiling. "It's a great place for Nina to grow up."

He nods and we keep on walking. It's my turn to ask a question.

"How's work?"

"Good. Although things may be changing."

I throw him a quizzical look.

"Don't say anything to Nina, but there's an opening at the *Inquirer*."

That means Philadelphia. "Wow," I say.

His brow creases. "You don't mind, do you? I mean, I think it will be better for us. For Nina. I mean."

"Yes." I swallow and it's like there's a stone lodged at the back of my throat. I feel like choking. "So, how serious a prospect is it? Would it be soon?"

"I think there's a good chance. They know I have family there. I could be in Philly by Christmas. Would you be okay with that?"

I realize he's nervous. "I think it would be wonderful! You're Nina's father. She loves you! And I know we all love this bridge walk but really? To have you so close to her and seeing her regularly? She'll be so thrilled."

122

"And you? And Dan?"

"Dan?" I wave a hand in the air. "Dan's so busy with his work. No, that's not fair. I mean, it's true he's busy but he's great with Nina. Always has been. I shouldn't be so flippant."

"Tough to change the habits of a lifetime?"

"Fair point." We walk on in silence. It's hard to process Booker's news. I never thought he'd leave Vermont. "What does Charmain think?"

"Ha." He nods and gives me a rueful smile. "Not crossed that bridge yet. I figured I wouldn't get her all worked up it until it's a sure thing."

"Like Nina." *Did I say that out loud?*

"Yes." And he nods again.

Talking with Booker about his mother, Charmain, is always treacherous, and comparing her to our ten-year-old is not exactly kind. I'm kicking myself, but he doesn't seem annoyed. If only he'd been so laid-back in the past. But no. I'm not being fair. While at the time I believed Charmain was pushing me out — and said so — his defense of his mother really was justified. I see it now. I made her the scapegoat for my own fears and insecurities about becoming a wife, about being a parent. Charmain didn't push me out. I ran.

"What's with the rings?" he asks.

Damn. I look at my hands. I'm wearing the cheap Amazon ring and our engagement ring, the one Booker gave me, the one that started the row that ended it all. *Damn.*

"Ah. Well, it's complicated." I glance at him. His expression is hard to read, especially with his sunglasses on. I hope mine are providing similar protection. This is going to be tricky.

"Try me," he says. "I'm assuming you would have told me if you'd actually gotten married."

"Totally! I am totally not married."

"Because it would be a bit weird, right? To get married wearing an engagement ring you got from someone else."

"Right! Of course."

"So, what gives?"

"You will think it's dumb. It probably is dumb. But I had some anxiety about moving into this new neighborhood. I wanted it to go well for Nina. For us to be accepted." I gesture toward her. She is yards in front of us now but has stopped to lean over the barriers and watch a flock of birds wheeling over and under the bridge.

"Go on," he says.

"The realtor said some of the neighbors weren't happy the home was going to be a rental. I wanted to fit in, not ruffle feathers. I figured it would be easier if our new neighbors believed Dan and I were married."

"But you're not."

"We're not."

"I'm struggling to see Dan agreeing to this."

I half-smile at him. "He was not totally on board with the plan."

"Not sure anyone would be. I mean, you're walking about wearing our ring. While living with him. Doesn't that seem kinda wrong?"

"He doesn't know where it came from."

Booker stops. "That's even worse, Jen!"

"I know, I know. Please. Keep walking." I grab his arm and pull him back into motion. My eyes are on Nina. She picks up on everything and I don't want her to see any tension between us when I have to say goodbye to her for a whole week in just an hour or so.

Silence settles between us. I hate it. "I'll stop wearing it," I say. "It was a mistake. I'll tell him I lost it. Or something."

"No."

"No?"

"That's just more lies."

* * *

We keep walking. I ponder the word "more". It hurts, but mainly because it's true. When he asked me for honesty, I gave him lies. Even in our last argument as a couple, I ended with a

124

lie. There were things he didn't know about me, I said. There were things in the past I didn't like to talk about. But I'd tell him, I promised. If he went to his parents' house for the night. If he just left me in our apartment with Nina, gave me that bit of alone time, then we could meet up in the morning and I'd tell him my secrets, every one of them. He looked at me. I'll never forget how he looked at me. Doubtful. Hopeful. Weary. Eventually he nodded and left, and the minute the door closed behind him I started packing. I took Nina and we got on a bus to Rochester and Jocelyn. I sent him an email (an email!) saying he could see Nina soon but the rest of it — us, being together, getting married — was all too much. I said he was too pushy, and his mom hated me. It would never work, I said.

The truth was, *I* didn't work. On the surface, I functioned reasonably well. I fed her, loved her, cared for her. She was tiny, beautiful, and perfect. But I had a lot of trouble sleeping. Having Nina made me revisit a past I'd been ignoring since the day we left Ithaca. Burying the past was all Jocelyn's idea, but I perpetuated it. Made a deliberate choice. I chose to go to college as Jen Silver, embracing the lies we had told in Rochester. I chose to forget I had ever been Genevieve Knox, to forget I had lived for twelve years in Ithaca, to forget I had a sister whose death never made sense and a mother who didn't love me enough. I blocked out my past entirely. And for a couple of years, it worked. I made friends, studied, took a side job, met Booker. My story, Genevieve's story, was erased. Until Nina.

Who can have a child without looking back at the past? Don't we tend to parent as we were parented? Or as we wish we'd been parented? Within minutes of giving birth, I was swamped by unexpected emotions about my own mother. Had she *ever* loved me like this? Had she felt the pumping adrenaline of love when she first laid eyes on me? I doubted it. I really did. She had felt that way about Lynette: that I could believe. But if she'd felt about me the way I felt about Nina, how could she ever have abandoned me? How could she? Unless there was something wrong with me.

125

My own thoughts became a kind of poison. I didn't deserve happiness when all day every day I pretended to be someone I wasn't. I felt unworthy. To be a proper parent to Nina I had to stop lying about who I was, but I couldn't tell Booker the truth. I had never talked about what happened. To anyone. If I couldn't be honest with Booker, how could I marry him? And so I ran back to the only person I didn't need to tell the truth to. Jocelyn.

I think all this, as Booker and I continue to walk. It's not new ground. I feel an urge to stop on this bridge and blurt it all out. It's physical. Like a fist has formed in my chest and I'm ready to spill, but up ahead Nina turns and grins. The fist dissolves. She calls Booker over, and he picks up his pace, leaving me behind. I watch him put an arm around her shoulders and pull her into his hip before they walk on, holding hands. What a fucking mess. I can never tell Booker the truth. It might be one thing, now, to tell him about my family, but what about Dan? What about Natalie Preston and the neighborhood move? How can I explain how Jocelyn forced me into it? I'm only just beginning to see how weak I am around her, how I've allowed her to manipulate me into this mess. Yes, I can tell him I went into it believing we'd find nothing out, believing I loved Dan, and was building a better life for our daughter. But do I? Am I? What's happening back in the neighborhood? And how does Booker moving to Philly fit with my plan?

I look at them, my daughter, and her father, moving as one, happy together. I swore I'd keep Nina ignorant of all the drama of my past. I've never wanted to burden her with it. She's another reason I've kept the truth to myself all these years. And when I see her happy and carefree? That's when I know I'm doing something right.

On the drive back alone, I call Jocelyn. She has a lot to tell me.

126

TWENTY-THREE

Dan
Now

Jen's back early. I do the math. Even with no traffic she can't have been with Nina's dad for more than an hour and a half. Good. Maybe what I said last night made an impression. Still, I'm anxious to make things right and get everything out in the open about Natalie as soon as possible.

"Hi!"

I'm at the island when she walks in through the garage. Everywhere is spotless. There's a baked ziti in the oven. Garlic bread baking. The house smells welcoming. Her nostrils flare just a little. Also good.

"How was the drive? Can I get you a beer?"

"Sure." She sounds okay. Maybe a little tired? By the time she's dumped her purse and hung up her jacket I have her drink in my hand and a contrite look on my face.

"Listen, Jen, I just want to say I'm sorry. For last night. You know. The way I spoke. It was wrong."

Her lips compress and her eyes scrunch. She's weighing me up. My expression, my words.

"You were kind of mean."

"I'm not proud of myself." I try for sheepish. "I guess I was jealous."

Her shoulders drop and she reaches for the beer. Our fingers touch. "Maybe I was too."

This is good. The charge in the air drops and it seems like we are past the awkwardness. Normal service is resumed. She tells me about the drive, about how hard it was to say goodbye to Nina for a week, but she knows it's the right thing to do. We eat. We drink some more. It should be a good evening. We should be getting ready to watch some Netflix or having sex with the bedroom door open because Nina's not there, and delightful as she is, there's no denying I love these weeks when she's gone and we can just *be*, without being parents — but no. I have this shit Natalie dropped on me to deal with. I *have* to talk to Jen about Ithaca. I wait till we're done eating.

"There was something else I wanted to say."

"Shoot."

"About last night."

Her brows snap together. "Okay?"

"About Natalie Preston."

Her face clouds.

"You know I love you, right?" I say. "And you know I don't really like talking about exes and so on."

"We agreed."

I nod. It was, after all, one of the reasons her already having Nina never bothered me. I wanted — still want — to be with someone who lives in the now, looking forward, not back. Jen has never been one for talking about her childhood or Booker and why they split. It's suited me. We've suited each other. If I learned one lesson from what happened to us in Ithaca, it's that turning the page and moving on *works*. You can get past anything if you decide that's where it belongs — in the past. I could kill Natalie. Really, I could.

"Natalie Preston was more than just someone I knew at school."

128

"Oh."

Her mouth actually forms an "o". I plow on.

"We were together at high school. For a bit. I may have been — well, she may have been my . . ." The words won't come.

"My God. You're telling me you lost your virginity to one of our neighbors?"

I look down at the island. "Yes. And I didn't say so right away because I was embarrassed. And it was years ago. But after last night I realize I should have. I need to be more open and honest."

I risk glancing up at her. This needs to work. Offers of openness and honesty. What woman doesn't love those words?

"But you're not interested in her now?"

"God, no!" I reach out and rub my hand over her knuckles. "Not at all. You know I'm here to be with you! I'm the one always trying to get you to marry me, aren't I?"

She smiles and tilts her head to one side. "Good. Because if you were seeing her behind my back . . ."

"Never. I've met her that one time, the other Saturday. I swear."

Jen closes her eyes for a moment. What is she thinking? Maybe relief? She grabs my hand and squeezes it. "Honestly, Dan, so long as you're sure it's all in the past, I'd understand if you wanted to talk to her." She looks me square in the eye and I stare right back.

"Nope. No interest."

"You say that, but it's like I said last night. You went through a lot together. Don't avoid her on my account. We can be grown-ups. I just met up with my ex. No reason for you not to do the same."

"How was he?"

"Booker? The same. Happy to see Nina. We didn't talk much. Just did the loop across the bridges."

She pushes back her stool and starts gathering the dishes.

"Here, let me help." I grab the empty ziti dish, take it to the sink and run the hot tap.

"Glorious garlic bread," she says. "Although I'm struggling for a zee word to go with the ziti, delicious though it was."

"I was thinking about this earlier. What about Zen? Zen ziti. Do you think Nina would approve?"

"We can ask her."

"I will. And I'll say sorry for not saying goodbye this morning. Did she notice?"

Her back is to me, as she stacks the dishwasher. "She didn't say anything."

"Good." I grab my phone and text the kid. "Wine?"

"Sure. Sounds perfect. I could do with some mindless TV to watch too."

"Also readily available." There's a smile on my face, genuine now. I've told her about Nat, and she's barely asked a question. My apology for last night wasn't too painful to deliver, either. I'm thinking we'll have a couple of glasses of wine followed by make-up sex. I might even apologize a bit more. See if it turns her on. She heads upstairs to change into PJs while I take the wine to the living room. We need to order some furniture. Her two-seater sofa from the apartment in Philly has seen better days. Maybe something leather, something substantial. I pick up my phone and look for ideas.

"We should shop for a sectional for in here," I say when she comes in. "Might be easier without Nina. Too boring for that live wire. I'm off on Wednesday. We could get lunch."

"Sounds good." She curls up beside me. Life is good.

"*Ozark*?"

Jen nods. It's a good show but I've already watched this episode. At the hospital there can be hours when I can't sleep or unwind. Shows like this one help. And then it relaxes me at home, watching something together that I've already seen. I let my mind drift to Natalie. I used to be so obsessed with her. What a fool. It was the chase, the conquest, that drove me, nothing about her is particularly remarkable. I looked at her today and felt nothing. She's not aged badly. Still fit and firm. Dyed hair but not a bad approximation of her natural color.

Whereas Jen is younger, and hotter, and also not so fucking bitchy. I think about Natalie mentioning Patrick. Only fair, I guess, since I brought up her father. The doctor in me should feel sorry for him, but I feel nothing.

On the TV a middle-aged couple are arguing. Some downtrodden man called Carl and his antagonistic wife. She's about to die. She's winding him up. Criticizing. Even starts jabbing a finger in his face, saying she should have married his brother. He's going to smack her and she's going to fall, tumbling over a low road-side barrier and down a slope into water. The first time I watched it, I never saw the Ithaca connection. Now it's all I see.

"Wow."

Although she says the word, I know Jen's not shocked. That's the kind of show this is, after all. But then she surprises me.

"Speaking of brothers," she says. "How's Patrick?"

TWENTY-FOUR

Jen
Now

As soon as we finish eating, I head upstairs. The lying bastard. I'd like to throw his ziti in his face and scream at him that I *know*. I know he met up with Natalie earlier, I know he has her cell number, I know that they're hiding something about my sister's death. I know it. Upstairs I change into my ugliest, oldest flannel PJs. He will want sex later and I'm not sure I can do it. Seeing Booker, having Dan lie to my face — it's a lot to take in. I'd like to go for a run but out here in the dark suburbs with no sidewalks or street lighting, it's not an option. Sharp longing for my cramped apartment in Philly brings tears to my eyes but I blink them away. I need to finish what I've started. And if Nina and I end up alone, back in those three rooms, sleeping to a backdrop of swirling lights and random sirens? So be it.

The generous glass of wine he's poured mollifies me a little when I get back downstairs. I sit in my usual corner of the couch and curl my legs up underneath me. Dan looks relaxed. He's internet shopping for furniture. In other circumstances I'd be all about it. But he's a liar. How much of a liar? Yet to be

132

determined. He puts on *Ozark*, our current binge watch, but it's hard to keep my mind on it until a woman's sharp, angry voice, rising up over a threatening audio track, grabs my attention. "I should've married your brother. He was three inches taller than—"

The husband shoves her, and she tumbles to her death.

"Wow," I say. And then I ask him how Patrick is.

He blinks a couple of times.

"Not great, as it goes. He got hurt at work. Broken ankle. I'm not sure when we'll see him next."

"That's terrible. Will he manage okay?"

He turns. "Why wouldn't he?"

"No reason, really. Only that he's living on his own." I take a big sip of wine. Dan's irritated and I'm not sure if that's a good thing or not.

The first time Nina and I met Patrick was at a basketball game. Someone Dan knew through work — a supplier of medical equipment, maybe — had a box. Dan had four tickets and chose to invite his brother, although he seemed to be regretting it before we even arrived. He'd wanted to pick Patrick up earlier in the day and drive us all to the game together using the one parking pass but no, Patrick had insisted on getting there on his own. That meant we were standing about outside the VIP entrance with hands in our pockets and steamy breath spiraling as Dan tapped out annoyed texts and paced back and forth. When Patrick did show up, he shambled over to us wearing a huge plaid overshirt, boots and a Seventy-Sixers bobble hat that at least fit the bill for the game, if not for the fancy box with free food and beer. Dan started in on him right away, not even introducing us until we were through security and on the escalator.

Patrick barely made eye contact with me. Nina, being Nina, stuck out her hand and Dan's brother did at least shake it, but whatever I'd been expecting, this wasn't it. Patrick was like a larger, lumbering version of Dan, socially awkward and an obvious introvert. He loved the basketball, though. While

Nina and I hung up our coats and were introduced to a couple of Dan's colleagues in the box, Patrick headed straight for the seats and didn't move for the whole game. He didn't take off his big plaid shirt, even as the temperature rose, and he didn't come up for any of the free food and drink. While Dan socialized, I fixed Nina up with chicken strips and a Sprite on a bar stool with a great view of the court. Patrick sat hunched over and focused. I remember thinking how different the brothers were and despite all the horns and music and lights, I had an intense longing for Lynette, for the chance to know how different or similar we might have turned out. What wouldn't I give for a chance to be irritated when she showed up late, for a chance to be annoyed with her?

"We should have him over for dinner," I say now. "When Nina's back. You could drive up and get him and he could stay over. You know how she likes him."

This is true. That first night at the basketball, Nina had slid down from her barstool while I chatted with some wives and slipped into the front row seat next to Patrick. She'd no real idea about the game but Patrick knew every player's name on both teams — I can hear Nina's voice saying "*both* teams" with great emphasis, as though Patrick were a genius or something — and he'd sat happily explaining offense and defense tactics, scoring, team history, everything her inquiring little mind had wanted to know.

"I don't know," Dan says now. "We'll see."

"Did he know Natalie, too?"

"What?" Dan's startled. He puts down his phone and twists around to face me. "Why would you ask that?"

"Why not? Hey. I thought we'd gone over this earlier. It's only a big deal if we make it one. I was just thinking about your brother and how you grew up together and it popped into my head that he might know Natalie too."

"He's older than me. He was out of school by the time I hooked up with her. And anyway, we weren't together long. Listen, are we watching this show or what?"

"The show! Sorry. I'll be quiet."

I shift around so that I'm fully facing the TV and do my best to look engrossed. In the corner of my eye, I see Dan pick up his phone again, although he's not texting, more swiping through some news browser or other.

"I can't wait to talk to Natalie properly about you guys, though," I say, eyes fixed on *Ozark*. "I'm going to get the full scoop on the young Dan Burrows."

I don't turn and he says nothing, but his movements change. He's texting now for certain. And I know who.

TWENTY-FIVE

Natalie
Now

I've been forcing myself to spend an hour in the room with my father every evening. Brad approves. It checks a box in his mind, confirming his wife is a good daughter, a good person. He doesn't say so, but it's all there in the way his hand pats my shoulder when I leave the kitchen to head upstairs and he makes a beeline for the family room, the TV remote, and whatever sports channel he's currently addicted to. It would never occur to him to come and sit up there with me and when Dan starts texting, I'm thankful.

> *If Jen asks if you knew Patrick, just say you didn't*

No *hello*, or *how are you*. No social niceties. Thanks, Dan. I purse my lips thinking of a few things I could say in response. I even start typing and then delete the words and put my phone down in my lap. Those three dots and then nothing will annoy him better than anything I could say would.

> *Nat?*

136

I do the same thing again, imagine him frowning, waiting, frowning some more.

I've told her we were together. Briefly. She's going to be asking about me/us. I need you to shut it down. Okay?

I take a long look at my dad. He could be sleeping, but it's hard to know anymore. Last week I found an old compact mirror that used to be my mom's and brought it up here. It sits on the window ledge behind me. I can see myself one day, maybe one day soon, picking it up and holding the mirror just above his mouth and nose waiting for a mist of breath, hoping there will be none. Dan has no idea about me or my life. I pick up the phone and tell him, okay.

Normally when I sit with Dad, I read a book on my phone or flick through Instagram. Not tonight. Tonight, I'm remembering Ithaca.

* * *

When Lynette first told me she was into Dan Burrows I didn't even know who he was. Well, that's not strictly true. His brother was friends with mine, and I'd seen him around. Dan was a nerd, but he played lacrosse and some of those boys were super-hot and popular. Dan wasn't popular but in a cool kind of way. Like he was on the edge by choice. Because he was hooking up with Lynette, I took a second look. She wasn't serious about him. She wasn't serious about anything. That was one of the things my parents hated about her. Or so they said.

I remember liking Dan's voice more than anything. His voice and his smile. He came across as kind of shy, but I caught him looking at me when he should have been paying attention to Lynette. She brought him to a couple of parties but kept abandoning him, probably on purpose, knowing her, and so when I saw him on his own it seemed like the nice thing to do to say hi and so on. Connor's house was where

137

most of the parties happened in junior year. It wasn't far from Mel's, so that's where I always told my parents I was. My mom believed me every time. And my dad? I'm not sure he cared where I was. He barely acknowledged I existed. Except when Lynette came over.

"Girls! How are we today?"

Wednesdays were the one night my dad came home early from work, and the one night of the week Lynette always ate with us. I thought of it as "fake Dad" night and found it pathetic the way he acted all nice when my friend was over. The rest of the week he came in much later and hit the scotch the minute his coat was off. Never on a Wednesday, though.

"We're good thanks, Mr. Eason," Lynette chirped. She'd been slouched at our kitchen table complaining about the way her English teacher had given them another closed book test when my English teacher let us have not just the book but also her handouts. It was a fair gripe, but when Dad came in, she straightened up and was all smiles. I guess I didn't mind. Lynette didn't have a dad. She envied me for mine, she'd said so directly, and so I let her think he was like this every night — and it felt good, for a few hours, to pretend it was true.

While my mom fixed dinner, Dad came and sat at the table next to Lynette. It was cringeworthy really, his small talk and teasing, his hints of what he was like "back in the day" when he was a jock (aka a jerk) and spent his days "working hard at school and play". The lift of his eyebrows on the word "play" set my teeth on edge and I glanced over at my mom. She had the whole works going on the stove — meat, potatoes, vegetable sides — but I'm sure she heard every word of his bullshit. Or maybe she liked it. Maybe, like me, she liked this one evening of happy families? I never asked her. Her answer might not have been something I wanted to hear.

"Nat has a new love interest," Lynette said, raising her eyebrows at my dad. "She's waiting for him to text right now."

I flushed. Wanted to kick her under the table. "Oh my God, Lynette."

"Language!" My mother *was* listening after all.

"Relax, Nancy." My dad shifted his chair closer to Lynette's. "Tell us more."

"His name's Dan."

"Please don't." I covered my face with my hands just as my phone buzzed on the table next to me. Lynette grabbed it.

"Hey!"

She flipped it open and showed the screen to my dad.

"He's sorry he missed you at school today," Dad said in a whiny voice with his lips pouted. I hated him for it.

"Give me my phone, Lynette."

She handed it back and threw me a wide-eyed stare. I had thought she didn't like Dan. Now I wasn't so sure. I stuffed the phone into my jeans pocket.

"So, give us the lowdown on the boy, then, Lynette," Dad said. "Is he good enough for my Natalie? What's he like."

"Super smart. A little . . . dull."

"Not your type, then?" Dad was grinning. It was embarrassing.

"Dad, can we drop this now? Mom, is dinner ready yet?"

"Oh, let me help, Mrs. Eason." Lynette pushed back her chair and jumped up, almost losing her balance. Dad grabbed her elbow to steady her. She flashed him a smile. I watched him watch her cross the kitchen and bend to pull four plates from the dish cupboard, wondering if I could slip from the room and text Dan back. My mother was not a fan of cell phones and limited my use of it. I had to plug it in every night in the kitchen and when I tried to sneak it upstairs she threw a major hissy fit. It was one of the few things my parents agreed on. They paid the bill. It was their phone, mine only on loan. My right to privacy was not up for debate. Even Sherri's parents let her have her cell phone in her room overnight and they were the most cautious parents we knew.

"I'm just going to the bathroom," I said.

"Going to text a boy, more like."

I ignored him. All that mattered was texting Dan Burrows.

The rest of the meal was unremarkable, but later I remembered it, almost like a scene from a movie. Because that's what Lynette became to me, after everything happened. My memories were a series of clips — short moments where I pictured her, heard her voice, remembered everything, from the swing of her long hair to the bitten fingernails she always tried to hide, to the threads of the friendship bracelet she wore on her left wrist. She was frozen in time and our friendship, prickly as it was, couldn't move forward. No more confidences. No explanations. No apologies. No forgiveness.

* * *

Dad's cough jerks me back to the present. I pick up his cup and poke the drinking straw between his lips. Until recently he's tried to lift his hand to the cup. Now there's barely a tremble of fingers. When I told the visiting nurse she gave me that wide-eyed gaze that says she's sorry, that she has seen this before, that it will not be long now. I school my features when I see her.

The drink settles him. His eyes are open but he's staring off to the window, looking right past me. They told me it would be good to talk to him, but God knows there's nothing I'd want to say to Dad that he wants to hear. I go back to my chair and check the time. Half an hour more.

* * *

Lynette's snark got worse the more I saw of Dan Burrows. And that just made me want to be with him more. He was kind of intense as a boyfriend, walking me between classrooms, even when his classes were two floors away from mine, dropping notes in my locker, texting me *good morning, beautiful* every day before I woke up. I'd be lying if I said I wasn't flattered. He made me feel special and isn't that what every teenage girl is waiting for? The boy that feels like "the one".

When his parents went out of town for the weekend it was only natural for me to spend the night. His older brother answered the door and looked at me blankly.

"Erm. Is Dan home?"

"Yes." He didn't move or open the door any wider, just stood in the gap looking like an older, heavier-set version of Dan with the same floppy hair and hooded eyes. There was something looser about him, though, as if his clothes were too large. He was wearing socks but no shoes and on one foot I saw his toes sticking out through a hole. *Not so like Dan, then*, I thought.

"Nat!" I heard Dan before I saw him and in seconds the door was wide open, and I was inside. The brother disappeared upstairs without an introduction and Dan was all apologies.

"Ignore him. Forget he's here. I do half the time. He'll stay in his room. Sorry. He's not very social."

"It's fine. You didn't tell him I was coming then?"

"No, I did. That's just Patrick. He's awkward. You know how it is."

I didn't. I loved my older brother, and wished he'd be home more, but I said none of that. I wasn't there to talk. Or I was, but I wasn't sure I could, at least not until after we'd done the thing we both knew we were planning on doing.

"So. What do you want to do? Watch a movie?" Dan rubbed his hands down the sides of his jeans, as uneasy as I'd ever seen him.

"Sure."

We were still in the hallway. His house was a little like Lynette's, although tidier, with a sitting room on one side that likely led into the kitchen at the back and a small dark dining room on the right, next to the stairs. I could see a big armchair in the sitting room, hosting a large marmalade cat bathed in what seemed to be the only light in the room.

"In there?" I asked. Dan was standing close to me. He bent his head.

"Or in my room."

It was a chance to back out. He was giving me that chance. But I had a backpack over my shoulder and a half bottle of vodka I'd pinched from the party at Connor's house the weekend before.

"Sounds good."

He leaned in and kissed me. His palm cupped the back of my head. He took my hand and led me upstairs.

The landing was small and dark. Four doors: two next to each other with a thin slick of light at the bottom. In Dan's room I could hear the blast and pop of his brother playing video games through the wall.

"Sit," he said.

"Have you got glasses?" I fished the bottle from my bag. "What's he playing?"

"Mario Kart. That music drives me crazy. Let me get the movie on. We can drown it out."

While he ran downstairs for glasses and some OJ to mix with the vodka I took in the room. Twin bed with a blue comforter. Old but clean-smelling. His room was super tidy with a stack of books on his desk and two pens lined up by them like soldiers. I pulled open the drawer on his nightstand. Paired socks. He'd only one poster on the wall, a blue-and-white graphic type thing of the Giants quarterback Kerry Collins which was kind of surprising as Dan had never so much as mentioned the NFL in the time we'd been hanging out together.

The vodka helped me chill a little. We heaped pillows and blankets and snuggled up in the dark with *Final Destination*. I'd seen it before, we both had, and after the first bit with the plane crash, we let the movie run and did the thing that I had come to do. It went okay, as far as I could tell, with nothing to measure by. I felt cold when he slipped from the room to get rid of the condom and was reassured when he returned and put his arm around me and kissed my hair. We drank some more vodka and at some point, I fell asleep.

In the morning it was kind of awkward. I felt weird taking a shower in someone else's house, and running into his brother in my towel was toe-curlingly embarrassing. But the way Dan walked into town with me holding my hand, the way he smiled at me when we said goodbye? He made me feel good. Like a grown woman. And I liked it, that feeling.

The only downside was, I'd told my parents I was sleeping over at Lynette's house. Which meant I had to ask her to lie for me if it came up at Wednesday dinner. It's another movie clip memory. Monday after school. At her house, in her room, door closed, music on loud. I'd come over with milkshakes from McDonald's to soften her up. We lay on her bed, like we always did, slurping the bottom of our cups as loud as we could.

"Oh, yeah. By the way. I told my parents I stayed here on Saturday night. You're good with that, right? It probably won't come up, but just in case."

The straw fell from her mouth, and she twisted around. I'd told her I was staying home on Saturday because my cousins were coming over. "Where the heck were you? Oh!"

My eyes fell from hers. I'd been half looking forward to this, wanting, but not wanting, her to know what I had done, but now that the moment was here the air seemed too thin and I felt nervous more than anything. What if she refused to lie for me? What if she said she'd lie for me and then didn't? A whole scene played out in my mind in under a second. Family dinner. My mom asking about our sleepover. Lynette's eyes going wide with fake surprise. A glance my way. A hand on her mouth. A silent betrayal.

She was still staring at me. "You were with him? All night?"

I nodded.

She stared at me still. And then her eyes softened. Her mouth split into a slow grin. "Natalie Eason," she said, "you're full of surprises these days."

* * *

What would she say if she could see me now? I've been staring into space, but slowly focus on my father, watching the glide of his eyeballs under thin closed lids.

What would Lynette have to say about him?

143

TWENTY-SIX

Jocelyn
Then

Officers Markham and Prentice came back the next day. Sal was up, although she looked like shit, and had barely eaten a mouthful of the soup I'd heated up. Genevieve wasn't doing much better. I'd seen her gnaw on a Hot Pocket but most of it had ended up in the trash. I seemed to be the only one with an appetite, but then maybe that was because I'd at least left the house and driven back to my place to shower and get some clean clothes.

Nothing about our situation felt real. Sal was coping by sitting by the phone, staring at the TV, and mopping up an unending stream of tears. Genevieve hid in her room, and I drove the streets, hoping to catch a sighting of Lynette. Ithaca looked entirely different suddenly. Full of twisting hills, thick with trees, crisscrossed by rivers and streams, overpasses and undergrowth — a hider's paradise, where each cold November night seemed darker and more threatening than the last. I drove and I looked, but I also took her photograph to the bus station, showing it to drivers and travelers because, while I'd never say it to Sal, Markham's suggestion that Lynette was a runaway was growing more palatable than the alternatives by the minute.

"Her friends haven't seen her," officer Prentice confirmed, once we were settled at the dining table with a mug of coffee each. My idea. She pulled out a notebook and flipped through the pages. "Natalie Eason saw her on Saturday, early evening. Lynette left Natalie's house and was supposed to meet up with Sherri Knowles at Connor Goodman's house but never appeared."

"Did you speak to the boy? Connor?" Sal leaned forward, and a little of the coffee she held spilled over the lip of her mug, landing on her sweatpants. She didn't notice.

"Yes."

"And?"

Prentice looked surprised and her eyes darted to Markham.

"We had a long chat with the Goodman family, Mrs. Knox," he said. "Both parents were present. I'd say that young Connor is a bit of a handful, but nothing out of the ordinary. He took advantage of his parents' absence to throw a party. Wasn't the first, won't be the last. But Lynette didn't attend it. Multiple kids agree. She wasn't there."

"No." Sal shook her head. "There's something off about him. I know it. He ran when we went to ask him about Lynny. Why run? Why?"

Markham shrugged. "Kids. He's the kind that's always up to something. Not to do with your daughter, though. I've plenty of experience of dealing with youngsters and he's as concerned about Lynette's disappearance as anyone." There was a pause, and he pushed his glasses up his nose before continuing. "Several of the kids we spoke to think it's very likely she's run off. To Binghamton, most likely, and then anywhere. She wouldn't be the first."

"No."

"People don't just vanish." Prentice's voice was soft, almost gentle. She spoke to Sal as she would to a child. "We've started speaking to bus drivers. No one remembers her yet, but she wouldn't have been trying to draw attention to herself, now, would she?"

"No." Sal was adamant.

"Is there anything missing from her room? Clothing? A bag?" Prentice asked.

"No."

Markham looked at me, eyebrows raised, asking for confirmation.

"It's hard to be sure."

The look Sal shot me was pure anger, but we'd already argued about this very question. Lynette's room was a mess. Sal didn't recognize half her clothes because the girl was in and out of thrift stores, and regularly traded outfits with her friends from school. As for a bag? If Prentice or Markham asked to look around the house beyond Lynette's room, they'd see every crevice from basement to attic was crammed with crap belonging to our parents. How could Sal know what was missing, when she'd no clue what was there in the first place?

"So, we can't rule it out." Markham nodded and got to his feet.

"Wait, what?" Sal's jaw was slack with surprise, as Prentice also stood up. "That's *it*?" Her voice rose, sharp and pointed. Her temper flaring. I knew the signs.

"You're still looking for her, here, though? In Ithaca?" I asked. They were moving toward the door, I tried to position myself between them and Sal. No point in antagonizing them. Poor Sal. In a flash I realized she'd believed the police were on her side, something I knew from day one they never would be. "When will you be back? Tomorrow? To keep us updated?"

"In a day or so," Markham said over his shoulder. Prentice was through the door already.

"What about Natalie Eason, then?" Sal called after him. I held her arms in the doorway, to stop her from following them down the steps and into the street. At least he had the decency to turn back. "Where was she on Saturday night?"

146

"With her boyfriend."

I felt Sal sag. She slipped out of my hold on her and turned away. I didn't need to look to know she was heading back to her seat on the couch, next to the telephone. I was about to close the door when I saw Markham pause at his car door, looking back up at me.

He didn't like me. Us. But I saw pity there, and a hint of something else. What? I pulled the door closed and walked down the steps to the sidewalk.

"No mother wants to believe their child has run off," he said in a low voice. "No matter how good or bad the mom, or the kid for that matter."

"She's certain," I said.

"But you're not."

"Not as certain as Sal is."

"Work on her," he said. "Make her see that's what's happened, most likely. You're a good sister. If Lynette has run off, there's every chance she'll come back. Get her to see it that way. Give her some hope."

TWENTY-SEVEN

Jen
Now

Book club is at Daisy's house. I expected Dan to make some joke about moms and wine and "book" club, but this morning when I told him the plan he just grunted. I can't decide if he's gone quiet because of Natalie, or if I'm reading into it too much and he's just pissed because we didn't have sex last night, even though Nina is away. It's on my mind, for sure, but I'm honestly so mad I don't know if sex would make everything better or worse. At least this evening he's at the hospital and I don't have to think about him. Instead, I can focus on Natalie.

She hasn't read the book. When I arrive, clutching my copy of *The Measure* under my arm and a bottle of Chardonnay in my hand, I see I'm the only one who's brought it. I immediately reset my expectations. Proper book clubs — in my mind, anyway — are about the book, and I love nothing more than flipping back through the pages, finding quotes or scenes, especially when it's a great read like this one. I've so much going on with Dan, Booker, Jocelyn, and Nina all jostling for attention in my head and driving me insane but reading *The Measure* has been a godsend. For all I've got on my plate, at least there's no little box on my doorstep containing a piece of string that measures out your lifespan. What a crazy novel. It ought to be perfect for a book group.

But Natalie's not the only one who hasn't found time to read it yet, and although Daisy and I declare we loved it, that's only half the room. Courtney is halfway through so we mustn't say a word — because "spoilers" — and Vicki says she's still got weeks to go on the hold list on her Libby app.

I'm last to arrive and take a seat in Daisy's generous living room. She has two beautiful white couches and an accent armchair, artfully arranged around a large square coffee table. There are decorative bookshelves on either side of an open fireplace, with pieces of kids' artwork, surprisingly not terrible, jostling for space between family photographs, books, and some ceramics. As I squish down on one sofa in between Natalie and Courtney, Daisy, in the armchair, is asking about swimming lessons. Lena has no issues, but her twin, Colin, is terrified of water.

Vicki's daughter swims for a team so she's ready with advice. "Call the Y. Request Emma Hill as her instructor. She's a high school sophomore. Beautiful, beaming smile. All the kids love her. She's a great kid."

"I will. Thanks!" Daisy takes out her phone and types in the name before jumping up to grab an open bottle of wine.

"So how are you doing without Nina?" she asks, handing me a generous pour.

"Good, thanks. Busy with work, though. You know how it is." Sitting in the center of this sofa is super awkward. There's nowhere to put my glass and nothing to do but keep sipping while the other women talk. I tuck my feet under me and try to look at ease. My smile feels like a grimace.

The upcoming homeowners' association meeting is high on Courtney's agenda so that's discussed next. I'm not really following the conversation. They're discussing other, older neighbors, dealing in names I don't yet recognize, and delving into the history of who has taken on which role, and who has never stepped up to the plate. I make a mental note to get something on the calendar so I can skip the meeting and let my mind wander to Booker. What would he make of this place, these people? What *will* he make of them? He texted earlier that he would drive Nina all the way home next weekend. He has an interview in Philly, so it works out. And it's only natural for him to want to see where we — *she* — is living now. Ever since I got the text, I've been imagining me and him and Nina living together as a family in a place like this. I can't see it. But is that because I can't see *us* as a family, or because I can't see us *here* as a family? Dangerous thoughts to entertain, with my trust for Dan evaporating. Enough to make me empty my wine glass way too fast. Daisy's quick to pour me a refill and take the opportunity to top up her own.

"How are your kids? All upstairs? Or out and about?"

"Two out, two in," Daisy says, rolling her eyeballs. "Once they start driving it's a whole new world."

"You can say that again." Vicki grins across at Daisy but in the corner of my eye I see Courtney's lips purse.

"There's also the country club for swimming," Courtney says, turning and patting the arm of Daisy's chair. My eyes flick to Natalie. She looks tense. Is it me, or is everyone ill at ease?

Vicki's phone rings and we all jump. She answers, and then walks from the room with the phone at her ear.

"I hope nothing's wrong," Courtney says.

"Jason probably can't work the stove or something," Natalie says. "He's hopeless." She sees I'm surprised and adds, "Don't worry. I'd say the same if he were here. And he'd admit it. Vicki's the boss. What about Dan? I imagine he's a bit more independent."

"For sure. He probably likes cooking more than I do."

"Geoff couldn't boil an egg," Courtney says, although it barely sounds like a criticism. I think about what Natalie said

150

about Courtney and Geoff. Courtney does not come across to me as a second wife, and certainly not as one who moved in here relatively recently. Vicki has been here since the homes were built and according to Jocelyn, Natalie bought her home in 2010. And yet it's Courtney who calls the social shots. Who'd have thought?

Vicki reappears, shrugging her shoulders. "I've got to head out, ladies," she sighs. "Madison's heading to camp tomorrow. She can't find anything and it's driving Jason bananas. A mother's work and all that." She hugs Daisy, squeezes Natalie's shoulders and gives Courtney and me a cursory wave as she heads out. Daisy takes the opportunity to pour more wine and Courtney switches into Vicki's chair so I hitch over to the corner of the sofa and have a better view of Natalie.

"So, is it just me?" Courtney asks. Her eyes sweep us all. I've no clue what she means.

"Don't, Courtney." Natalie pinches the bridge of her nose and looks pained.

Daisy, on the other hand, is amused. "You don't think she's gone to help with Madison's packing?"

"No! And neither do you, Nat." Courtney leans forward and puts her glass down on the coffee table. "If I know Vicki, Madison's been organized for a week."

"So, what's going on?" I ask.

"Thomas Price."

"You don't know that." Natalie shakes her head and folds her arms across her chest.

"What? What?" Daisy is all in, her face a little flushed from the wine.

"Look, Courtney, if you've got to talk about it all, at least let me leave the room." Natalie stands up. "I'll be in the kitchen. Come get me when you're done."

She leaves and for a second; I'm conflicted. Naturally, I'm curious to hear whatever axe Courtney wants to grind about Vicki's son, but the opportunity that's just opened up to speak to Natalie? I can't not take it.

"Bathroom break for me," I say. "Let me catch this story another time." As I follow Natalie out, Courtney crosses the room and pulls Daisy into a conspiratorial whisper. I hope I never hear a group of adults talk about my kid this way.

I take a quick trip to the powder room and then join Natalie in the kitchen. She's leaning against the island, studying the photographs tacked to Daisy's fridge.

"You didn't stay to hear Courtney's story?"

"How interesting can it be?" I shrug. "Kids fall out all the time."

Her brows contract a little, into a half-frown. "True."

"Yeah," I say. "I had these three best friends at school in Rochester. We were bonded, inseparable." I'm winging it here. "And then there was a boy. He dated one of my friends — this girl, Claire — for three months and the rest of us hated him. We weren't quiet about it either. So, no surprise, they split, but then one of the other two — Mia, who'd been maybe the worst of us about how terrible he was for Claire—"

"She started dating him?"

"Exactly. And Claire could not get past it. Who could blame her?" I shrug again. "But when it came down to it, we were just kids."

"Kids can make mistakes, though. Big ones." Her face is somber, and I know she's thinking about Ithaca. About my sister. There is guilt there — in her face, her voice, everywhere. How can I get her talk? How?

Right behind her on the corner counter I see a bottle of vodka, a full one. Alcohol, I think. It's not nice. But life's not nice, as I know all too well.

I grab the bottle. "Let's do a shot."

At first, she recoils, shaking her head, but I can be persuasive when I want to be. "Come on. Live a little. We could have a toast. We have a lot in common." I'm grinning as I say it, keen to put her at ease. My smile comes easily. It is kind of a funny situation. I mean, I know she knows I know. I'm as sure as I can be without laying eyeballs on his phone that Dan has

152

texted her since his "confession" the other night. "You know, Dan's not a talker," I go on, "but I did get the impression you two were quite the item back in the day."

Her cheeks flush and she nods at the vodka bottle. "Why not," she says. Natalie's familiar enough with Daisy's kitchen to lay her hands on a couple of shot glasses and we take a hit. Then another. She clutches her chest, and I stick my tongue out, like I'm breathing fire. We're both laughing.

"Was he a mistake, then?"

"What?"

"You said kids make mistakes. I know I did. Was Dan one of yours?"

She shrugs. "Yes and no. He was kind of intense. Is he still?"

"About work, yes."

"Brad's the same."

"And does it bother Brad? Dan, I mean? Being here?"

"No!" Natalie's smile is warm and genuine. She reaches for the vodka bottle. "Just one more. Then we'd better get back in there." She knocks it back. "Brad thinks it's hysterical. Says he can't wait to meet him."

"Lucky you. Dan is not a fan of my exes. Well, one ex in particular."

"Nina's dad?"

I nod. Maybe the third shot wasn't such a great idea. I'm supposed to be bringing up Patrick, not Booker. "He's going to be here soon. He's bringing Nina home. I haven't told Dan yet."

Natalie pulls a face. "I can see that being awkward. You maybe want to prepare him. The Dan I knew did not like surprises." She scrapes back her stool, ready to head back to join the other ladies.

"I thought maybe I'd invite his brother over. To be, I don't know, a buffer or something. Did you know Patrick? Back in Ithaca?"

"No." She's rinsing our glasses in the sink and has her back to me, but I see her face in the kitchen window. Her eyes close and then open again. "Never met him."

153

TWENTY-EIGHT

Jocelyn
Now

The problem with Jen is she's too nice. She sees the best in people. I. Do. Not.

Sure, Dan texting Natalie behind her back has her rattled, but Jen's seduced a little by this new lifestyle, I can tell. She wants answers about Lynette still, but if the truth is ugly? If Dan and Natalie were somehow involved? Jen can tell me she's prepared until she's blue in the face, but I've known her all her life and she's always been a dreamer. I, on the other hand, am a do-er. It's time to shake things up.

I've met up with Sasha almost every day since our fun excursion to NYC. For some reason she's obsessed with iced caramel lattes, so the local coffee shop is our go-to meeting point and, despite some reservations at the cost, their iced mocha has won me over. When I meet her on Tuesday morning, she has already gotten my order in, bless her, and she has her laptop open. I hang back at the door for a moment, however, as one of the servers stops by Sasha's table and talks to her for a moment or two. The girl is tall and skinny, and I know exactly who she is. Thankfully, it's not long before she's back where she belongs behind the cake pops and croissants.

We get to work.

As always, our topic is true crime. Sasha wants to be a journalist. It's one of the things we talked about on our little NYC adventure, and I threw out a few breadcrumbs about citizen detectives, as we like to call ourselves. She ate it right up. Since then, we've been exploring various cases via websites and forums, and she's desperate to show me some new "avenues" she's looking into.

Much as I'd wanted to set Sasha on Lynette's case, I'd thought it best to warm her up to cyber-sleuthing with a case I knew she'd see progress on. No point banging your head on a brick wall until you're so hooked you can't feel the blood until it drips in your eyes, after all. She has binge watched *I'll be Gone in the Dark* and *Don't F**k with Cats* and then I got her started looking into the case of Susan Maynard. I already know all there is to know about Susan's disappearance, but Sasha doesn't know that.

I've been to CrimeCon and attended a workshop on the case where her daughters made a special appearance. It was pretty moving. Susan was a forty-year-old mother of three, no history of mental illness or addiction. Divorced but not dating. Working in the office at a local gardening business. Driving her teenage daughters here and there. And then gone. No missing clothes. Susan Maynard streamlined her wardrobe when she downsized after the family house had been sold. The girls had helped her do it. I believed in their certainty on that point.

At CrimeCon, I'd briefly imagined Jen up there, talking about her dead sister, and her mother, and me. She would stir up the crowd, invite the hive mind in the room to find answers the police had failed to supply. It would never work, though. Jen comes across well but I'm not sympathetic enough and if I'm brutally honest, neither were Sal and Lynette. The police never warmed up enough to care back in Ithaca. I don't believe the true crime folks would now. They're a pretty accepting bunch, but I rub a lot of people up the wrong way. It's just a fact.

Sasha, on the other hand? She doesn't seem to see me like other people do. She's quick and she's curious and she can't wait to show me what's happening in true crime on TikTok. That girl plays her phone like it's a musical instrument, her fingers tapping and swiping at a pace too fast for my eyes to follow. I'm here for her enthusiasm, though, and when I'm done cooing over TikTok, and hearing her new theory about Susan Maynard, I ready myself to deliver the words I've planned to say.

"By the way. Did you hear anything about this girl one of your neighbors knew?" I keep my voice casual and my eyes on my laptop screen, pretending to look for any new threads about Susan Maynard.

"No. Who?"

"My daughter said one of the women — I forget her name. Not the one who runs. The other one?"

"Miss Natalie? Miss Vicki is a runner. They hang out a lot, walk their dogs together."

"I'm not sure. Anyway, one of the moms on the street went to school up in Ithaca with some girl who went missing. Terrible, really. I'm not sure if my son-in-law might have known her too. He's from up there."

"Terrible, yes, but wow, Miss Jocelyn. Don't you want to know more? I mean, we might have access to a witness. Two witnesses. Think about it!"

"Well now, Sasha. Slow down. Don't make me wish I hadn't mentioned it." I put my hand on her arm, eyeing her over my glasses. "People don't always like to talk about the past. I don't think we should be stirring things up."

"Is it on Websleuths?" She opens a new browser.

"I'm not sure . . ." I have a hard time not smiling. *Of course*, it's on Websleuths. I put it there.

"What was her name?" Sasha's eyes are bright. Her fingers twitch. I know the feeling, but she's going to have to work for this.

"No clue. Look, all I know is Jen mentioned that one of the moms got all upset when you and I took that little trip to the city. It brought back memories from when they were teens. I can't ask more. Jen's sensitive about being new here. She'd be furious if I started asking questions."

Sasha nods. "But I'm not new." She grins and it's infectious. I let myself smile back. Yes, I'm using her. But I like the girl.

"What are you thinking?"

She looks off into the distance and takes a moment before answering. I take in her profile, her round cheeks, her pink hair. Sasha's not conventionally pretty and the pink hair tells me she knows it. But she's not cowed, like I was when I realized I'd never fit in like Sal did. I envy Sasha her hair, or at least the confidence it took to dye it.

"Why don't I talk to Miss Natalie?" She leans back and crosses her arms. "I just told Erin I'd be over later to lend her some summer reading books for school." She nods her head toward the counter, and I feign confusion. "Miss Natalie's daughter. She works here. Anyway, I can say it's for a school project. I'll get the victim's name and we'll go from there. What do you think?"

What I really think is, how wonderful it is to watch a plan fall into place. Natalie Preston knows something and Sasha asking questions will put the pressure on. By the time I'm done with her, that woman is going to spill it all. I just need Jen to make sure she's there when Natalie loses it. Because lose it she will.

"Why not?" I say. "Although don't be a nuisance. Here." I've bought my own copy of Michelle McNamara's book, signed by her husband. I waited in a line for forty minutes for Patton Oswalt's signature, thinking of all the things I could say to him about the death of his wife and the long road ahead of him, bringing up their child alone. I knew a thing or two about that road. There were difficult days — months — when it was just me and Genevieve. Moving to Rochester, changing

157

her name to Jen, dropping her last name Knox — that part, at least, had brought some low-level satisfaction — had been difficult, but necessary. I knew about grief. About single parenting. But in the end, I'd said nothing to the poor man. Just watched him write his name and mumbled I was sorry for his loss. He didn't need advice from someone like me. But I could put the book to good use. Sasha was thrilled, even traced his signature with her finger.

"This is amazing. But really I shouldn't—"

She's a well brought up girl, no doubt about it. "I have two," I say quickly. "I'm not taking no for an answer."

"Really?"

Of course, not really. Who would have two signed copies of the same book? But Sasha's as human as the rest of us. Doesn't matter if it makes sense, if it's what we want to hear, most of us will accept any old bullshit.

"Really," I say.

I'm rewarded with a hug.

* * *

Not long afterwards, I leave Sasha busy imagining a future life of sleuthing and true crime bestsellers and drive over to Jen's house. She's made a big deal about me keeping away from the neighborhood, but it's only Natalie Preston I need to avoid. Her Facebook feed is a mine of information and I've had a fake account that's friends with her for years, set up in the app's early days when no one was savvy about who they were friends with or what their privacy settings were. Back when Natalie's kids Erin and Reid were still at Fairfax Elementary, I set myself up pretending to be someone who had kids at the school. I went through Natalie's friends' list and, over time, friended a whole bunch of them. Plenty accepted my request and when I decided it was time to friend Natalie, I knew she'd see multiple people she knew were friends with me already and hit accept. It worked like a charm. I've watched

Erin and Reid grow up. I've seen Halloween in the neighborhood, Fourth of July cookouts, and family Christmases back up north. I read the tribute she posted when her mother died last year and know that her Tuesday yoga class is her favorite part of the week, particularly as it's always followed by lunch at the country club. Natalie's never in the neighborhood on Tuesdays. As she drives out, I drive right by her. Her eyes are on the road. She doesn't see me at all.

Jen looks less than thrilled to see me walk in through the garage and, without even saying hello, rushes to the living room window, presumably unable to take my word for it that Natalie Preston is out of the neighborhood and will be for hours. I join her and we stand looking out for a moment or two. It's hard not to see the appeal of living there. Every garden is manicured, the mailboxes all match. There are basketball nets on most driveways and other than a slew of bikes leaning against the garage at one house a couple of doors away, everywhere is uniformly tidy. I think it's unnatural, but then maybe not every home is full of kids. Up past Sasha's house, an older couple are chatting with another older man who leans heavily on a walking stick. This is the kind of place families come to raise their kids. And then the kids leave, and the parents grow old without even knowing it. On a sunny day, when the humidity isn't too horrible, it seems like a nice enough place. But there's a storm due in a couple of days and I'll be glad to be back in the apartment with Seinfeld. There are way too many trees here, planted far too near people's homes. It's not difficult to imagine the tremendous damage they could do.

"What day is Nina due back? I'd like to see her."

"She'll be home on Sunday. I'll bring her down to visit next week."

"What about the weather? Have you seen the forecast?"

"Yes. Booker's bringing her earlier than planned to be on the safe side."

"Bringing her here?"

Jen looks a little uncomfortable and so she should. Now Nina's father is allowed a visit whereas my presence is barely tolerated? But I've no time for hurt feelings. "What did you learn from Natalie? Anything?"

"Nothing. She said she'd never even met Dan's brother. And I've been thinking, Jocelyn. What if I can't get Dan to talk? What if I can't get Natalie to talk? I mean, ever. I'm beginning to think it was all very naive. Did I really think we only had to bring Lynette up and one or both of them would suddenly start telling me about something they may or may not have done over twenty years ago? Where has all this got us — beyond me living here with a man I'm not sure I can trust? Maybe it's time to tell him the truth."

"Don't be ridiculous." Jen threatening to pull out of this whole operation is something I've been expecting. Over the years, I've found the best way to deal with her when she's like this is by ignoring her. Dismiss and distract. "It's time to go to work on the brother."

"Did you hear what I just told you? That Natalie never met him?" Jen lets out a long sigh. "I was thinking. Maybe you misheard their conversation. Maybe you heard what you wanted to hear."

I don't like her tone, or the way she's looking at me, but I know just how to shut her up. I walk back into her pristine white kitchen. "Come look at this," I say, bending to fish my laptop out of my bag. I flip it open, and it connects quickly. I already have the page open on my browser. Sensing her behind me I push it to her and wait while she settles herself on a stool.

"What's this?"

"What does it look like?"

"Yearbook photographs. From 2000. But why that year? Oh. Am I looking for Patrick? Is he in here?"

I consider a slow clap but resist. *Just a little more patience*, I tell myself. She will see it soon enough. Give her time. Let her find it. Her fingers slide down the bar. It doesn't take her long.

"Okay. Patrick Burrows. Fuzzy photo but definitely him."

"What does it say beside the photo?"

"You already know what it says."

"Read it to me."

"Oh, for God's sake." She wriggles on her stool. "It says, *When asked who or what he will miss most about high school, Patrick Burrows said: 'The E-dawg. He's been a solid friend since elementary.'* And your point is?"

"Keep looking through. Look for kids whose last name begins with an E." Jen throws me a sharp look, as if she doesn't quite trust me.

"Oh." She grips her lower lip between her fingers. "Is this what I'm supposed to be finding? Natalie's brother? John Eason?"

"Yes. Read what it says next to his photograph."

Jen shifts again and I sense her reluctance. When she does read it, she sounds lethargic. "*What was your most memorable moment at Ithaca High? My boy Patrick scoring a touchdown and taking us into the divisional champs in junior year.*"

I say nothing. Wait.

When she speaks her voice is heavy with disappointment. "Natalie is lying. Just like Dan has been lying. Sounds like their brothers were friendly for years. God, I'm so sick of this."

"Which is why we need to find the truth, Jen. Which is why I'm here. I think it's time you had a little talk with Patrick Burrows. And since he doesn't live in this neighborhood and has never laid eyes on me in his life, I'm coming with you."

TWENTY-NINE

Jocelyn
Then

I leaned into the idea of Lynette running away. Not for myself, but for Sal. I moved back into the house in Ithaca and started working on her. No one vanishes, I said. Not in Ithaca. She must have gotten on a bus. Slipped on, maybe, so none of the drivers remembered her. I reminded Sal of the time she took the bus to New York City when she was fourteen. She had ridden all the way to the city, and then panicked and come straight back. I'd been furious. Our parents barely noticed. She'd gone on impulse, and I reckoned if Sal had done it, Lynette was certainly capable of doing the same. That was the first time she looked me in the eye and said, "Maybe". Every night until the "maybe" night, Sal had been downstairs pacing in the dark when she thought Genevieve and I were fast asleep. We were weeks into Lynette being gone by then. Even if we were wrong, I figured, at least she could sleep now.

Weeks became a month. Sal called out of her job at the gas station up on Danby Road so often they fired her. When she put the phone down after they told her, she simply sighed and kept on watching the TV. Genevieve went back to school, and I guess it was rough on her. She never said much but I knew the other kids treated her differently after her sister went missing. If TV shows were Sal's favorite distraction, books were Genevieve's. In those first weeks I'd look in on her in her room every once in a while, but she was always either doing homework or curled in her bed with a book. She was fine, she'd say, and who was I to say she wasn't. They hadn't been close, her and Lynette, not as far as I ever saw. Not like me and Sal.

TV and books didn't do anything for me. I hated being back in that house and felt angry at Lynette. My sister didn't act like my sister anymore, and staring at the door didn't make Lynette walk back through it, any more than staring at the phone made it ring. But after she warmed up to the idea that Lynette had run off, Sal slowly started to get her act together. One day when I came home from the store, I found her in Lynette's room straightening things up.

"So, Lynny feels welcome when she comes home," Sal said, lining up a collection of stuffed tigers the girl hadn't so much as looked at since she was seven. I said nothing. At least Sal was off the damn sofa.

Genevieve slid past the doorway. I almost collided with her.

"Watch it, kid," I said. Or something like that anyway. She threw a glance into her sister's bedroom and bunched up her lips at the sight of her mom smoothing down the comforter and then lining up the tigers all over again. "Lynette will be back. Your mom's getting everything ready." But Genevieve just shook her head.

After that Sal started spending more and more time in Lynette's room. I'd come home from work and find her in there, or sometimes she'd even be in there when I came down in the morning to put the coffee on. One day I noticed a new hot pink blanket on the bed, and a couple of framed photos on Lynette's now tidied dressing table, pictures of Sal with

Lynette as a baby. Perhaps they gave her comfort. What did I know about having a child, after all? And, of course, she was in there on the Saturday afternoon when the police finally showed up in person for the first time in nearly two damn months. It was on the tip of my tongue to call them out for it, but when I opened the door and saw their expressions, I knew they'd found her, and that it wasn't good. I just wasn't ready for how bad it was. None of us were.

THIRTY

Now
Jen

Patrick lives about forty-five minutes from our house, north of Philly toward Allentown. I've no idea how he ended up there. Dan has always been vague about his brother. There had been a brief stint in the services which "didn't work out too well", and I know he works multiple jobs, mainly construction, and sometimes security, although it's never clear who for or who with. He buys and sells stuff online a lot, whether legit or not I have no idea, and there's no one else on the scene — no wife or partner, male or female, no kids, not even any pets. I've never visited his house, but I do know his birthday is around now, and he's been stuck at home since breaking his ankle. Jocelyn and I — by which I mean Jocelyn — cook up a story that we were up that way at the King of Prussia Mall and decided on a whim to drive on up to his house and bring a bag of groceries and a cake from Trader Joe's. She figures Patrick will be taken aback by our surprise arrival, and we'll have him at a disadvantage. If Dan finds it weird, she says, I can tell him it was all her idea. And anyway, by the time he learns about it we'll have been and gone, and he can think what he likes. Easy for her to say.

My mind strays again to Booker as we drive up to Patrick's. He'll be on the road a few days from now, bringing Nina home. His plan is to drop her off in the neighborhood and then head into Philadelphia for the night before his interview on Monday. I imagine him looking at apartments and wonder where he'll land. He'll be looking for a two-bed. Nina will have her own room, that second-home-bedroom kids from divorced families tend to have, except me and Booker never quite got that far. Thinking of how far we never got, I remember I'm still wearing his ring. I won't be on Thursday when he arrives.

"I'll do the talking when it comes to Ithaca," Jocelyn says.

I'm not arguing with that. This is her idea, her show. I'm just the driver. I glance left. Her eyes are on the road, her right hand grips the handle in her door. She's tense and seeing it, I'm flooded with a sudden sense of anxiety.

"Maybe this is a bad idea." I can't see her expression, but sense she's pulling a face and press on. "You never think things through. We've never thought any of this through. Have we? I mean — say Patrick really did have something to do with Lynette disappearing. Say he has something to hide. I don't know him well, Jocelyn. You don't know him at all. He's a big guy. What if we make him angry?"

"There are two of us. And besides . . ." She rummages in her purse. "I have this."

My eyes flick from the road to her lap. She has a taser. At least I think that's what it is. Jesus H. Christ.

"Where the fuck did you get that?"

"Online."

Of course, online. I am a living, breathing face-palm emoji.

"When?"

"Months ago."

"And does it work? Do you know how it works?"

"Yes."

166

I know every nuance of Jocelyn's voice. "You've never used it, have you?"

"No. But I've read the instructions. It's not complicated. Keep driving. Trust me."

* * *

Patrick's home is depressing. It's a ranch, low, squat and brown, and you don't need to be an expert to see the roof has seen better days. The bug screen has fallen off the window nearest the front door and leans drunkenly against mossy wooden siding. We pull up in front of a short lawn full of crab grass and dandelions. Weeds choke the border and the path to the front door. He's home. His garage is open, his truck is there. We walk up the driveway and take a look in the garage. It's such a mess. There're at least three washing machines, a home gym in several pieces, a ride-on lawn mower that looks about fifty years old and an old brown two-seater sofa patched with thick black tape. Shelves of sagging boxes fill one wall. A dirty gray off-cut strip of carpet leads to an interior door. We exchange a look and take the path to the front of Patrick's house.

"I was never much of a housekeeper," mutters Jocelyn, "but if that's the garage, I'm going to need a shower after this visit."

The bell doesn't work, so I knock on the door. There are glass panels on both sides of it. I see a carpeted hallway but not much more. We wait.

"He has a busted ankle. What if he can't make it to the door? Maybe we should . . ." My voice fades away as Jocelyn reaches out and turns the handle. The door opens. She glares at me, expectant.

"Patrick?" With no choice, I step into the hallway. There's a smell of pizza. It's so quiet I actually hear the carpet crunch under my feet. "Patrick, it's me, Jen. Are you home?"

No answer. I look at Jocelyn, but she shakes her head. There's a door ajar to our right, light spilling from it. My heart throbs in my chest as I push it open and walk into his kitchen. It's a mess of unwashed plates, unopened mail, and trash. Milk cartons, pizza boxes, crumpled empty cans of beer, a pile of coffee grounds in the sink. Wait. Not coffee grounds. Ants. Completely gross.

It's bright in here, though, and when I turn to the patio doors, I see him. Patrick is outside, leaning back in a wicker chair, possibly asleep. Jocelyn gestures at me to open the door. I'm worried we'll scare the crap out of him but what's the alternative? My teeth clench as I do what she wants. The whine of the door sliding open is enough to rouse him.

"What the—"

"Sorry! Sorry! Sorry, Patrick, it's me, Jen. Just me."

His confusion is evident. His eyes dart around, and I feel terrible for intruding on him like this. He runs a hand through his hair. Such a rumpled version of Dan. It's impossible to imagine two brothers more different. I can't imagine what Dan would make of Patrick's kitchen.

"I brought you some groceries. We were nearby. Dan said you'd hurt your ankle . . ." I can't finish my sentence. Patrick is standing. Patrick, in fact, jumped to his feet when I pulled open the door. "He said you'd broken it." I look down at his feet and he looks down too.

"Oh that?" He waves a hand in the air. "Busted ankle. Yeah. That's right. But not broken, just you know, a sprain." He shifts his weight to his left leg and pats his right thigh. "I'm out here resting it. Took a couple of sick days from work. Here, why don't we all take a seat?"

Patrick gestures to a small round glass table and chairs behind me on the deck. "Can I get you ladies anything? Coffee? Water?"

"No, nothing. Please, you need to sit."

He nods and shuffles to the chairs with Jocelyn following.

"I'm Jen's mom," she says. "We haven't met."

Small talk ensues. I talk brightly about the shopping I've brought and offer to put everything in his fridge before I go. Jocelyn asks about his accident and he's vague in the way someone not accustomed to talking about themselves can be, but I'm not buying it. If, and it is still an if, Patrick knows something about Lynette, it makes perfect sense that Dan wants to keep him away from the neighborhood and Natalie Preston. Against my better judgment, I feel a spike of excitement. Although how to get him talking about it? I glance at Jocelyn. She's asking him about his job, telling him how she worked for years in various Dollar Tree stores, how she could still tell you the price of every variety of Tasty Cakes, twenty years later. Patrick seems to be listening intently, and then I see a change in his eyes. His eyes narrow.

"What did you say your name is?" He smiles at her, perhaps to soften the interruption. "I can't call you 'Jen's mom', now, can I?"

"Jocelyn Silver. Call me Jocelyn."

"Thank you. I will," he says. He tilts his head. "Are you sure we've never met before?"

"I don't think so."

He looks unconvinced but doesn't say more. My mind races. Could he recognize Jocelyn? Could he have known her back then? I think of the funeral. It was small. We've always been certain Dan wasn't there, but Patrick? It's possible. I jump in to change the subject. "Nina would love to see you soon. When your ankle's better."

Patrick smiles. "That girl. How's she doing?"

"She's been with her dad this week. He's bringing her back on Sunday."

"Nice. Bet you miss her, though."

"It's certainly quiet without her."

He asks how Dan is and we talk a little about their parents who recently moved to a retirement community in Ithaca.

"Ithaca?" Jocelyn sounds all perky and bright. Totally fake. "I had some friends who used to live in Ithaca. Now, what was their name?"

Patrick and I watch Jocelyn pat her cheeks and drum her fingers on the table in a pantomime of forgetfulness.

"I know! Eason," she says. "Jane Eason was the woman I knew. She had a daughter. Maybe a little younger than you. And a son. I can't remember his age."

Patrick sits up in his chair. Leans forward. "You sure I don't know you?"

"Yes."

I can tell she's unnerved and I don't like the way Patrick has gripped the arms of his chair. He's a step away from recognizing her. I'm suddenly sure of it.

"Look at the time!" I say. "We need to get out of your hair." I stand and lock my eyes on Patrick, trying to turn his attention my way. "Why don't you show me where I can put these groceries? It's nothing fancy. Just a couple of meals you can throw in the microwave."

He gets to his feet. "I'll come and get them from your car."

I can't look at Jocelyn. She might be mad at me. Or she might be relieved. All I know is we really, *really* need to get out of there. I follow Patrick round the outside of the house, past his truck and to my car where I pull two bags of shopping from the trunk and hand them over. He's not even pretending to limp and his expression has been shuttered since Jocelyn mentioned the Easons. The tension is unmistakable.

"You shouldn't have gone to all this trouble," he says, but it sounds a lot more like *you shouldn't have come*. He nods at us both, his eyes skimming away from Jocelyn and settling on a point somewhere between us both. "I'll let you get on."

He doesn't move. I feel like I should hug him. In the past I've hugged him goodbye. I should do that now. That would be normal. But the moment is not normal, the visit wasn't normal. In fact, it feels like a colossal mistake. We get in the car. As I pull away, I see him, in the rearview mirror, just standing there in the road, watching us go. We don't speak until we hit the freeway.

"Do you think he recognized you? I think he recognized you."

"I don't know. Let me think."

"Let you think? Jesus, Jocelyn, did you see the way he was looking at you? I was afraid. *Afraid*. Weren't you? And when you said the name Eason his whole demeanor changed."

"I know, I know. But why? What does it mean? And now because you ran us out of there we can't even ask."

"You're saying we should have stayed? Are you crazy?"

I glance at her. She puts her hands to her face. "Yes. No! I don't know." She slams her hands against the dashboard. "Damn it!"

"What if he calls Dan?"

"Is that likely?"

"I don't know. We shouldn't have gone."

"Well. So what if he calls?" She's trying to rally me, rally herself. "Dan's the one that told you Patrick broke his ankle. And that was clearly bullshit."

"What if he's recognized you and he calls Dan and tells him? What happens then? What the hell happens? What am I supposed to say? Oh my God — Nina. I can't have Nina coming back into the middle of this. I should never have gotten involved with your craziness!"

"Just be quiet and let me think."

Rage billows up in my chest but I swallow it somehow and keep my eyes on the road. "Well, I hope you're thinking about how we've upended my daughter's life and connected her with people we have no idea if we can trust."

She doesn't reply. I feel a wave of self-loathing. Nina. I have one job — *one job* — of looking after my daughter and this is what I've done. I was wrong about Dan. He has lied about his brother's ankle to keep him away from the neighborhood. From Natalie.

I'm driving. Changing lanes, checking mirrors, following directions home but I'm also seeing Patrick's hands grip that chair and hearing his voice when he asked Jocelyn if he knew her. What if Patrick has a dark side? Natalie Preston has lied about knowing Patrick to my face. And yes, the truth about

Lynette's death has tormented me as much as it has Jocelyn, but whatever she says or decides now, I know I need to call Booker. I need to tell him to keep Nina in Rochester. He will have work. He'll need to make arrangements — shit, he has an interview in Philly on Monday. I feel like smacking my forehead off the steering wheel. But his mother will help him. I'll call Charmain myself if I have to. I'll beg. I'm not proud. I can tell them I'm sick. A wave of sadness hits me. I'd much rather tell them the truth. But the lies have gone on too long, and I've brought Nina along with it. They'll never understand it. I'm not sure I understand it myself.

We drive in silence.

"I can't let it go," Jocelyn says eventually. "I want to. For Nina's sake. You know I love her."

Does she, though? Really? I guess as much as she loves anyone. "Which is why we should drop it."

She shakes her head. "Which is why we should finish it."

I'm overwhelmed with frustration. This has been so much of my life. Jocelyn — bullish, determined, stronger willed than me, overbearing and relentless.

"Hear me out," she continues. "What's the worst-case scenario?"

"The absolute worst case?" I don't know why I'm allowing the conversation. Except that she is Jocelyn, and this is what we do. "Worst case, one of them killed her. Or they know who did. Absolute worst? Dan killed her. I've been living with a murderer. Nina and I have."

"Does it seem likely?"

"No!"

"Good. Look. I think we need to not overreact."

My foot hovers over the brake. If we weren't in the middle of a three-lane highway I'd pull over and throttle her.

"The goal," she says slowly, "is to find out how Lynette got in that river. Natalie lied at the time. She feels guilty enough to still be lying about it now, calling it an accident, even to a stranger. We've learned Dan knows more than he's saying. Natalie's name touched a nerve with Patrick. Maybe they were drinking. Maybe there was an argument. They were teenagers. Teenagers make mistakes. Maybe she went off and met someone else who hurt her. We just don't know. I've never thought you or Nina were in any danger, and I still don't. Was Patrick unnerving just now? Yes. But he's an odd fellow at the best of times. You said so yourself. We rattled him. He reacted. That doesn't put Nina in danger. Look at the way he spoke about her. He likes her. Dan loves her. You know that."

Some of the anxiety leaves me. Just a little. Like air from a balloon. Seeping away.

"They both love her."

"Which makes her safe."

"I don't know. I don't feel good about it. About any of it."

"If you don't let Booker bring Nina back to you on Sunday, what's Dan going to think? He'll want to know why. Booker will want to know why."

I don't have an answer.

THIRTY-ONE

Jen
Now

Surely Patrick has called Dan. I pace the kitchen, waiting for him to come home from the hospital, waiting for the inevitable argument. We've not had many disagreements in our three years together. None about Nina, as he's always left her to me to deal with, a fact I've appreciated. There have been a couple of times he's shut me down when we're talking about his work, but generally only when he's been drinking more than me and feeling stressed. I'm not holding those against him. We can all get on our high horse about our own fields. I'm a real grammar Nazi and have been known to raise a few hackles in meetings when someone doesn't know their *Chicago Manual* as well as they think they do.

It's something I've liked about Dan — our not arguing — but now I question it. It has been an easy relationship. What if it's been too easy? What if we've just stayed in our own lanes, running parallel, without ever truly being intertwined? Take this new house. We've made our own spaces. The kitchen is mine. Plants chosen by me. Photos on the fridge, chosen by me. The maple leaf coasters I bought on our trip to Canada, the fruit bowl I picked out for Jocelyn to buy me for Christmas last year. Yes, his shoes are in the cubbies by the back door and there's a box on the shelf where he keeps his keys and leaves his wallet but pluck those things out and he disappears. I head upstairs to our room.

He's more visible here, mainly in the furniture. It's his bedroom set, from a big box department store that's never been in my price range. My old bed and dresser from IKEA are still in the apartment in Philly, waiting for my final decision. I told Dan they belonged with the flat, figuring I'll solve that part of this move equation when I call Joe with my final word on it in a couple of weeks. One other thing in this room stands out as his, though. It's a print, a big one, that he had up opposite his bed in his old apartment and hung up in our new room here on the day we moved in. When I think about it, it's the only picture he's hung. I've done all the rest. I look at it now and remember the first time I saw it — that first night together.

* * *

"Look at that," I said, gesturing toward the picture on his wall. Dan's apartment was tiny, the room held his bed, a wall of fitted mirror wardrobes and a dresser. I'd managed to avoid looking at the mirror wall while we'd done the deed, and now he lay between me and it, so I was spared the temptation to fret about my bed hair or peer at myself trying to see how much mascara had slid down my face during the — let's face it — pretty athletic and successful jump in the sack we'd just finished. Keeping my face away from the mirrors leaves me with nowhere to look but straight ahead and this print — this big, framed print of a mythical creature. It's certainly a statement piece.

"Cerberus, right? Am I in your chamber of secrets, then?"

"Would you be horrified if I said I'd never read Harry Potter?" He stretched, a delicious unfurling of skin and muscle. "Or seen the movie. I bought it in London. On a trip not long after I graduated college."

"Is it William Blake?" Full disclosure, I knew it was. I was an English major and William Blake's drawings are so distinctive. The grays, the shading, the swirl of pink and lick of yellow? Instantly familiar. I knew all about Cerberus guarding the gates of hell in Dante's *Divine Comedy*.

"I'm impressed. Not just a pretty face, are you?"

Okay, so his response was clichéd, but I didn't care. I'd opened with the Harry Potter reference because for some men, a woman being smart doesn't seem to equal sexy. Now, though? Now Dan's fingers traced my rib cage. Now his lips bent to my shoulder. I closed my eyes on the three-headed dog at the gates of hell. This was nothing like hell. His lips grazed my shoulder. Jocelyn, I thought, had finally done me a favor, harrying me into this crazy hook-up with someone from Lynette's high school class. This was a man I wanted to see again. A man I was going to see again. And again.

When his mouth reached my hip bone I turned and watched us in those wardrobe mirror doors. I liked what I saw.

* * *

And yet, if I'm honest, I'm not too keen on the Blake print. Back then our shared knowledge about it implied compatibility. I wonder if we both took it as more of a sign that we were good together than it really was. It's not as if I even like it to look at. I mean — a three-headed dog, all jaws and claws and rolling eyeballs? It's kind of unpleasant when you think about it. And yet it's the most "Dan" thing in the house. That and his big recliner.

My watch buzzes. A text. He won't be home for hours. A new case in the hospital. I feel a flicker of relief, quickly followed by guilt. My reprieve from seeing him comes at the cost of someone, some family, who needs Dan, a brain doctor. They are probably good people. And he will be a great doctor for them. He could be saving a life right now. All while I'm worried about the situation here which is a) all of my own making and b) something I wish I'd never started. What I *should* do, is just come clean on the whole mess. I should sit him down, before Nina gets back, and tell him who I am and what I want to know. It will be the end of us — of this — I know that. My mind spools out into imagining the consequences. I see me and Nina back in the city. And I think about Booker being in Philly too.

It's like hitting a wall. How can Nina and I move back the second I hear Booker's going to be there? It will look like I want him back. Like I'm chasing him, for Christ's sake. He's already caught me wearing his ring. He'll run a mile. And if he ever finds out that I got together with Dan because of Lynette, I just know he'll never forgive me. His mother's face and voice swim up from my memory, although I haven't seen the woman in over nine years. She's not the ogress I made her out to be back when Nina was born. That was all just part of my excuses for leaving. But Charmain would, for sure, have a lot to say if she knew about this, and none of it in my favor. I couldn't even blame her. She wouldn't be wrong.

My mood is dark. Drink won't help but it's what I reach for. I won't come clean with Dan just yet, and I can't have Booker knowing the truth. If I decide Nina and I are better off back in the city, I'll do so when he's two hundred and fifty miles away, back home in Burlington. Nina can go and stay with Jocelyn — another reason why it's so difficult to face cutting her out of our lives altogether — for a few days if I need to end it with Dan. And then I'll make it clear to Booker that the move has nothing to do with him, or any of the lingering feelings and regrets I'm harboring.

I pick up my phone looking for distraction. It comes in a text message from Daisy.

Wine open. Kids upstairs. U free?

Thank God. I reply:

C U in 2!

* * *

Daisy brims with gossip as she ushers me into her kitchen. My mind spins to Natalie, lying to me about Patrick after we did shots in here the other night, but Daisy is talking and handing me wine, and I force myself to focus.

"You didn't hear what Courtney had to say about Vicki's son, Thomas, at book club, did you?" I shake my head, and she launches into the story. "Well. Here's what she told me. She said Geoff's daughter Paige won't set foot in the neighborhood, all because of Thomas. The story is that Thomas was 'overly friendly' to Paige. And there were a couple of times when everyone was hanging out on someone's patio — and you know how that goes? It's dark, the adults are drinking, the kids are running around — and Thomas started singling Paige out. No one noticed, Courtney said. But then one night when they were supposed to be playing flashlight tag, he talked her into going off with him. Said he had something to show her."

I feel this in the pit of my stomach. How bad can it be? I think of the way Daisy greeted me. She was excited to tell me this. It can't be as bad as I'm imagining. Unless Daisy is a whole different person than I thought she was.

"What was it?"

"A dead cat. He'd put it on her swing set in Courtney's back yard. Creepy as fuck, don't you think? I had no idea at the time. I mean, I remember the night. We were hanging out at Natalie's, and Paige came up howling for her mother who, of course, wasn't there. Courtney and Geoff couldn't calm her down. They took her home. I think Geoff's ex had to drive over and get her. We all thought she'd been spooked in the dark. I'd never heard about this cat business until the other night. Courtney said when the adults went to look it wasn't there. Vicki insisted Paige must have made the whole thing up, but Courtney believes her."

"How old is she?"

"Same age as Nina."

"And what do you think? Would she have made it up?"

"No clue. But I thought I'd ask my older kids a bit about him."

"And?"

"Poppy said that he's weird, for sure, but she didn't know much. Actually, I felt kind of bad about it — like, what was I doing, talking about some poor teenager? It's a tough age, right? I decided to forget about it. And then Casey brought him up over dinner tonight, without any prompting." Her eyes are wide and shining. We have got to the part she's dying to tell me. She leans in. "Casey said he was thinking about changing his course selection. They have a window right now where the kids can go in and change their courses. Never mind. High school is *waaay* in your future. The point is, he said he was thinking of dropping art. He said the teacher sucked, and only ever paid attention to a couple of kids, including guess who? Thomas Price."

She pulls up and takes a deep swig of her wine. "And that's when I remembered the end-of-year exhibition. They do it every year — it's cool, really — all the kids' artwork out on display. Some of it's amazing. But last year there was one set that really stood out and not in a good way. This one kid had painted nothing but dead animals, roadkill mainly. Incredible brushwork. Grim, though. There was a deer, a raccoon . . ." She's nodding as she's talking and I say it, even though I don't want to.

"And a cat?"

"Hanging by the neck. On a swing set."

"Jesus."

* * *

I'm asleep when Dan gets home. In the morning he's a slumbering lump beside me in the bed and I ease my way out from under the covers without waking him. After I left Daisy I drank another couple of glasses of wine, sitting in the dark in his chair in the living room, just watching the lights in the neighborhood slowly blink off. I decided I wouldn't wait for him to bring up Patrick. I'm not going to sit about worrying, waiting to see if Patrick has told him about our visit or not. I am Jen Silver these days, not Genevieve Knox, and I need to act like Jen would if she really knew nothing about Ithaca and Lynette. While he sleeps, I do some work on my laptop and drink coffee. When I hear noises and know he's awake I pour him a cup and head upstairs.

"Hey. How was last night? How's your patient?" I am all smiles as I hand him his drink.

"Thanks." He stuffs a pillow behind him and sits up in bed. I climb in beside him. "Things went well, I think. How have you been?"

"Good." I launch into Daisy's story about Thomas Price, and he agrees with me that we don't want Nina anywhere near him, just to be on the safe side. He suggests I have a chat with Sasha — if she's continuing driving Nina around for the summer it seems like a good idea to say something. Although presumably she knows the story since it's her stepsister who had the problem with Thomas in the first place.

"Speaking of siblings," I say, "Jocelyn and I had kind of a weird visit with Patrick yesterday."

Dan sips his coffee. His face is blank. "How so?"

"We went up to his place. It was a spur of the moment thing. Maybe we shouldn't have. But we were over that way at King of Prussia, and he came up in conversation. I told her about his ankle, and she got it into her head that we should take him some groceries. You know how she is when she gets an idea."

He says nothing, just rolls his lower jaw.

"So anyway, we went. And for one thing, I don't think there's anything wrong with him. If he did hurt himself, he's fine now. But why would he make something like that up? He wouldn't lie to you, would he?"

"He would not."

"Well, so that was strange and then, honestly, he was pretty weird toward my mom. He kept asking her if he knew

180

her, which, of course, how could he? But he was kind of weird, almost angry. And so I was just worried that maybe there's something going on with him that you don't know about? What do you think?"

"I think he doesn't like visitors. He never has. He's shy, Jen. You know that. It was stupid to go up there."

"We meant well."

"You might have. I'm not so sure about Jocelyn."

I let that pass. He finishes his coffee and climbs out of bed. How do I feel? I'm relieved that I've brought up Patrick and World War Three didn't just break out. But also, I'm a little surprised he's getting up and heading for the shower. Surprised, relieved, but also worried. The sex is one of the best things about me and Dan, always has been. The fact that he's not interested shows how things have changed. For a minute or two I sit on the bed, listening to the rush of the shower and wondering how this all ends.

Not well, I think. *Not well*.

THIRTY-TWO

Jocelyn
Now

On Sunday morning, Sasha texts me. She has spoken to Natalie. We agree to meet in the new library in town, in case Erin has a shift at the coffee shop and might hear us talking about her mother. Sasha says she's been volunteering as a language tutor and knows how to book a room in the library. Anyone seeing her with me will assume I'm a new student. She'll say I'm an immigrant from Eastern Europe. Most of the people she works with are South American, but people might think I'm Polish, she says. I debate what that says about my appearance for all of two seconds. I want to know what Natalie has told her.

The library is all glass and exposed brick and there's a wrought iron staircase with a mural of a tree winding around it so that climbing the stairs feels exciting, at least to the two small girls in front of me, who scramble ahead of their mother and squeal most inappropriately. Not that our parents ever took us to the library when Sal and I were that age, but if they had, we'd never have had the nerve to make a sound. It's airy and spacious upstairs, with different areas painted in a range of bold colors. I head for yellow, as instructed, and soon find Sasha in a small, windowless room with a clean desk, two chairs, and the chance of privacy.

"Well?"

"I hardly know where to start!" Her eyes are bright, and she leans across the desk, gripping a Moleskine notebook. I tap it.

"You took notes? When you were with her? Or after?"

"With her. I asked if I could. I can't believe how ready she was to talk. I mean, it took a bit for her to agree. I thought she was going to send me packing at the start, but then something changed — hard to say what — and yesterday she basically told me her whole life story, and this girl's story. It was a lot. I think I might be good at this, Jocelyn."

I held up my hands. "Good. Great, even. But maybe stop for a breath? And, you know, start at the beginning?"

"Right." She flushes and puts her hands to her cheeks, looking suddenly very young. I remember Jen at her age, always so serious and quiet, with none of Sasha's enthusiasm. Not that I'm blaming her. Jen was a quiet kid even before it all went to shit. But afterwards? In those early days after Ithaca? Then she was quiet on a whole new level. It was only when she got to be Sasha's age that I had any hope for her future at all.

"Okay, so she wasn't home when I dropped off Erin's books the other day. But yesterday I saw Miss Natalie on the street walking her dog and went over to her. I said what we discussed — I had a summer assignment for psychology where I needed to research a traumatic event, and I wondered if she might help me. She looked blank, but I kept going and said I'd heard neighbors saying she'd had a friend at school who had died. I said I didn't want to be nosy, or upset her, but it would really help me out if I could interview her about what had happened and how she'd been impacted by it. Honestly, I thought she was going to say no."

"But?"

"She asked me how old I was. And then she said nothing for a bit."

"And?"

"I asked her how old her friend was when she passed."

"The same age. Good." I'm nodding. I see how this went. Sasha is a smart girl, maybe even smarter than she understands herself yet.

"Her whole face changed color. She went pale, then red, then pale again. I felt bad. I almost said to forget it. I literally thought she was going to cry."

Sasha's eyes are wide, like she's still shocked by Natalie's reaction. I put my elbows on the desk and slide my fingers under my sweater, feeling for my pulse.

"Take your time. Tell me everything."

"Okay. So, I started off asking her about school. It didn't sound that different from my school, to be honest, although it was more in the center of town and, she said, when they didn't have many sports or whatever, a lot of the kids would congregate in cafés in some area called the Commons. She said, around sophomore year the parties started and she would go, but always with three other girls because there was safety in numbers. Her friends were—" Sasha flips open her notebook. "Sherri Knowles, Mel Parks, and Lynette Knox.

"She knew Mel since elementary. I asked if they were still in touch and she said no. Mel had gone to college in the south — Alabama, Auburn? — she wasn't sure, and anyway, she said, after everything that happened, who could blame her? They all wanted to get the hell out of Ithaca, she said."

"Where did Natalie go?" I ask, knowing full well she went to Binghamton, although she dropped out after her freshman year.

"She didn't say. We didn't talk about what she did after graduating high school. Should I have asked about that?"

"No, no. I was just curious. Go back to this friend group. They were close?"

"I guess. I mean, it sounded like there were some tensions."

"Like?"

"Miss Natalie and Mel were friends the longest. In middle school they both got friendly with Sherri. Sherri was the

184

nicest person, she said, but shy. They were in the same English class. Sherri and Mel were both smart, smarter than she was. She said they didn't like it at first when she got friendly with Lynette Knox. She said . . ." Again, Sasha reaches for her notebook and makes those annoying air quotes: "Lynette was the kind of girl that would say anything to get a rise out of a teacher. It was attention-seeking, I see that now. But at the time, she seemed edgy and brave. Two things I wasn't. I wasn't anything. Not as smart as Sherri and Mel. Not as sharp as Lynny."

"Good-looking, though," I say. "Which never hurts."

She looks uncertain. "I guess so. I don't think she had a bad time at school. Until everything happened. She made out life was kind of ordinary. Sherri and Mel weren't keen on Lynette, but then Lynette stuck up for Sherri when some boy barged into her in the lunch hall. She said Lynette had a hard outside but when you knew her, she was a loyal friend."

"There were tensions, though? What about?"

"Boys."

Sasha says this in a withering tone, as if she knows more than she wants to about how boy drama causes upset between girls in high school. Good for her. When I look back on my high school days, I see myself on the edge, or on the wrong side of an aquarium glass. Sal was always in there, swimming with the big fish, going to parties, kissing boys. I was not.

"In junior year, not long before it happened. Lynette was dating a boy called Connor Goodman. It caused a few arguments. Lynette was always over at Natalie's house at that point, she said, but when Connor came on the scene, she dropped them all, and they weren't too happy with her for it. She said it was so obvious, even her parents noticed and kept asking where Lynette had gotten to. I got the impression that Connor wasn't the greatest influence, maybe? He had a lot of parties — he was that kid whose parents didn't care what happened at their house. Anyway, when he dumped her, Lynette went a bit off the rails. Miss Natalie wasn't clear how — maybe I should have pressed her on that — but she was just kind of talking and I didn't want to interrupt. As soon as this Connor dropped her, Lynette acted like it had never happened, and the girls were mad at her, you know, feeling like Lynette thought she could just pick them up and drop them. And then Miss Natalie said *she* started seeing someone — Miss Natalie, I mean." Sasha stops and looks across at me a little anxiously.

"Dan Burrows? Don't worry. I knew that already."

"Does Nina's mom know? I mean, that's got to be weird, right?"

"It was a long time ago, Sasha. I think Jen's fine with it."

"Okay. Good." She flips the pages of her notebook. "This is where it all got pretty sad."

I nod encouragingly.

"They had an argument the day Lynette Knox went missing. She's haunted by it. Completely haunted. When she told me about it her eyes filled up, her voice was unsteady. It was difficult to sit there, to be honest, and I thought, you know, my God, she feels guilty, really guilty. It's not much of a jump to think Miss Natalie feels she caused what happened, is it?"

I want her to stop right there. I want to take her stupid notebook and throw it in her face. The anger's rising. Why did I send this stupid girl in there? It should have been me in that room, dragging the truth from Natalie Eason, making her say what she wouldn't or couldn't back then with her mother and father breathing down her neck. I don't want to hear Sasha's conclusions, her *jumps*. I want to know the truth.

"She told you the girl killed herself because the two of them had a fight?"

"No." Sasha shakes her head, her eyes wide and bright. "No. That's what was so weird about it all. Because — suicide? That's what they said at the time, but no. Miss Natalie wasn't having it. She said whatever happened to Lynette Knox, it was never a suicide. And no one who knew her had believed it for a minute."

THIRTY-THREE

Jocelyn
Then

Lynette's death crushed Sal. Crushed her like a car in a scra-pyard. It rendered her unrecognizable. My own sister. Gone.

Markham and Prentice sat us down at the dining table. Genevieve too. Prentice looked paler than I remembered, and I wondered if she'd changed her makeup. Crazy the things that go through your head at times. Soon enough, I knew why. After Markham went through the basics — a body found in the creek down by Titus Avenue, definitely Lynette, look-ing at the clothes, the hair (not *her* clothes and hair, *the* clothes and hair. Such a small thing but telling) — Sal began sobbing. I did the expected things — grabbed tissues, offered coffee, pressed down any reaction of my own by grabbing Sal's hand and rubbing her knuckles.

"Can we see her?" I asked.

Markham's eyes flicked to Genevieve, and I was hit by a wave of nausea. It had been two months. How long had she been in the water?

"Genevieve. Room. Now."

Her lips parted, as if she was ready to argue, but the look I threw her brooked no arguments. She went. I waited until I heard her door click shut.

"Tell us. We need to know."

"She was found yesterday," Prentice began, "by a woman walking her dog."

I squeezed Sal's hand. "See, Sal. Another good reason never to have a dog."

Prentice drew in a sharp breath. Had I shocked her? I didn't care. She didn't understand me and Sal. How it was my job to keep her spirits up. To keep my baby sister going.

"Just tell us," I said.

"The body was recovered and taken for examination. We're not requiring a relative to confirm identity at this time."

"What we're saying is that you don't want to see her." Markham's sympathy was worse than his sneer. "A body changes in water. You won't see the girl you remember. But it is her. And we'll confirm it with forensics."

I swallowed. "She was fully dressed?"

"Yes."

Tears fell from Sal's eyes, and I reached for more tissues.

"Had she been hurt? Assaulted?"

"It's hard to say at this stage."

"Right." I swallowed again, battling nausea. "But you're thinking . . ."

"It's too early." Prentice leaned toward Sal, hand outstretched, her eyes shiny with tears in a way that made me angry — angry because my eyes were dry, and she was no one to us. No one.

"Fuck off," I said to her. "Don't fucking touch my sister."

"That's uncalled for."

My gaze swung to Markham. "Is it? You come here. After all this time. After telling her, telling us, Lynette had run off somewhere. Was what? Living her best life in New York City? But oh no, she's found by some poor woman and her dog because you lot couldn't be bothered to look for her. And now

188

it's been two months. But it's too early to say what happened to her? She was in the river, for Christ's sake. How did she get in there? How?"

"Speculating helps no one."

"Speak for yourself! Speculating is all you're leaving us with. What? You're just going to roll in here, say she's dead and then roll on out again? We need to know. Need to."

"And you will. In good time."

"There'll be an autopsy?"

"Happening as we speak."

"So, you'll be back with the results of that?"

Markham nodded. "We will."

"And in the meantime?" I glanced at Sal. Her eyes were still down. Tears still flowing. "If you had to guess. To speculate. What are we talking about? Murder? An accident?"

Prentice was shaking her head, getting to her feet, signaling to Markham that it was time to go. But his eyes were on mine, and I was daring him, goading him to give us something. Anything.

"Suicide," he said, his voice flat and low. "Teenager. Difficult background. A bust-up with friends. Impulsive action."

He got to his feet and held up two hands. "You did ask."

THIRTY-FOUR

Natalie
Now

I regret talking to Sasha Wallace the moment she's gone. She's a nice kid but agreeing to sit down and talk to her about Lynette? With Dan living right across the street? What was I thinking? She caught me off guard. At a weak moment. All the time we were talking I was gazing at her, wishing to tip out of my body and into hers so I could feel again what life felt like before it all happened. I often have the same feeling around Erin. She doesn't know it, I don't think. I'm just her mom, looking at her, like moms do — all misty-eyed and what not. That's all it should be. But I don't think I look at Erin like any other mother would. Yes, I'm proud of her, and excited to see where life takes her and what choices she'll make. But there's this extra layer of looking — of searching — going on. I look for myself in Erin, for my old teenage self. The "before" girl. The one that didn't know death and tragedy. The girl who thought her best friend was hard to like at times. Who thought she was in love with a boy. Who didn't like her dad, without being quite sure why. Before.

Telling Sasha about the argument was a mistake. For hours after she leaves, I pace the kitchen going over and over the conversation in my mind. At night, I can't sleep. But what's done is done. I tell myself it's fine. It's for some school project. No one who matters will know I even spoke to Sasha about it. I see that notebook, though. And her neat hand-writing. What did I say and how did I say it? Nothing bad. Nothing revealing. At least I don't think so. I was emotional. I do know that. Should I blame myself? Should I? It's been emotional, it *is* emotional. As if it wasn't bad enough having Dan Burrows appear in the neighborhood, I've been strug-gling with constant reminders of life in Ithaca ever since Mom died and I had to take care of Dad.

When the alarm on my phone goes off at 10.30 a.m. the next morning, I trudge upstairs. Four hours have passed since I was last in his room. I've been doing everything in four-hour windows for the last five months.

"There was a girl here yesterday," I say. His eyes track me as I move around, twitching his covers, pouring water into a glass he can't reach. "She came to talk to me about Lynette."

My voice snaps on the double "t". His eyes widen, then quickly narrow.

"We've never really talked, have we?" I sit in the chair by his bed and lean forward so my elbows are on his mattress and my chin rests on my hands. I'd love to rip the mask off his face right now, but I won't. This is a cold anger. Very cold.

"I mean, you told me your version of events at the time. And I believed you." His eyes flick away. He can't turn his head, but he can disengage with his eyes. Shame for him that ears don't work that way.

"For years, I refused to believe you had anything to do with it. I mean, you were what, forty-eight, something like that. And she was seventeen. I believed you when you said you just saw her on the street. It's a small town." The machine keeps his oxygen supply steady. It hums along. "And yet at the same time, I think I always knew it was more. The way you

191

were when her aunt came looking for her. The way you never said her name, when she'd been such an obvious favorite.

"Did you do something to her, Dad? Did you? Was it all your fault?" My voice is a whisper. I'm thinking of the years that followed, of the fights between my parents, the divorce, the succession of younger women, of the reconciliation and their "second time around" together that turned my stomach even as it made some naïve part of me feel mended. I sit there for a while, saying nothing, weighing his non-response. We are two people in a room. One sick, one not. Father and daughter. Nothing out of the ordinary happening, not on the surface.

When I'm ready, I rouse myself. I take off the ventilator and push the buttons that make the bed rise so he can sip his drink. Solid food is a thing of the past. He can't chew. Swallowing is difficult. If I left him alone with this smoothie, he could easily choke on it. I push another pillow behind his head wondering if I'm a monster to think such things about my own father. I set him up with his drink, placing the straw in his mouth, feeling his lips cold to the touch. He says nothing. Twenty years ago, when I challenged him, he tore right into me. Anger, recrimination, and loud resentment were his stock in trade. Now he says nothing.

Twenty years ago, he swore it was an accident. Swore there was nothing he could do. Leaving "the scene" — I can hear him saying those words, remember hating it — was for the best. Best for him, for my mom, for me, he said. It was better if no one knew he was there. I'd found him in the dining room drinking whiskey and confronted him, wild with anger, but wholly unprepared for the questions he'd then have for me.

The next day, the family came looking for her.

And I lied.

192

THIRTY-FIVE

Jen
Now

Booker is due to arrive with Nina in the next hour, and should be here well in advance of the storm we're expecting. Dan has rearranged his schedule to be here although he's been sitting at the island, frowning at his laptop, and looks like he wishes he were anywhere else. It occurs to me he might be nervous. Not a quality I generally associate with him, but not out of the question given the circumstances. They have never met. I would have made sure they didn't meet this time, either, but I had to tell him Booker might be moving to Philadelphia. Had to, before Nina did. Booker and I agreed he'd tell her last night, before the drive down. Not that it was a done deal, but that he was having an interview, and his moving here was in the cards. She had texted me from her iPad, an all-caps, emoji-ridden burst of excitement. And so, I'd told Dan. His response was muted, and he didn't ask me how I felt about it, which was just as well because I've no idea what my answer would be.

"Oh, by the way," I say now. "The stone fell out of that cheap engagement ring." I have my back to him, unloading the dishwasher, so I can't see his face and he can't see mine. I'm still wearing the wedding band, but I can't have the other ring on when Booker gets here. This is the best lie I could think of.

"Piece of shit, anyway."

He doesn't say anything else, and I don't turn. I hear him typing. I'd been worried he'd start talking about buying me a real one again, but there's clearly some work thing going on and I'm just relieved.

Normally I can't wait to get Nina back after a week up north. I've gone through the motions of preparing — changing her sheets, making mac and cheese, buying strawberries for dessert, and popping a bag of sour patch candies on her desk like I always do — but the idea of having Booker and Dan in the same space has me entirely on edge. Two months ago, I think I'd have been fine with it. But having Booker nearby — part of our lives on a regular basis — at the same time as everything has changed between me and Dan? It feels like too much. It's all I can do to pick up my phone and look at the radar on my weather app while the minutes tick by. And then they're here.

"Mom!" Nina barrels in through the garage door and into my arms. I look down at her dark curls and love swells in my chest.

"Hey, baby. How was the drive?"

"Awesome. We were listening to a book and — oh, well, but I'll tell you later. I want to show Dad everything."

She twists away from me. Booker is in the doorway and Dan has already moved to greet him. I watch them shake hands. Booker is taller by a couple of inches, but I'm jolted to see that they're more similar than I'd realized, both slim, clean-shaven, even similarly dressed in khaki shorts and close-fitting tee-shirts. They both look far more relaxed than I expected. I should feel good about that. But I don't.

"Nina!" Dan opens his arms, and she leans into him but quickly steps back and grabs Booker's hand.

"Can I show Dad my room, Mom?"

"Let's give him the full tour," Dan says. "How was the drive? Can I offer you a coffee? Or a beer?"

It's surreal watching them interact. Dan's grouchiness has disappeared, Booker is smiling and agreeing that coffee would be good as Nina pulls him from the room.

"I'll get it," I say, and watch wonderingly as Dan follows them into the hall, smiling as Nina babbles on to Booker.

Once the tour's complete we have coffee out on the patio. The sky is clear but it's humid. The closeness in the air is the only hint that a storm is coming. Everyone but me seems relaxed. Booker has got Dan talking about his work and is nodding away as Dan recounts a story I've heard multiple times about a boy he calls Jack, although that's not his real name. Jack was hurt as a child. Dan's always vague about that part, talking about "non-accidental" brain injuries that caused the boy to develop severe epilepsy, as well as limiting his eye-sight and impairing his motor skills. He had been adopted by a caring family, and neurologists had worked with them for over two years trying to find a drug regimen that could control or at least reduce the number of seizures Jack experienced each day. Nothing worked. Eventually, Dan had carried out his surgery — a functional hemispherectomy — where he basically disconnected the malfunctioning left side of Jack's brain.

"Wow." There's nothing but admiration in Booker's voice and I see how that's loosening Dan up. I sounded just like Booker does the first time I heard this story too. But now? Now I hear it different. Dan sounds full of himself. He's showing off. And it's irritating.

"But not every day is like that one, surely?" Booker says. "There must be heartbreak, in among the miracles."

"Of course," says Dan. "And believe me, when something doesn't go well, you hear far more about it than when it does."

"Internal politics?"

"Some. But also keyboard warriors, ready to criticize and insult. Even when they have no idea what they're talking about."

"Ouch. Sounds irritating."

"It is. But you must have similar experiences, surely? As a writer? Aren't the comment sections on any media platform just a cesspit of accusations and hyperbole?"

"You know it." Booker leans back in his chair and smiles. When he turns to me, I feel heat rising in my chest. "This is a great home for Nina," he says. "I can see why you made the move. I thought you'd always be a city girl, but this," he spreads his arms wide, "this is pretty darn nice."

"More coffee?" Dan disappears into the kitchen to fetch the pot.

"Nina likes him," Booker says nodding at the house. "You could have done worse."

"Thanks." He's smiling a half-smile I recognize. Like he's about to tease me or say something provoking — I can still read him. "Spit it out," I say.

"I've a message for you. From my mom." He's still smiling. "Go on, then."

"She asked me to tell you she thinks you've done a great job with Nina."

"Wow."

"Uh huh."

I'm pleased. I can't help myself. I'm smiling back at him.

"I knew that," I say. "But it's good to know Charmain knows it."

"She's always known it. The fact that she asked me to tell you so, now, that's the interesting part."

"What do you mean?"

"I mean, she realizes that if I move down here, she'll be coming to visit. She started talking about Nina's gymnastics and piano and then even about prom, of all things."

"Prom! Whoa. We are light years from prom."

"Tell me about it. But she's thinking ahead and wants to be in Nina's life. She wants to mend fences. I'm hoping you do too." There's a mix of confidence and uncertainty in his voice. I rush to reassure him.

196

"Please tell her I said thank you. Tell her . . ." my voice trails off. "I'm a different person now. I can see things differently. As a mother. Tell her that. I'd be happy to see her again. Say that too."

He nods and looks satisfied. Dan returns with the coffee and Nina appears with a pack of cards. We play Uno, all four of us, and it's not anything like I imagined happening, but it's strangely okay. Of course, I'm comparing Booker and Dan, and mulling over what he's just said about Charmain. Not for the first time, I wonder how different things might have been if I'd told him about my family. If I'd have told Booker and his family about my mother and sister, would everything have gone differently? Could I have seen Charmain's involvement as help, rather than interference? Could I have built a relationship, instead of destroying everything? If I had stayed in Burlington with Booker, it's not hard to imagine that we'd have been happy. And Jocelyn and her search for the truth about Lynette would have been — what? Nothing. Nothing to do with me.

"Are you okay, Mom? It's your turn!"

I blink to put my focus back squarely where it should have been all along. On Nina. But as I lay down a card, I feel myself shiver and notice where a minute ago we were in bright sunshine, it's suddenly much, much darker. We all look up. And a sound has us all turning our heads toward the neighborhood.

Thunder.

THIRTY-SIX

Jocelyn
Now

Sasha's phone rings as we are finishing up in the library. I can hear a woman's voice, rapid and urgent, and Sasha's face changes color.

"What is it?" I say, but she's still listening.

"I'm still at the library. Wait." She steps out of our little room and I follow. Rain is slashing against the library windows. "Okay. I'll come now." She ends the call and grabs her notebook. "I have to go home. Right now. It's the storm. My mom is freaking out."

She's already out the door and I have to move fast to stay with her. "Shouldn't you wait it out? That rain looks heavy."

"Mom says the storm already ripped through the neighborhood. There are trees down. She wants me home now."

I think of the tree right in front of Jen's house. And of Nina, coming home in this weather.

She turns left as we leave the library, heading for her car. Mine is in the multistory in the other direction. Even though I know Nina's with her dad, panic squeezes my chest. My hands are shaking. How can I just drive home? I can't.

I'm drenched by the time I get in the car and the ten-minute drive to the neighborhood takes twice as long as usual. Water is already pooling on the road at several points and I'm driving near blind, my wipers slamming back and forth to little effect. I call Jen, but she doesn't pick up. My heart is thumping; I'm sure if the rain wasn't hammering the roof I'd hear it, and I breathe in deeply, trying to get a grip. I just need Nina to be safe.

The rain has stopped as I turn into Jen's road, but the storm damage is obvious. A tree is down on the garage at number two and there are leaves and branches everywhere. Sasha's car is back at number four and as I stop near the bottom of Jen's driveway, cold relief floods me. The house is fine. The tree hasn't budged. Ahead of me, I see a knot of people, neighbors out to see what the damage is. I'm looking for Jen, but first I see Nina and the rush of emotion brings tears to my eyes. She's back. She's here. She's safe. I stop the car just next to them and jump out calling her name. Within a minute she's in my arms.

"What are you doing here?" Jen puts her hand on my shoulder and squeezes. It hurts. I let go of Nina and widen my gaze. Behind Jen there's Dan and next to him a tall, calm-looking Black man. I've seen him from a distance, and in photographs, but he's more handsome in real life and he looks a lot like Nina, which surprises me somehow. Other figures register. An older woman, about my age, staring down into the cul de sac where another large tree is down, crushing an old blue minivan. A tall, slim woman in shorts and a vest, with a kid holding each hand. A couple of teens stand just a foot or so to one side of her, whispering. Noises register. A house alarm. The hum of generators. Jen takes my elbow and steers me toward their house.

"What are you doing here?"

"I was afraid. You didn't answer your phone."

"I must have left it inside. It was pretty terrifying. I've never heard lightning strike before." She shivers and runs her hands up and down her arms.

"Look." Jen turns when the tall woman speaks. A woman — I think the neighbor called Vicki — is having a heated conversation with a tall teen boy as they look at the damaged car on their driveway.

"Thank God no one was in it," I say. "Although she looks pretty mad about something."

"Maybe we should leave them to it," the other woman says. I hear her accent. This is the Australian neighbor. "Bring Nina and come to mine while the power is out. You don't have a generator, right?"

"Right." Jen nods. I can see how hard she's working to keep it together. I grab Nina's hand while Jen tells the men what her plan is. I see them nod and wonder if Booker will leave now, but no, it's Dan who turns toward his own house and Booker and Jen join me and the other woman and her kids. We're almost on her driveway when I turn back and look at my car. It's parked across the driveway of the house between Jen and Sasha's.

"I'd better move my car," I say to Jen. "I'll just put it on your driveway."

"Okay." Everyone else walks inside, leaving me and Jen on the doorstep. She keeps glancing around, looking at all the trees, and especially that pine in front of Nina's bedroom window. Words aren't needed. I know how she feels because I feel it too. Another near miss. Another reminder of how thin the line is between okay and not okay. A better person might hug her, but that's never been my style. Besides, if it wasn't for me they wouldn't be here. We're both thinking it, I'm sure. I watch Jen walk into the house and head to my car. My hands on the door handle when there's more noise down the street.

The woman standing beside the destroyed Honda Odyssey has started shouting. I can't make out her words over the groan of all the generators. But she's pissed as hell at her kid — to the point where she puts both hands on his chest and pushes him up against the car, knocking him to broken branches and clusters of leaves. For a split second I think I should step in, although that's no more my style than hugging Jen is, and so I'm relieved when another figure comes out of the Vicki woman's house, rushes over and grabs her by the arms, pulling her away from the boy. She sends him inside and then holds the woman by the shoulders, speaking intently. I should move before she looks up and sees me staring, but I don't. And then it's too late.

Because, of course, I'd know her anywhere. She's Natalie Preston.

THIRTY-SEVEN

Natalie
Now

When the storm hits I'm at Vicki's house drinking green tea while she complains about her husband's snoring. It's exactly what I need after overthinking everything about Ithaca and Lynette, and my dad. We're both used to the wildness of Pennsylvania summers, but this thunderstorm comes in fierce and fast, lightning flashing at her kitchen windows only seconds after the first crack of thunder. We go to her front room and watch the rain bounce against the road. It drums so loud my neck shrinks into my shoulders. We're standing right there when lightning strikes the tree only meters from us, and we clutch each other in shock as it falls, crushing the old blue minivan Thomas drives around in. Thank God he's upstairs. Thank God he's not in it. The car is almost split in two with the weight of half a tree lying over it. Windows are smashed. The whole trunk is buckled and broken open. The next few minutes are a bit of a blur as the power goes out in the neighborhood and the texts start flying. My kids are fine. Reid's at a friend's house and Erin is home. The generator is already on, she texts. I tell her I'll be back over soon.

The rain stops and the sky clears nearly as fast as it darkened. The smell of wet grass and leaves is in the air as Vicki goes out to look at the damage. I'm about to follow but Thomas pushes out the door in front of me and for some reason I hang back. He's always been kind of sullen, and I'm guessing he's not going to be too happy about his car, so I decide to wait in the kitchen while Vicki deals with him. It's only when I hear raised voices that I step outside. And at first all I see is Vicki, wild with anger at Thomas. It makes no sense, so I separate them and send him inside. I grab Vicki's arms, trying to find out what on earth is wrong, and that's when I look over her shoulder. When I see her. It's Lynette Knox's aunt. I'd know her anywhere.

"Don't look!" Vicki says, and I'm confused, for a split second, thinking she knows who I've just seen on our street, but it's the car she's steering me away from, not the aunt. I'm suddenly afraid that there *was* someone in the car, and so I peer round her and feel my eyes widen.

"What the hell, Vicki?"

I can see fur, different colors, maybe three separate animals, lying dead in the back of the vehicle. I see a little pink collar on one, bright against white hair, matted with blood. I'm trying to process it as she drags me back indoors.

"Wait in the kitchen."

The next few minutes are surreal. I sit at my familiar spot at her island while Vicki grabs garbage bags from under the sink and picks up her car keys. She doesn't make eye contact, but bustles out of the room. I hear low voices and the door opening and closing. She comes back in and crosses the row of cubbies beside her garage door. She leans into the garage, and I hear her huff because the electricity is out and her generator doesn't power the whole house. She has to open the garage door manually and when she comes back in, she's red in the face. I don't need her to tell me what's going on. I don't want her to talk to me about it. But she does.

"It's not what you think," she says, "I mean, it's not great. I'm working on him about it. You must know that."

"Vicki . . ."

She leans across the island and squeezes my arm, just above the wrist. It's a reassuring gesture. In normal circumstances.

"He's not a bad person," she says.

"Of course not." It's an unwritten rule of friendship between mothers. We don't criticize each other's children. But I don't want to look at her. I can't look her in the eye.

"Jason has no idea. You mustn't say anything to him. Or to Brad."

Ugh. There's a heavy feeling in the pit of my stomach. We have been friends for years, Vicki and I. My mind goes to Courtney, and to her story about Thomas and the dead cat on the swing set. I can hear Vicki dismissing it. Calling Courtney a liar, a drama queen, neurotic.

"How long has this been going on?" I ask.

THIRTY-EIGHT

Jen
Now

Dan goes home to make some calls. The storm will have caused chaos on the roads. That's bound to impact the hospital. Booker and I head into Daisy's house and Nina is swept into a game upstairs with the twins. I'm trying not to show how rattled I am. But I can't get the image of Vicki's son's smashed car out of my mind. Can't stop imagining that pine tree smashing through the roof over Nina's bed. It's just like the other day with the deer.

"Well, that will cramp Thomas Price's style," says Daisy, standing at her living room window, looking out toward their house. "Looks like they're having quite the argument about it. There's definitely something off about that kid."

Booker looks from me to Daisy. "Off? Like how?"

She tells him then, about the cat and the swing set, and Courtney's conviction that Thomas is some kind of serial killer in the making.

"*And* he's a lifeguard?" she announces. "Gross, right?"

"Some people call it 'the link.'" Booker picks up his phone and starts scrolling. "I read about it a while back. There's a definite link between animal abuse and person to person violence."

I don't know why, but there's something about the two of them silhouetted in the window, and the casual, almost disinterested way they're talking, something about the sounds of the storm when the wind tore through the neighborhood, and the destruction all around — all this rattles through my brain like one of those flicker books, except the images don't turn into something watchable, they just jar or repeat until I have my hand over my mouth and find myself sinking onto Daisy's sofa and gasping for breath. The neighborhood was supposed to mean normality. It was supposed to be safe. This is how panic feels. This is looking over the cliff edge. There's a tremendous hissing noise. And then black.

* * *

"Here. Try this."

I'm on Daisy's sofa. Booker's arm is around me. I'm aware of a fresh scent. Lemongrass, maybe. He brings a glass of water to my lips, and I sip it slowly, enjoying the cooling sensation as I swallow.

"I fainted? Wow. I haven't done that since I don't know when." My brain clicks slowly back into gear. Dan is at home, Nina is upstairs. Booker is closer to me than he has been in years. "Where's Jocelyn?"

Daisy's back at the window. "No sign of her now. Her car's gone." She looks to her left, toward Vicki's house. "Well, Thomas might be weird, but at least no one got hurt. He's driving off in Vicki's Tesla right now."

* * *

No sign of Jocelyn. No sign. It's not lost on me that I've just had a panic attack and the person who's here for me is Booker. Not Dan. And not Jocelyn. I feel a flare of anger toward her, and at the way I have let her direct my life, in some misguided gratitude to her for getting us out of Ithaca, and some foolish daydream about Nina having the normal family I was denied. It's her obsession that has brought us here. For the longest time I thought it was harmless. When did it all change for her? When did she start pushing me toward Dan Burrows and moving here?

When Lynette vanished I was young, only a few years older than Nina is now. I didn't see, or perhaps understand, what was taking place in the months when she was gone. Fingers were pointed, of course. Connor Goodman came in for the worst of it. I don't remember him from Ithaca. But I remember the day Jocelyn told me he was dead. I can picture her, as clearly as if it was yesterday, sitting at her computer desk in our tiny home in Rochester. Clicking away, all night long, the wash of blue screen light across her face, rocking back when she "found" something. Connor Goodman died from an accidental overdose, she announced. Jocelyn was almost gleeful about it, reading aloud from an article she'd found online. I hadn't cared. I only knew he'd been Lynette's boyfriend at some point. He'd gotten years more of life than my sister and what had he done with it, only to end it in drugs or alcohol, or both? Anger was all I felt when Jocelyn told me about it. Anger at his wastefulness. At his inability to appreciate what he had. What my sister did not.

Maybe he'd killed himself out of guilt, I'd said to Jocelyn. Maybe any answer she was looking for had died with him. But she wasn't having any of it. Because she was all fired up about a new lead, as she called it. She'd found a name. Jocelyn was going to find out everything there was to know about this boy Natalie Eason had been seeing. Dan Burrows.

And I, to my eternal shame, had gone along with it.

THIRTY-NINE

Jocelyn
Then

The formal ruling of Lynette's death as a suicide sent Sal over the edge. She went somewhere, in her mind, after that, and nothing I or Genevieve did or said was enough to bring her back. She was on so many meds during the funeral I don't think she knew what was happening. I kept it small because my sister was barely in a fit state to get through the service. There were a couple of teachers there. Natalie Eason with her parents. A few other girls. A couple of people at the interment I didn't recognize. Funeral tourists. Wackos.

Suicide. All my talk of Lynette running away had done more harm than good. Sal was totally unprepared for Lynette's body being found. Even then, an accident, she might have come to terms with. I thought so anyway and woke up every day for months with a ball of rage in my chest about it. Talking to her didn't help.

"I still think it's bullshit." I had the day off. Sal was on the sofa staring out the window. Genevieve was out at school.

"Does it really matter?" Her voice was soft as worn leather. It annoyed the hell out of me.

"Yes, it matters. Fucking cops. First, they said she'd run off, then as soon as they found her, they said suicide. He said it here. In this house. On that day."

"Because that's what happened."

"You don't think that." Sal didn't turn and look at me. I had to go and put myself between her and the window. Even then, it felt like she was looking through me, not at me. She shrugged. "Like I said, Jocelyn. What does it matter?"

"We should have insisted on seeing her."

"No."

At least there's an edge in her voice when she says no. I latch onto it. "No?"

"You wouldn't understand."

"Try me."

"Sit down."

This felt like progress. I sat next to her on the old two-seater, angled toward her, our knees touching. She took my hands in hers.

"Close your eyes," Sal said. "They said her body was a mess because of the water. Do you remember that?"

A mess. Yes, they had said that, and more. Cuts, contusions, torn clothing, water damage, skin sloughing, animal activity. She was found in shallow water, but the police were confident that wasn't where she'd been for the two months she was missing. They'd tracked upstream and found clothing further up Six Mile Creek and concluded she likely entered Well's Falls at the bridge on Giles Street. It would have been quick, they said. The force of the water. The rocks. But then the body snagged somewhere downstream, perhaps where the scraps of her jacket were recovered, before becoming dislodged and drifting to where she was discovered. Teens were impulsive, they'd said, over and over. And our family wasn't exactly known for mental stability.

"I see her, you know," Sal said. "She looks beautiful."

"Sal . . ."

"Keep your eyes closed. I'll help you see her."

I said okay, but I was lying. I couldn't do it. I wouldn't. Instead, I watched my sister's face as she spoke, her eyes closed, her lips almost smiling, her features relaxed and peaceful. "She's in her room, lying on her bed. She's wearing those shorts I bought her last summer. And that sweatshirt from Long Beach Island. She's just had a shower and gotten dressed. Towel on the floor, of course." There was a lift in Sal's voice. A stronger smile forming. "Her hair's wrapped in a tee-shirt and her skin is pink and warm. Can you see her?"

She opened her eyes and I shut mine, but not fast enough. Sal snatched her hands from mine. "You didn't do it."

"I don't get it. She's not there. How does it help to think she is when she isn't?"

"I want you to go."

"Sal . . ."

"I mean it. Get out, Jocelyn. Get out and give me some peace." There had been anger in her eyes, but it had flared out and now she just looked empty all over again.

"I'll go to the store," I said, getting to my feet. "I'll get something for dinner."

"Whatever."

* * *

But I didn't go to the store, not right away. First, I drove up to Well's Falls. I parked across the road by the wildflower preserve and walked back up to the road and the view over the water below. There were a few tourists taking photographs of the abandoned pumping station beside the falls. It was an eerie spot, and I remembered our father taking us there for a picnic one summer. There was the rock we sat on, down off the road to my left. I remembered scrambling down the side of the falls with him, trying to be brave, hiding how the rush of water made my stomach tingle, how the boarded-up windows seemed to lean across the river, as if the deserted old building wanted to eat me up.

The pull of the water. I felt it. A person could roll themselves over this low bridge. They could. They'd hit the water.

Bang their head. Break bones. The cold would be biting. But brief.

I leaned over.

Yes, I could see it happening.

But not to Lynette.

Not by choice.

FORTY

Natalie
Now

Here's the thing about Vicki. She's always had a blind spot when it comes to Thomas. Brad and I have discussed it often enough. Thomas was a weird little kid. He used to walk the neighborhood in the dark until the Kauffmans — the couple who used to live in Jen and Dan's house — brought it up at the homeowners' association when Thomas was nine or ten. Before that there was an incident with a BB gun. All through elementary he had an assigned seat at the front of the bus. Vicki said he "struggled socially" but there was gossip about vandalism of school bathrooms, and he was asked to leave his travel baseball team for talking back to the coaches. Then the issue with Geoff's daughter. That caused a real rift and I saw how Vicki was with Courtney — shutting down, hearing nothing. The same expression is plastered on Vicki's face now. She has worried about him for years, but lately has been more upbeat, talking about his talent for drawing, and an art college in California.

"There's nothing 'going on'," she says, her jaw set, and her arms crossed.

"Vick, Thomas has just driven off in your car with a bag of . . . of . . ." What do I say here? Dead cats? Pets?

"Animals," she says. "Roadkill."

"Roadkill," I repeat. My mind feels blank. This conversation is surreal. If you can call it a conversation. Vicki is the only one talking.

"Look, I'm not saying it's ideal," she says, "but animals dying on the road are a fact of life around here. How many times a week do you drive past a dead deer? Or a racoon? Squirrels, even. Remember when you hit that squirrel on the back road by the country club last month? It wasn't your fault. Okay, you felt bad for it, but what can you do? You drove on like anyone else does. But that's not what Thomas does. It's art. He's explained it to me. It's all about man and the environment, and recording the damage. His paintings are amazing. Visceral. They're ugly too, but a lot of life is ugly, Nat." Her voice has grown stronger, as if hearing herself defend him has propped up her belief in him. But I saw her face when she looked in the car. She was as shocked as I was. As I am.

"So you're saying he collects roadkill? And paints it?"

"I am."

"But Jason doesn't know."

Her expression falters and she spins away from the island, beginning, of all things, to empty her dishwasher.

"Jason doesn't really get Thomas. You know that. I can't tell him. I want my son and husband to have a good relationship. Fathers don't always understand. He hasn't spent the time with Thomas I have. He might be critical. I don't want him pushing Thomas away."

"Have you talked to anyone about it? His art teacher?"

"Of course. He doesn't see a problem with it." She doesn't make eye contact when she says this. And I know Vicki.

"Does the teacher know Thomas is painting from life? Not from pictures?"

Her lips purse. She shrugs. She shrugs like it's not important and I think about that white fur and that thin pink

213

collar I glimpsed in the trunk of Thomas' car. Someone's pet. Beloved, most likely. I think about all the times I've driven past posters about missing pets, and all the Facebook images of lost animals, and all the unhappy families not knowing where their dogs or cats or whatever have gone, or what has happened to them. And, of course, I think about Lynette going missing. Guilt swamps me. And anger.

"He had a cat in the car, Vick. Wearing a collar. Did he tell you where he found it? Did he even try and find its owner? That cat isn't just *roadkill*."

She stops what she's doing with the dishes and stands up straight. Her posture is awkward and I see that this is a burden she's carrying. That Thomas is a burden.

"He's my son," she says, her voice raw and bleak. "My son. I don't love that he has this, this 'interest', but you know how it is, Natalie. It's my job to protect him. To protect my family. I've done the research. He's not killing these animals. He's not torturing them. He's from a good home. He's a good quiet boy. No one needs to know anything about it. I'm asking you, as a friend, to just please forget what you saw. It's for the best. Honestly. It's for the best."

* * *

I realize several things in this moment. Firstly, that Vicki isn't sure that Thomas really is simply finding these animals in the road and stopping to throw them in the trunk. Secondly, I understand our friendship is on the line, because protecting her child, whatever the truth about him may be, is her priority, beyond all reason. And thirdly, I know I need to get away from her as fast as possible. Because the reminders of the past, the echo in her words that takes me back to my father and the night Lynette disappeared, are overwhelming.

Somehow, I make it home without throwing up.

I can't go up to Dad. If I did, I might do something terrible. Instead, I sit at my kitchen table, open a bottle of wine, and wonder what the hell Lynette's aunt was doing in the neighborhood today.

FORTY-ONE

Jocelyn
Now

I know she's recognized me. The way she went still and just stared? There's no question Natalie Preston recognized me. I panic. I jump back in the car and hightail it out of there. Driving away, I feel — what? Anxious? But also elated. This must be what it feels like to lay a bomb and walk away. The coming explosion is going to hurt. It's going to hurt Jen and maybe even Nina, for which I'm sorry. But overall, Natalie Preston recognizing me is an adrenaline hit. I just need to control what happens next.

There's a strip mall not far from Jen's fancy house. A big Walmart, Chipotle, TJ Maxx, Ulta, and a Hallmark gift shop. It takes a bit of a detour to get there, navigating past fallen trees and someone's trash can, blown into the middle of the road. I park but stay in the car.

For years I've wondered if Natalie Preston was once a nice girl. Wondered what scars she carries. Finally, it's time to find out. I put the car in gear and head back to the neighborhood.

I don't turn in, though. The place is a shitshow, with a couple of trucks arriving to start the clear-up, so I continue on and park in the next neighborhood. It's similar to Jen's, although the houses are bigger and there are fewer of them. They won't like my car sitting here — I can already imagine a text chain lighting up about this strange car in their pristine, safe bubble — but hopefully I won't be gone long.

There's a bit of an incline and no sidewalk between here and Jen's neighborhood. With my knees the way they are and the glaring sun, so bright it's hard to believe the storm ever happened, the walk is unpleasant, but I'm fired up. The street is quiet. Less damage here. The wind that whipped through Jen's front yard seems to have barely touched this street.

No one answers at Natalie's house. She must still be with her neighbor. Sitting on her doorstep in plain view of Jen or Dan doesn't seem like the best option so I slip round to the back of the house. They have a deck patio, freshly painted, and a new-looking set of wicker furniture I can wipe dry with my sleeve. It looks inviting. Don't mind if I do.

What is her life like? I imagine Natalie Preston sitting here on a Friday evening drinking wine with her husband. Perhaps they're having another couple over for drinks, or something on the grill. It's the life Jen is looking for and who knows, maybe she could pull it off. I know I couldn't. If I had a deck, which I never will, I'd only need one chair. Or maybe two, but only for the cat. Loneliness becomes me. It's taken a lot of years for me to reach this understanding, but I know I'm my own best companion. I don't have the knack for other people. Sal did. And for a while she carried me along with her. But once she was gone, I was left to deal with Genevieve. That's when I really learned about my own shortcomings. Jen is better off without me. When this is over, I think I'll leave them alone. My only regret will be Nina. Although, of course, she's better off without me too.

The light in the kitchen flicks on, the patio door to my left is suddenly a rectangle of yellow. Natalie's inside and she's alone. I watch her for a while, sitting at her island, drinking wine in the middle of the day, thinking God knows what. She doesn't so much as glance my way. In the end, I get up and bang on the glass.

"Jesus!"

I hear her squeal through the closed patio doors. Do I enjoy watching her hand go to her chest and her knees buckle because of the fright I've given her? A little bit, yes, I do.

Once she gets over the shock and opens the door, we stand looking at each other. She's taller than me, and appears older in close-up than in photographs, but she has good skin and a largely unlined face. The twenty years haven't changed her dramatically. She's wearing the same kind of workout clothes Jen always has on these days. I don't say anything. I want her to speak first.

"You're Lynette's aunt, aren't you? I'd know you anywhere." She gestures to the seat I've just vacated and sits opposite me, rubbing a hand across her brow. "Why are you here?"

"I want to talk about Lynette."

She nods slowly and then makes a noise, almost like laughing. "Of course, you do. Wow. What a day. You're here. Looking exactly the same. It's kind of mind-blowing. I think I need another drink. Do you want a drink?"

She doesn't wait for me to answer, just heads indoors, and in a minute she's back with the bottle of white wine and two glasses. She pours us both a drink and takes a long swallow. I don't touch mine.

"You remember her, then?" I ask. "Lynette?"

Her brows snap together. "Of course! My God, she was my best friend."

"Did you think about Lynette's family? Us? Back then? What my sister went through? When her daughter disappeared?"

She closes her eyes. Coward. "No," she says. Her voice is small and sorrowful. "I should have. But I was seventeen."

"True." I'm surprised to find myself nodding. "I won't go so far as to say I don't blame you. But you *were* only seventeen."

"You've barely changed. I'd know you anywhere."

"We never saw you after the funeral."

"No."

"My sister, Lynette's mom — she really struggled."

Natalie Preston takes another swig of her wine. "I'm sorry for your loss."

I hate that phrase only marginally less than the "thoughts and prayers line" every politician in this country trots out week after week as we lurch from one mass shooting to another, from one natural disaster to the next. "I don't think you have any idea."

I say it sadly, my voice as empty as her platitude. She doesn't seem offended.

"Probably not. I only have a brother, and we're not close these days."

Her phone is on the wicker table between us. I can see text messages flashing up on the screen and my own phone is vibrating away in my pocket. That will be Jen, but she can wait. I tilt my head to Natalie. "Don't mind me."

She grabs the phone and scans her messages. "Just my husband, checking in after the storm," she says. And then she surprises me.

"Why was Sasha over here asking about Lynette?"

I choose to say nothing. People find silence hard. I'm not great at asking questions, but I do a mean silence.

"Have you *met* Sasha? Did you — I don't know — did you send her over here somehow?" She frowns and keeps staring at me, and I keep right on saying nothing. "Does Dan Burrows know you're here? Have you been here before today?"

She's getting worked up, but not in the way I was hoping. Time to press her buttons instead.

"You say she was your best friend. But you never really gave a shit, did you? That first time I met you, at your house, I came away thinking you were one cold bitch."

"I did care! She *was* my best friend!"

"Was she? You were a good friend to her, were you? There for her?" Tears fill her eyes and I lean forward. "You lied to me about that night. I've always known it. Lied to protect

218

someone — yourself? Connor Goodman? Dan Burrows? Someone else? Who?" I'm on the other side of the table but I'm right in her face, just with my words. The pressure's working. Her face is wet with tears. Her hand goes to her mouth. I'm ready for this. "Maybe your father?"

And then I'm surprised. When I mention her father, Natalie Preston's eyes flit toward the house. Immediately she's shaking her head, and trying to regroup, but I know what I saw.

"My God," I say. "He's here?"

FORTY-TWO

Natalie
Now

It's a total nightmare. First Vicki. Now Lynette's aunt. I can't even remember her name, and that makes me even more wretched. One minute I'm swollen with disgust at the way Vicki's so obviously covering for Thomas, the next I'm confronted with the aunt. The shame of it all burns me. I think a glass of wine will help, but I don't even taste it and she lets her glass just sit there, condensation prickling up on its surface as we sit on my deck, Lynette's aunt and me.

She says she wants to talk about Lynette. That much is surely obvious. What's not obvious is how she got here, what she's doing in my neighborhood and how this all connects to Sasha's questions and the fact Dan has recently moved back into my life.

Right away, though, she makes me feel guilty. I don't feel in control of the conversation, and she's so on the money in her accusations.

"My father lives here now, yes. He's sick."

"How sick?"

"Very. He has ALS. It's degenerative. He—"

"I know what ALS is." There's no hint of sympathy in her gaze. "And it was him? You were covering for your father? How did he even know her?"

I feel something let loose. I want, I need, to be honest. "She was my best friend. We were in and out of each other's houses. He saw her every Wednesday. We had family dinner once a week." If this woman had been here yesterday, I would have stopped speaking at this point. I'd have been polite. I'd have stuck to the usual story and sent her on her way. But today I've seen Thomas Price's collection of roadkill, and worse, have witnessed how far Vicki is prepared to go to cover for him. And so, I'm done with the usual story.

"My father had a thing for Lynette. It was probably obvious, although I didn't see it. But my parents divorced and since then I've seen my dad with a lot of younger women. So, yes, he had a thing for her, yeah. Disgusting as that is."

"What happened on the night she disappeared? You said you had a fight about homework. She left. And then you hung out with your boyfriend on his porch."

The aunt has fat fingers, and she stabs her palm each time she makes a point. Her intensity is just as intimidating as it was twenty years ago, but now Mom's not here to have my back. But neither is Dad glowering in the doorway.

"We did argue. But not about homework." I'm not sure how much of the truth I'm prepared to go with here, but undoing the first lie is liberating.

"What about?"

"My boyfriend. I thought she was just jealous, but looking back later? Maybe it was something more."

"That makes no sense."

"No? You knew Lynette. It makes perfect sense. Teenage girls. You know what they're like." I watch her digest that. She rubs her forehead.

"Not really. You'll have to explain it to me."

221

I let out a deep sigh. "She had been seeing this boy. It was nothing. Casual. Everything with Lynette was casual. She took nothing seriously. When I look back at it now, I wonder about that. About why she was like that, and whether at least some of it was an act. Anyway. They weren't serious and I liked him. We got together and Lynette was fine about it. I totally thought she was fine about it. But then I slept with him." I pause and drink some more wine. The aunt doesn't look shocked. I wish I knew the woman's name, but how to ask? "I stayed overnight at his house. I needed Lynette to cover for me, and say I was at hers. My mother was bound to ask her. Bound to. And Lynette was just a complete bitch about it."

The aunt nods. It's a relief, but I rush to clarify. "I don't mean she was a bitch. I loved her. She was my best friend. She was the funniest, sassiest, smartest person I knew. I was devastated by what happened. I hope you can believe that."

She pulls a face. Kind of like she's thinking about believing me, but the jury is still out. My glass is empty but hers is full and sitting right there. "Don't you want that?" I ask.

"No." She slides the glass across the table to me.

"So that was what the fight was about. I thought she was mad I'd slept with someone. But maybe it was because it was him in particular. She was winding me up, saying I was asking a lot for her to lie to my parents. She came out with this whole spiel about how kind they were with their Wednesday dinners and the extras of everything my mom always gave her for her sister. She said how lucky I was to have a dad that cared. You can imagine it, I'm sure."

"Where were you? How did the fight end?"

"At my house. In my room."

"And you didn't see her again?"

I think about this. About how far I'm prepared to go. I picture Vicki. And my father right now, lying upstairs. "I saw her out the window. On the driveway. She was talking to my dad. They looked . . . friendly. I didn't like it. I banged on the window. They both looked up. I never saw her again."

"And later?"

Can I tell her about later? I want to. But can I?

"It was like I said at the time. I was with my boyfriend." She stares at me until I plow on. "But when I came home my dad was sitting in the kitchen. He said he was waiting to speak to me about what I'd seen out the window. How I shouldn't misconstrue it. How he had seen she was upset and was simply checking on her. But there was more to it, I was sure. He talked about his reputation and how gossip might damage him. And how that would affect Mom, and me and my brother's future."

"He was threatening you?"

"Maybe. He came in the room the next morning when you were there. Do you remember?"

"Of course."

"Well, that was to make sure I kept my mouth shut."

"About what?"

"What he told me." I let out a sigh. Am I really going to say this? I am. "He told me she'd been in an accident. He told me she'd been hit by a car."

"Where?"

"I don't know. All he said was he saw it happen but couldn't stick around. For our sakes, he said, for the family. He left her there. Said it was 'for the best.'" *Roadkill*, I think. *My friend. Roadkill.*

She doesn't speak and I think this has gone okay. I could say more. I could tell her the whole truth and it would be like lifting a stone from my chest, I know it would. But I'm not sure I'm ready. I'm not sure what good it would do. Or what further damage. This is not like Vicki's situation. Maybe once, but not now.

I see a movement in the kitchen. It's Erin. She comes out to say hi and my love for her hits like a wave. The precariousness of life is overwhelming.

"The storm was crazy," she says. For once she's happy to be folded into my arms. She smells of grass and sweat. Not unpleasant — in fact, pleasantly real. She is flesh and blood. Here. Safe. I touch her hair, kiss her forehead. I'll do the same when Brad picks up Reid from his friend's house on his way home from work. He'll be less tolerant of my affection. Or maybe not. Maybe he'll be as shaken as the rest of us. It's hard to know with boys.

"Mom?" Erin has stepped back and is looking at my visitor.

"Oh. I'm sorry. This is my daughter, Erin. Erin this is . . ." My voice trails off, I still don't know her name.

"It's Mrs. Silver, right?" my girl says brightly. "You're Nina's grandma, right? I've seen you at the coffee shop. With Sasha."

"Nina's *grandma*?"

I've enough wits about me to shoo Erin back indoors as the meaning of what my daughter has just said explodes in my mind.

"Nina's grandma? That means . . . that means . . . Oh my God, she's Genevieve."

FORTY-THREE

Jen
Now

Nina is happy to stay with the twins, but I sense Booker's itching to get out of Daisy's house. I don't have the bandwidth to keep up a conversation between them and I'm thinking, very tentatively, maybe this is the moment to tell him about Lynette. Living dishonestly isn't working for me any longer. The thought of the lies makes me want to vomit.

"We need to get out of your hair," I say, and although it's clear Daisy's in no rush to be left alone at her window watching the family at number two survey the damage to their garage, I persist, and Booker and I walk back over to my house in silence. Dan's car has gone, to work presumably. Another good reason for me to confide in Booker. If I'm ever going to do it, this is the moment. We sit at one corner of the kitchen island. It feels both strange and familiar, sitting here with him.

"Something tells me that friend of yours will be pouring herself a glass of wine right about now. Are you sure Nina is okay over there?"

"I'm sure. I mean, you're probably right. Daisy is a drinker. But her kids are good kids. I don't think she has a real problem. She's just unhappy."

"Oh?"

"There's something going on with her husband. I've never seen him. He's not been here since we moved in. She says he's over in Australia. That his mother is sick. But I don't know. I feel like there's more to it."

"Have you asked her?"

"No. What would I say without offending her? I can't just come right out and say, *hey Daisy, so has your husband left you and your four children for good or what?*"

He laughs a little. "It's not always easy to know what's going on in someone else's head."

We fall silent. It's a giant lake of silence waiting for me to fill it.

"There's something. I—"

"But you know, this place, these people, it's not really you. You know that, right?"

"What?" It's like he's snapped an elastic band in my face.

"That Aussie woman's a hot mess. She clearly has a drink problem. The kid down the street is probably dangerous. And Dan? I mean, I get that he's successful. And a good-looking guy. He's even good with Nina. But my God, what a bore."

My mouth drops open. "Are you kidding me?"

"No." He leans back and looks around the kitchen I'm so proud of. I don't like his expression. "I'm not kidding. Come on. This isn't you, Jen. All the granite. So sterile. The fancy appliances." He practically leers. Like appliance is a naughty word. Like lingerie or vibrator or something.

"I love this kitchen!"

His handsome face dissolves into incredulity. "You might think you do. But believe me. You don't."

"Please don't tell me what I think, Booker." The threat of tears is real. I get up and go to the sink, gripping its edge, hunched, defensive. I hear his stool scrape. He must be standing. Maybe he'll just leave. But he doesn't.

226

His hand rubs my back. "Okay, look I'm sorry. Truly, Jen. I shouldn't have said all that. I just think that in trying to do your best for Nina, you've forgotten to think about yourself."

It crashes in on me then. I can never tell him the truth. Booker thinks I'm better than I am. A better mom. A better person. I've tried to tell myself this move was good for Nina, but we came here because Jocelyn made me. Because I *let her* make me.

"You're giving me more credit than I deserve," I say. "And I know this place is a little different for me, but it's a good different, can't you see that? This is the kind of place people raise good kids."

"I know, I know. And I want to respect your choices." I raise my eyebrows, and he grimaces. "I should have kept my mouth shut." We're standing so close together, I can feel his breath touching my face. "Maybe I'm just envious."

That breaks the spell. "Envious? You? Booker, you think you know me and what I want? Well, I know you. You've never envied anyone or anything in your life. I've never met anyone so grounded. If I could see Nina grow up to be the same way, I'd be a happy woman."

He smiles at the compliment but then his brow furrows. "I am, though. I'm envious of Dan Burrows."

"No, you're not." Even as my heart leaps, I make light of it. I go to push his chest and step away, intending to get some distance from him and this conversation we shouldn't be having, but he grabs my hand and holds it there.

"I could be moving down here soon. As soon as Labor Day maybe."

"I know. I'm happy about it. For Nina."

"What about for you?"

"I . . ." I've a crashing sense of frustration. *Why now, Booker?* I want to scream. Why not a year ago, a month ago, why not before we rented this big house, before I dragged Nina so far into Jocelyn's schemes? "There are things I need to talk to you about. I'm not sure," I mutter.

He releases my hand and steps back. I sway a little, tempted to move toward him, but a noise stops me. A door bangs in the utility room. Someone's coming in from the garage. I've time to think it must be Nina, but then the door is thrown open and it's not her at all. It's Natalie Preston.

She strides across the room, ignoring Booker entirely. Before I can form actual words, she grabs me by the shoulders and stares into my eyes. There's so much emotion in her face. Anger and shock. Disbelief. But also, something softer? Something . . . hopeful?

"Genevieve," she says at last. "It really is you. Genevieve." And suddenly her arms are around me. I can't see Booker's face. I'm not sure what's more shocking. Natalie knowing, or Booker being here for this. What I do see is that a slightly breathless Jocelyn has followed Natalie Preston into my kitchen. She's leaning in the doorway.

"You *told* her?"

"It was more that she guessed."

Natalie's arms unlock and she leans away but her hands still clutch my shoulders. "I can't believe I didn't see it. Even when we talked about her, I never made the connection. But you do look like her. You do."

She's smiling broadly and I smile back, feeling warmth spread, tasting the pleasure of hearing someone, beyond Jocelyn, speaking of the sister I lost. But, of course, there's another person here. And he wants to know what's going on.

"Who?" he says, speaking clearly and calmly, but his voice is a little louder than normal, "who exactly does Jen look like?"

Natalie turns her gaze away from mine. "Like her sister," she says. "Lynette Knox was my best friend. I've missed her every day since it happened."

228

FORTY-FOUR

Booker
Now

Whoa. Whoa.

Genevieve Knox?

I'm not gonna lie. There's always been something Jen's held back. When we first met, I liked it about her. She was a little elusive — although now I'm thinking evasive would be another word for it — and it was appealing. I'd been feeling swamped by my family; my four loud older sisters, my opinionated, fun-loving mother, my smiling father who liked nothing more than sitting back in his chair with a cold one in his hand and listening to his wife and kids holler and laugh. I couldn't afford to go away for college and living at home was driving me nuts. Jen was an oasis of calm. We read books together, walked, took photographs, listened to music. I liked to watch her, lying in bed reading, while I played my violin. My sisters had literally thrown things at me when I practiced as a kid. Jen made me feel like a grown-up.

She told me she had next to no family. Only her mother, back in Rochester, New York, who had suffocated her. Going to college in Burlington was freedom. She called her mom Jocelyn, emphasizing her independence, I thought. I could tell Jen didn't love easily. Which made her loving me, choosing me, even more precious. When it was just us in her tiny studio, we were wholly ourselves, she said. And I'd believed her.

Now I feel my brain jamming. Jen has — no, had — a sister. Wait, not Jen, Genevieve. And not Silver either. Her last name is Knox. Which means Nina's name should be . . .

"What the hell is going on here?"

"I'm so sorry." Jen starts around the island toward me, but I hold up my hands. I can't have her touch me. I don't even know who she is. She jerks back like I've slapped her in the face, and wavers uncertainly, before pulling out a stool and sitting. She props her elbows on the granite and covers her face in her hands.

The blonde woman who burst in has the grace to look embarrassed. Her eyes flit from Jen to me. She doesn't need to be a rocket scientist to figure I'm Nina's father and that this whole sister-and-name thing is new to me. And so, I turn to Jocelyn.

"Well?"

"Let's all sit," she says. "I think I need a glass of water. Anyone else?" The blonde shakes her head and Jen doesn't move. Jen's mother bustles around finding glasses and running the tap. Even though I didn't respond, she pours me a drink and sets it down on the island as far away from Jen as can be. She nods toward the drink meaningfully and pulls out a stool by Jen for herself. The other woman shrugs and takes a seat. Jen doesn't move and it's infuriating. I need to see her face.

"Natalie," says Jocelyn, "this is Nina's father, Booker. Booker, this is Natalie Preston. She lives across the street."

We nod at each other. I've an urge to laugh. Or shout. Probably shout.

"When I arrived in the neighborhood earlier this afternoon," she continues, "Natalie recognized me. The last time we saw each other was nearly twenty years ago. In Ithaca. At my niece's funeral."

"Your *niece*?"

Jocelyn nods and looks toward Jen. "There's no point in hiding anything," she says, although I've seen no reaction from Jen so far. "You see, twenty years ago Jen's sister went missing. Lynette was seventeen. She went out one night with friends . . ." her eyes slide to this Natalie woman, ". . . and never came home. My sister, Sal, was out of her mind with worry. Genevieve was devastated. We all were. I was certain someone knew the truth, but it was like she'd vanished into thin air. The police decided she was a runaway. Nothing we could say changed their minds. Two months later a woman walking her dog found Lynette's body in shallow water. She'd been there so long, they said it was hard to know if she'd drowned or died some other way. My sister was told she couldn't view the body. Lynette's death was ruled a suicide. I don't know if you know Ithaca, but there's a lot of water there. Lots of waterfalls. Bridges. Some of them have wire cages to prevent suicides. Some don't. But Lynette didn't kill herself. And I don't believe it was an accident either."

"So, you're Jen's aunt? Nina's great-aunt. Where's the mother?"

Jocelyn doesn't like my tone. Her face stiffens. I hardly know this woman — we've never exchanged a word. I've seen her, of course, when Jen was back living in Rochester. When I'd drop Nina off or pick her up, Jocelyn would sometimes be at the door, or working in the yard. Jen had called her a semi-recluse, an oddball. She was in no rush for us to meet, Jen had said, and I'd assumed it was probably a race thing. My eldest sister had dated a white guy in high school and although the boy had been fine, Ellie had reported all the veiled and not-so-veiled remarks his parents had made about having fun and not settling down, or about finding people with more "in common". If Jen's mother was the same way, it wouldn't be Jen's fault, I'd reasoned. But it looks like I've read the whole story entirely wrong. Hard to swallow for a journalist who prides himself on his intuition and people skills.

"Lynette didn't kill herself," Jocelyn says slowly. "But my sister did."

Like a match to a cloud of gas, her words kill my anger. Natalie Preston has gone red in the face and starts to weep. There's a rawness to it, her face full of emotion, in contrast to her so put-together appearance, from her designer sunglasses to her Tori Birch flip-flops. Jen still doesn't move. I want to ask how the mother killed herself, but that seems too cruel.

"Not long after that, Genevieve and I moved to Rochester. Ithaca was too full of memories. She wouldn't — or to be more accurate, couldn't — set foot in the house. I sold it. We needed a new start. Genevieve Knox couldn't function. But Jen Silver — Silver is my name, Sal's maiden name — was gradually able to start again at a new school where no one knew her story, in a house without bad memories."

"I'm so sorry." Natalie Preston looks anxiously at Jen. Tears have seeped between Jen's fingers and Natalie rips off a couple of sheets of paper towel and slides one over to her. "We didn't know the damage — the *further* damage — we were causing."

"You were involved? I thought you said she was your best friend?" I try to keep my tone light. "Who's 'we'?"

"Well, Dan, obviously."

"*Dan*?" I look at these three women and watch Jen's hands drop from her face. She dries her face with the paper towel and finally looks me in the eye. She doesn't speak, though. It's her mother/aunt who talks, her voice low, almost monotone.

"Dan Burrows and Natalie were an item. He had been Lynette's boyfriend first, though. I have known in my bones for twenty years that someone hid the truth about Lynette's death. We need the truth, Jen and I, we need it. Nothing else matters."

"Not even Nina? Jen?" The implications of what this woman has just said blooms like ink in water. "Does Dan Burrows know who you really are?" She shakes her head. She's looking at me so sorrowfully. Her eyes are huge. I scan her expression looking for some sign that she's going to contradict me. That she can explain. That this isn't what I think it is. Finally, she speaks.

"We found him using social media. Natalie too. Jocelyn did it. I met up with Dan. I was to get him talking about Ithaca. About my sister and what happened to her." She shrugs and dread grows in my guts. "Things spiraled."

And now it's not just that I don't know this woman's name, it's that I don't know her at all. The Jen I know wouldn't do this. No one would. Or at least not someone with a child. With my child, the child she took from me to run back to Jocelyn, and the past.

"Spiraled? Interesting word choice," I say. "Not sure Dan Burrows will like it." She frowns and looks confused, but I feel clear, very clear, about what is going to happen next. "You need to tell him, Jen. And if you don't, I will. But Nina won't be here to witness it."

"No!"

"*No*? Jen, have you lost your mind? You have. You have lost your mind. You — her mother — have been lying to the man you both live with about who you are and why you're here. I mean, you're not denying that's why you're here, are you? Why, out of all the neighborhoods in America, you just happened to move to the one where this woman lives?" I watch Natalie Preston react to this. It's obvious by her expression that she hasn't made that leap, but now she's staring at Jocelyn, who is the most composed of us all, somehow. "He's not going to like it. Even if he loves you, how can he forgive you?" My voice twists a little. Damn it.

She reads me like she always has. "I was starting to tell you. Earlier. Over by the sink." We both look over. I can see us standing there, her hand on my heart. Me all but asking her to leave Dan and try again with me. It's true. She had been going to tell me something. But it's not enough.

"You've had years, Jen. *Years* to tell me who you were and what you were carrying."

She says nothing, because, of course, there is nothing to say. In all these years, she's never trusted me with the truth of herself. She's given me the shell, never the center. I shake my head, aware of the tears stinging my own eyes in the knowledge of the wounds I'm about to inflict. I've always loved Jen Silver, but I'm Nina Silver's dad. And getting her out of this neighborhood is the only thing that matters right now.

"I'll give you some time without Nina. You'll tell her you want her in the city while the power is out. We'll go to my hotel. I'll get Mom to fly down so I can do my interview. In the meantime, you resolve this. Whatever *this* is. We'll see what's best for our daughter after that."

FORTY-FIVE

Jocelyn
Now

The moment Natalie Preston admits her father knew something about Lynette's death, I know my next move is to get in his room and confront him. I think of nothing else even as I follow her over to Jen's house, cursing myself I haven't left something behind I can suddenly remember about and have to pop back to fetch. I'm so busy thinking about him, I barely register the fall-out between Booker and Jen, but thank goodness for it, because Booker's decision to take Nina away gives me the very chance I need.

When Nina returns home and she and Jen are upstairs packing a bag, I gesture to Natalie that I'm heading up to help them. Booker doesn't look up from his phone. In the hallway, I simply slip out of the front door. I bend low as I follow the path to Jen's driveway but with all the shrubs, I'm not worried Natalie will see me. Someone would have to be really staring from the kitchen and through the dining room to spot me slipping past. I'm much more worried about who is in Natalie's house and my chances of making it upstairs without getting caught. But she'd said her husband and son were out and, with any luck, Erin will be like any other teen, holed up in her bedroom with headphones on. The garage is open and the door to the kitchen isn't locked. There are plenty of lights on but no one on the first floor. So far so good.

My plan is to slip off my Skechers and carry them, but Natalie has so many rugs covering her hardwood floors, I'm able to walk around without making a sound. Thick carpet runs up the stairs and along the upstairs hallway. Thank God these houses are so similar. The master is clearly to my left. To my right, one room is in darkness, likely the boy's. Lights are on in the room opposite, and the door is ajar just enough for me to see a strip of pink wall. Erin's room, I decide. That leaves the door at the end of the hallway, opposite the master. I walk slowly toward it, noting the line of light at the bottom of the door.

He doesn't turn when I enter. His bed faces the window and isn't up against a wall which makes sense given the monitors he's hooked up to. There's an armchair but I'm guessing he hasn't made it as far as that for a few weeks now. As I step up behind him, the first thing I see is how thin and wispy his hair is. He was a good-looking man back in the day. He had thick hair, the kind of head of hair any man in his forties would be proud of, and he was. He had that swagger about him, I remember it very clearly. He had nice forearms, I had thought, and then hated myself for thinking it, when my mind should have been on nothing but Lynette. Now my eyes glance on and off his still form. I move slowly round the bed, expecting him to at least try and turn, or speak, but then I think maybe he's sleeping and frown. I don't have much time. The blinds are open, and I glance over at Jen's house. I'm pretty sure Natalie will be there for a while. Discovering Jen is Genevieve seemed to make her emotional, in a way I don't expect I'll ever understand.

I'm next to him now and good, his eyes are open. They look watery, and weary. I wonder how much pain meds he's on and if, in all the upset of the day, Natalie has missed giving him something. His face is drawn, cheeks sunken, and his lips are too colorful for his otherwise faded face.

"Do you know who I am?" I ask, turning my back on the window and leaning across the bed, forcing my face into his line of sight. "Do you?" He does. I see it in the way his chin trembles. The way his lips part a fraction. I hear the hitch in his breath. "I've come for truth this time," I say.

His eyes kind of bulge out and as he makes a weird noise from the back of his throat my heart sinks.

"You can't speak?"

He blinks once. Oh, great. Here we go. I feel pressure building at my temples. I don't have time for this shit.

"Is it true she got hit by a car?"

Two blinks. Is that a yes or a no? Christ, this looks so easy when people do it in the movies. I think fast. "Your daughter is Natalie?" Two blinks. Okay. That's a yes.

"Was it you? Did you hit Lynette with your car?"

One blink. Not him.

"You were there, though?"

Two blinks. A sphere of water slips from the corner of his left eye. I doubt it's a tear — unless it's for himself. Frustration runs like a drug through my veins, and my eyes slip from his face and to the snaking clear tube that runs from the drip beside his bed and to the cannula in his inner elbow. This is getting me nowhere fast.

"And after she got hit, what did you do? Did you try and help her?"

One blink. Water leaks from both his eyes now. I think maybe he is sorry. There's a cross on the wall. Maybe he's religious these days. Maybe the thought of meeting his maker has him feeling scared.

"Who hit her, then? How did she end up in the water? Do you know?"

One blink. No. The disappointment is physical. I sag back and have to lean against the wall and close my eyes. When I open them, I see his IV bag.

The decision isn't difficult. In fact, it's not really a decision at all. This has to happen. The moment Natalie said her father saw Lynette hit by a car and then abandoned her, I knew what I'd do, given the chance.

It only takes a moment to unhook the IV bag and lay it on the bed. He can't see what I'm doing, even though his eyes swivel like he's some frightened cow. I can't stop my hand from rubbing my own neck. It must be terrible to be a prisoner in your own body in this way. I smile at him, kindly, because, in a way, it is kind, what I'm doing. If it works, he ought to thank me for it. It will be a sweet release. I tap the bag. Shake it up a little. Then I hang it back up. There should be enough air in there to kill him now, I think. It's time for last words, but my eyes flick nervously across the road to Jen's house. How long have I been gone? Too long. But he needs to hear my voice. There are names for men like him. Ugly names for ugly men who prey on young women and who cheat on their wives. I want him to have something to think about until the air enters his bloodstream, but names won't do it. I lean over him and whisper.

"You will not be missed."

* * *

Minutes later, I'm back across the road at number six. Jen is still upstairs with Nina and won't have noticed I was gone. No surprise there. Invisibility has become my secret weapon. I used to think it was a weakness. No one liked to look at me; from a young age I knew it, watching eyes drift away — teachers, my dad, people in shops — talking to some unknown spot over my shoulder instead of to me. I'm not the kind of person people smile at when they're walking by, or hold doors for, or make room for in an elevator, or let step on an escalator first. I've been brushed past and pushed in front of all my life. People don't see me. They don't know or care if I'm there.

Useful, on a day like this.

FORTY-SIX

Jen
Now

It pains me, how readily Nina agrees to go with Booker, even though it makes sense. He is her dad, and they're close. She's already told me what a great time they had up north with all her cousins and her gran, chattering in Spanish and doing volunteer work with a citizenship program through her local library. The city is familiar territory to her also. If anyone knows the appeal of retreating to the familiar when life becomes chaotic, it's me. As I watch them drive away, I know it's the right thing. I feel like I'm stabbing myself in the eyeball, letting her go when she's only just back, but I can't have her here when Dan comes back.

Booker barely looked at me when they left, and how can I blame him? It's too much to expect him to understand. I can excuse myself for not telling him in the first place, back in Burlington. He was new, our relationship was new, and above all, I was new. I was happy to be Jen Silver. I liked her, especially with him. You don't know when you meet someone how long they're going to be in your life. I didn't know we'd have Nina, or how that would change me. I should have talked to him when I was pregnant with Nina. If I'd told him my history then, who can say how different things would have been? He read my insecurity as a parent as insecurity about him and his family. When he offered me a ring, I panicked and ran. I blamed his mom. Said she'd never approved of me and never would. I ran back to Jocelyn. And then I let myself get sucked into her obsession with the past and gotten involved with Dan. That's what Booker isn't going to forgive me for. And especially not for taking it one step further and moving here. Because of Nina.

Two things are very clear to me. I must end things with Dan and cut ties with Jocelyn. Nothing less will do. Booker and I will continue to co-parent in some form or another. But that glimmer of something between us back then in the kitchen before Natalie and Jocelyn stormed in? That's gone.

As Booker's car turns out of the neighborhood, I take one last look at the tree down on the garage just four houses away. I think of Courtney, and of Daisy, and of Vicki, and of Natalie. Booker is right. They are not really my kind of people. But Natalie is inside my house right now, and if the truth about my sister's death is ever coming out, this might be the time. Jocelyn may have forced me here, but a part of me is every bit as invested in the past as she is. Natalie owes us some answers. I'm going to deal with Dan, with Natalie, and with Jocelyn. And then focus on getting my daughter home. Wherever home might be.

* * *

"We've been talking," Jocelyn announces as I walk back into the kitchen. Natalie looks pale and anxious, but Jocelyn's eyes are bright. There's confidence in her voice, a briskness, telling me *she* has been talking and Natalie has been listening, nodding and agreeing because sometimes the force of Jocelyn's will just does that to you. "Natalie has some things she'd like

240

to tell us about Lynette. She's already told me some of it. But now *you* are here, she may even have more to tell."

"Okay." I look cautiously from one to the other. I can handle this, I think. Although there's one thing I want to know up front. "I have one question, first."

"Go ahead." Jocelyn's smiling. Something about her is off but I don't have time to consider it.

"Did Dan . . ." I begin, with a lump forming in my throat. "Did Dan kill my sister?"

"No." Natalie looks me right in the eye when she answers, and I believe her. It feels like all the liquid in my body just hit the floor and bounced back up through me again. My hand goes to my chest. "Does he know who did? Do you?"

She swallows. "It was an accident, I think." Tears flood her eyes. Her hands are trembling. "I'm so sorry. I'm so sorry."

I push away an urge to wrap my arms around her. It's hard to watch someone in such obvious pain. But it's not answer enough.

"We need more than 'I think,'" says Jocelyn, like a hound scenting blood. "After all this time we need — we deserve — more than that."

Ideas, theories, questions, race through my mind. "You and Dan lied about how well you knew each other in Ithaca. Why?"

Natalie doesn't answer, even though Jocelyn's eyes are laser-sharp on her. She doesn't seem to feel it, though. Instead, she stares at me.

"She loved you, you know," Natalie says. "I know Lynette came off as mean sometimes, but she wasn't, not really. We all thought she was so strong, but as I look back at it, now I'm older, I think I was wrong about her. I was so wrapped up in my own shit. We had a terrible fight, that night. I've never forgiven myself."

This knocks me off-kilter. "I don't even know what the last thing she said to me was," I say, the urge to offer this woman something, some kindness, suddenly as urgent as hearing the truth about Lynette. My sister loved me. Hearing Natalie say it feels like a gift. "It wasn't your fault. You were a kid."

"I still can't believe it's you. Lynny's sister." She shakes her head slowly.

"You must think I'm insane. This. I mean, it is kind of insane. I saw it in Booker's eyes. He thinks I'm a lunatic."

"I don't think so," she says softly. "He was shocked for sure. He asked me a little about your family. Lynette. And your mom."

"He did?" I glance at Jocelyn. She won't have liked that.

"It was when you guys were upstairs. Packing. He was very respectful. Seems like a good guy."

I nod, grateful again to this woman, despite everything. "You will tell us what happened, won't you? We just really need to know, you know."

"I know. I'm realizing that today. I was at Vicki's house. There's a lot going on with Thomas." She shakes her head and hurries on. "I can't talk about it, but she's covering for him. The ways she spoke about it? I felt so angry with her. But then also ashamed. Because I knew. I knew that Lynette was dead. And I didn't tell." Her voice trails away to a whisper.

"She was missing for two months," I say, accepting the wave of anger that rolls over me as she bites on her lip. But the anger doesn't last. Instead, the enormity of this moment billows in my chest. We're going to find out what really happened. Finally. Finally, we'll know. "Okay," I say. "Please. Just tell us what happened to her."

"To who?" His voice catches us all off guard.

Dan.

"The road to the hospital was closed, but I called at the store and grabbed some ice so we can keep the fridge cool."

He ambles in, a bag of ice under each arm, but stops dead as he takes in the three of us around the island. I see his expression change, rearrange, his brows snap together. His gaze settles on mine. Suddenly there's no warmth there. Only wariness. And I know it's time.

"To my sister, Dan," I say. "To my sister, Lynette Knox."

FORTY-SEVEN

Jen
Now

He blinks it in. I feel an urge to laugh, watching Dan digest what I've just said. He could probably tell us in fine detail about what's happening inside his head. Neurons firing. New pathways being created. Links made and broken. Memories reframed in the context of this new information. Somehow, though, I know the shock is purely mental for him. Not emotional. The things I have felt for him? The love expressed between us? It's like it never was. No, it's worse than that. It actually *never was*. As the silence stretches, he's not the only one who's re-drawing their understanding. This has not been love. Not for him and not for me. Because my heart's not breaking as I tell him our whole relationship has been a lie. It's just not. I reach down and tug off the wedding ring. Natalie watches me, eyes wide.

"We're not really married," I tell her. "It wasn't all an act. But that was."

"Good to know you were able to draw the line somewhere," he says.

I don't respond.

"Natalie was about to tell us what happened to Lynette," says Jocelyn.

"Great. Looks like I arrived just in time, then," he says, packing the ice in the fridge before fishing out a beer and taking a stool. "Let's hear it, Natalie."

"Okay," she says. "Jen, I already told your aunt some of this."

My eyes flick to Dan. He mouths one word at me. *Liar.* Then his gaze swings back to Natalie.

"I had an argument with Lynette. Over Dan. I had . . . we had . . . slept together and she wasn't happy about it."

"News to me," says Dan. "I never thought she gave two shits about anything."

"That's my sister's daughter you're talking about," snaps Jocelyn, but he just takes another swig of his beer.

"Anyway, Lynette stormed off, but I saw her talking with my dad on our driveway. There was something not right about it. And then later that night, when I knew Lynette was missing, Dad and I had a fight. He told me she'd been hit by a car."

There's more to this than she's saying. It's clear from her expression.

"But? The truth now. When did you know something had happened to Lynette?" asks Jocelyn.

Natalie tilts her head toward Dan.

"When he told me she was dead."

I feel a wave of nausea. My sister. Some days I can barely remember her face. Other times I can hear her voice and picture every detail of her, from her bitten fingernails to the scar on her knee when she cut it open at recess in the second grade.

Dan sets down his beer. "All right." He takes a few moments, as if he's gathering himself. Does he feel cornered? His eyes flick to Natalie and I wonder if he'll try to contradict her. She's not lying, though. And we all know it. Dan sighs deeply.

"Are we really doing this, Nat?"

"There have been enough lies. If you don't tell them, I will."

There's another beat of silence, and then he talks.

"My brother was involved. They were arguing. Your sister. And her dad. Natalie's father pushed Lynette in front of Patrick's truck. Patrick panicked and drove off. Wait." He holds up his hands. I can see the pain in Jocelyn's face. Dan points at Natalie. "*Her* father disappeared. Patrick went back. He found Lynette alone, lying bleeding on the ground. He picked her up and put her in his truck. He should have called 911. He should have driven her to the ER. He didn't. He drove to our house."

I can't speak but in my mind I'm screaming. How did they not call 911? Jocelyn is crying, now. Natalie too.

"Natalie was with me, at our house. My parents were out. Patrick took me out to the car." Dan lifts his head and looks Jocelyn right in the eye. "She was dead. A head injury. It was probably instant." His gaze moves to me. "I've always believed she didn't suffer. The more I've seen things as a doctor, the more certain I've become."

"What happened next?" Jocelyn asks, dragging her sleeve across her face.

He takes a long pull on his beer and wipes his mouth with the back of one hand. I think about his hands. Touching me. Touching my sister.

"I'm not proud of this," he says.

Jocelyn glares at him. She's done with tears. Anger comes off her in waves. Natalie is looking down at the island. Her phone is nearby. It's vibrating, but she ignores it.

"He's my brother. He's not like other people, but he'd never hurt anyone."

"You put her in the river. Didn't you?" Jocelyn's voice is cold, almost robotic. Dan doesn't need to answer. It's written on his face, and Natalie's. Dan Burrows took my sister's body and hid her in the Six Mile Creek.

It's all I can do to get out of the room and into the bathroom before I start throwing up.

* * *

I take my time. It's cool in the little bathroom. I lean my forehead against the mirror. Even though I clean up right away, the scent of my own vomit hangs in the air, revolting — and yet I'm in no rush to go back to the kitchen. Going back in there means looking at Dan. Speaking to Dan. Dealing with how completely, totally, wrong I have been about Dan. I'm thankful Nina is miles away. Once I'm sure I'm not going to throw up again, I splash some water on my face and run the cold tap on my wrists. I can't stay in this little washroom forever, but right now, the thought of what's on the other side of the door is overwhelming.

But when I do drag my ass back into the kitchen, there's no one there. Jocelyn's car isn't on the driveway and when I look across the neighborhood, I see every light blazing in Natalie's house.

Where the fuck is Dan? I stand still by the island and listen. There are footsteps upstairs. He's probably getting changed or something. I can't even imagine looking at him again. The pain when I think about what he did to her? It's physical. Only Jocelyn can feel the same. But she's not here.

Has Jocelyn really just *left*? I don't know what I was expecting when we got to the truth of things, but I know it wasn't that she would vanish. I had this idea that we were in this together, but it looks like we were not. She's left me here and it's making me angry. I should be angry with Dan — I am angry with him — and with Natalie — although less so, it must be said — but it's this, this *desertion* by Jocelyn, that's really hurting me right now.

I go outside, right through the garage to confirm that her car really has gone. I call her phone, but it goes straight to voicemail. I walk to the bottom of the driveway and stand for a few moments. There are tree guys looking at the damage at number two and number nine. It's nearly dark and this damned house doesn't have a generator. I'm going to have to dig out candles before it's too dark inside for me to find them. What a joke.

A wail of sirens cuts through the silence.

When I see an ambulance turn into the neighborhood, my heart stops. I can't think what it means and stand there rooted to the spot as it rolls to a halt. Natalie's front door opens. She's there, with her husband, one moment framed in the doorway, the next bustling along her front path. The ambulance turns into her driveway, and she rushes up to them. There's a conference between the EMTs, Natalie and her husband. I can't make out what's being said. In another moment they all turn and go indoors.

My phone buzzes in my hand. A message from Courtney. Erin has told Sasha her grandfather just died. Courtney's letting everyone know. Natalie's dad has passed away.

* * *

It's too much to take in. I walk back up to the house, shaking my head, trying to process it, while I grab matches and assemble every candle we have on the kitchen island. Natalie was just over here. She must have gone home, checked on her father and — what? Found him dead? The thought that he was taking his last breath while we sat in my kitchen talking about him and my sister blows my mind. It's so unlikely. He was ill, yes, but for this to happen, at this time? It's incredible. I stop, match in hand, about to strike. I'm a word person, after all. Incredible. As in *not credible*. It is just not credible that this man should die, not today of all days.

Jocelyn. Where the fuck is Jocelyn?

My brain starts making connections. I replay my conversation with Natalie. We talked about Booker's reaction to finding out my real name. And when I asked about Jocelyn, Natalie said she was out of the room, upstairs with me, helping get Nina ready.

Only she wasn't.

My hand goes to my mouth. I'd thought Jocelyn was downstairs. They believed she was upstairs. I take another leap of thought. Where exactly is Jocelyn right now?

My hands are trembling as I grab my phone. I tap in my password and swipe to the Find My iPhone app. I'd consented to location sharing with her reluctantly, and never thought to use it before this moment. At first it says she's here, in the neighborhood, but I can see it working and wait for it to update. Please God, let her be on Route 1 somewhere, heading back to Havre de Grace to feed the old cat she looks after. Please, God. But no.

She's heading north. Toward Allentown. Toward Patrick.

FORTY-EIGHT

Jocelyn
Then

I was at work when Sal hanged herself. I'd left the house around eleven for the twelve-to-eight shift at the Dollar Tree. Before, I'd have been back by nine at the latest, but those days I didn't want to go home. I'd gotten in the habit of stopping at the bridge on Giles Street most days. It must have been dark when Lynette went in, and I'd go there and think about it all. Some nights suicide even seemed possible. Something — or someone — could have upset her. She might have stormed off. They'd found alcohol in her bloodstream, after all; she'd never forget Markham shaking his head over it, as though no teen in Ithaca ever drank underage. In a college town? Sure. What the alcohol said to me was that she went somewhere after she left Natalie Eason's house. Maybe to the party at Connor's? Although surely someone who had seen her there would have spoken up. If not there, where?

All this was still rattling round my head when I got back to the house. It was around ten thirty, and the lights were off in the living room, so I figured Sal and Genevieve had gone to bed. There was nothing strange in that. They both kept to their own spaces pretty much. Sometimes one or other of them would watch TV with me after dinner, but I don't think they'd spent any time just the two of them since Lynette disappeared. And that was coming on for eighteen months ago by then. I was tired. I left my purse and my shoes near the door and went straight up to the bathroom. I saw the light seep through the gaps at Sal's door but figured I'd leave her be. We hadn't been talking much. There didn't seem much to say.

But just as I padded past her door, I heard a funny noise. It wasn't sobbing, not exactly, more like the kind of whining noise you might make from the back of your throat, somewhere between a whimper and a cry.

It didn't sound like Sal.

It wasn't.

It was Genevieve, balled up on the floor next to my sister's dangling feet. Sal had used the hanger for the Christmas wreath and one of our father's ties. Genevieve had a piece of paper clutched in her hand. Some permission slip for school. If I'd have been there, she'd have asked me to sign it. But I wasn't. And she'd gone upstairs and found her mother instead.

* * *

I'd been angry for a long time before this happened, but there weren't words for the rage I felt when Sal was gone, and even if there were, there was no one to say them to. Genevieve was a mess — silent, sleepless — and I wasn't much better. Soon enough I realized we had to get out of the house, out of Ithaca altogether, and see if being somewhere else — hell, even being someone else in Genevieve's case — gave us the chance to at least function.

It worked, after a while. Genevieve went to school in Rochester as Jen Silver and I kept my eye on her, because I owed it to Sal, because she was all I had left. But then came college, Burlington, Booker, and then Nina. Sure, she came back to me with Nina, and things were good again. But by then I'd already promised Sal and Lynette I'd find the truth of what happened if it killed me. I was committed. I had the names Genevieve had written out for the police back on that terrible day, when she was just twelve years old: Natalie Eason, Mel Parks, Sherri Knowles, and Connor Goodman. I'd find them, and the truth. Nothing else mattered.

FORTY-NINE

Dan
Now

I hear Jen calling my name. She bursts into the bedroom and looks less than happy to find me lying on the bed sipping another beer. Good. If she's unhappy, I'm happy.

"Look, we've got a problem," she says.

My left eyebrow hitches higher than the right. "There is no 'we', *Genevieve*."

"The problem is Jocelyn."

"Your problem. *Your aunt.* Not mine."

That fires her up.

"Since *your* brother didn't get proper help for *my* sister, and you — *you* — decided to hide her body so that my aunt, my mom, and I went out of our minds over what had happened to her, I can tell you that Jocelyn very much is your problem. And she's also Patrick's. Because she's on the way to his house right now."

"She's *what*? Are you sure?"

"After what you just told her about Patrick and Lynette? I'm pretty damn sure."

252

"Fuck." This is not what I planned. I'd plan to sit here drinking, watching Jen pack her shit and get the hell out of my life. "Let's go, then," I say. "You're driving."

* * *

There's an ambulance outside Natalie's home as we pull out of the neighborhood.

"More trouble?" I ask.

"No idea."

Of course, we both stare at the tree cleaving the garage roof at number two. It's a miracle no one got hurt in the storm. Although if they had, what would it have meant to me? Our dramas are so intense, but also so personal. Human connection is constantly overvalued. When everything happened with Lynette, I remember how strange I felt, even walking down the street. Everyone looked different to me, and yet they were going about their lives as if nothing had happened. It was surreal. When the person next to you stumbles and falls, you've no choice but to plow on. That was how I saw things in Ithaca. It's how I see things now.

"We could have just called the police," she says. "Got them to check on Patrick."

"Patrick doesn't do well with authority. This way is better."

"Right."

We fall silent again. The road is dark. There's no street lighting here so I can only see as far as the headlights illuminate. Locust and black walnut trees hang over the road, lush, dark green fronds reaching for us as we sweep by. Thankfully the storm didn't hit here like it did the neighborhood. Still, I'm glad she's driving. I can't afford to get pulled over and breathalyzed, not with my job.

"She's a fool," I say. "Driving up to Patrick's. What's she playing at?"

"She's angry. She's been angry for a very long time."

"You've probably blown this whole thing out of proportion. You're as crazy as she is."

"Fine." We've stopped at a set of lights, and they've turned green, but she doesn't move. "Let's forget it, then. You can't get a hold of Patrick. Maybe he's not home. Maybe she won't find him."

"Can you just fucking drive?"

"So, you don't think I'm crazy?"

"Let's check my brother and Jocelyn are okay, shall we? Then we can wrap this whole thing up and move on."

"This whole '*thing*' has been my whole life since I was twelve years old. You do realize that?"

"Yes. Okay." I'd calculated a swift admission in the kitchen was the way to go. It had even felt good to talk about it. But this feels like overkill. "Look, if I could rewind the clock, I would. But hasn't she — haven't you both — got what you wanted now? Natalie's dad was involved with Lynette. They must have been somewhere together. She'd been drinking. They had a fight. She had a short fuse. You knew that, right? And he wasn't the kind of man you messed with. Natalie was scared of him. It's his fault Lynette died. No one else's."

Jen goes silent. Concentrating on driving hopefully. But no. She's not done.

"What was she like? My sister."

"Seriously? You're going to ask me that?"

"Why not?"

"Because you've lied to me straight for three years, *Genevieve*. That's why not. I've told you what happened to her. You've got what you wanted. I'm not in this car for you."

"I know that. And, for what it's worth, I'm sorry. It wasn't all an act. I never meant it to go so far."

"Then I guess we both have regrets." It's not a lie. I've never been exactly happy about it. I conjure up Lynette Knox, the person, in my mind for the first time in years. "Actually, she was a lot of fun. I liked her."

"She was fun when we were younger," Jen says. "Not so much in the couple of years before she died. I've always thought maybe we'd have grown close again."

"I'm sure you would have." Again, I think, that's enough now. But Jen keeps talking.

"It's kind of a weird coincidence, don't you think, that it was your brother who hit her?"

"Jesus, Jen." I want to shut her down but she's not a fool. I shouldn't have had those beers. I'm scrambling for what to say.

"What are you not telling me?"

"Nothing."

"It's not nothing!" Her voice is sharp. "My God, Dan, just tell the truth."

"Look. It's nothing that changes anything. It happened just like I told you both. But okay, maybe it wasn't a coincidence that he was there. He liked her. Lynette. She and I had hooked up briefly. She had met Patrick at our house. Been nice to him."

"And he was — what? Following her? Stalking her?"

"Which was why I did what I did, Jen. I'm sorry for it. I'm sorry for the months of waiting and for the years of unanswered questions. Truly I am. But at the time — at the time all I saw was she was dead, and he was in trouble. You know Patrick. Imagine him if the cops got a hold of him. He'd incriminate himself in a second without even trying. My parents had no cash for lawyers. I didn't think about you, or Lynette's family. I thought about mine."

She doesn't say anything. My story makes sense. Thank God.

"Try my phone," she says. "Try calling her again. And him. If we can just talk sense into one of them . . ."

"Straight to voicemail. Both of them."

"And you can't see his location?"

"No. You know Patrick and I don't do shit like that."

"Where is she now?" Her phone glows in my hands.

"At his house. And we're still, what? Twenty minutes out?"

"Yes."

We drive on in silence.

FIFTY

Natalie
Now

The ambulance crew are remarkably efficient. They confirm my father has passed away. Because it's a sudden death, even though he's terminally ill, they tell us his body needs to be taken to the hospital for a post-mortem. Just routine, one of them says. The other nods. We are all in the room, our spare room, standing around the body of someone who is no longer there. He looks like he's sleeping. I thought he was sleeping until I shook his shoulder trying to wake him up and tell him I've finally acknowledged what he did to Lynette. How I know he pushed her. And how other people know it too. I was ready to tell him how much I've hated him. But he didn't wake up. I explain to the ambulance men. I saw right away his chest wasn't moving. He wasn't breathing. And I called 911.

Later, when I've hugged the kids, and told Brad I just need some time alone, I go back to the room and sit down beside the empty bed. What a day. The storm, Vicki, Genevieve, and now this. Now this ending. I sit and think of the questions I'll never ask him, the confession he'll never be obliged to make. I think about Dan and Patrick. About the night Lynette disappeared.

* * *

We were up in his room, and I was half-undressed. Dan had unhooked my bra, and our pants were on the floor although we were both still in underwear and tee-shirts. I wasn't sure I liked it — doing it — but without saying a word, Dan made it clear he had expectations. If I wanted to have a boyfriend, I understood this was part of the deal. And I did like some aspects of it. I liked the weight of his arm around my shoulder when he lay still afterwards. Maybe the rest would improve in time. We'd gone for pizza and then he'd said the party at Connor's was of no interest. His parents were out. Even his brother had been going out more lately. As soon as we got back to his house, we went straight upstairs, and the lights were off. It was quiet. And I was glad about that. Until I wasn't.

We both jumped when the front door slammed.

"Patrick," Dan said under his breath. "Don't worry, he won't come in here."

"Dan!" His brother's feet pounded the stairs. I grabbed for my pants and we both scrambled up.

"Hang on!" Dan flicked on a light as his brother crashed through the door. "What's your problem, man?"

Patrick's face was pale, and he was shaking. "Oh my God, Dan. Oh my God. In the truck. In the truck. I didn't mean it. I did-didn't."

"What the fuck have you done?" Dan pushed him from the room and slammed the door behind them, leaving me alone with no clue what was going on.

I thought about following. Their voices grew quieter. I heard the front door open and close. A traffic accident. It had to be. Patrick was in a bad way for sure. I wondered how long it would take for Dan to calm him down. I fastened my bra and lay down. Having a few minutes on my own felt nice. I considered texting Lynette again but decided against it. She'd come around in time.

We'd had the plan for tonight fixed all week. Chill at mine after school, go for food, hang on the Commons till about nine. Buy some vodka. Head to Connor's party. But then Dan had said he'd come eat with us. And when I'd told Lynette, it was like she went cold. She started up with the whole thing about covering for me with my parents and we argued. She grabbed her stuff and lit out. Did she hate Dan now, or just hate me being with him? Hard to say.

"Natalie?" Dan stuck his head around the door.

"Is your brother okay? Do you want me to come down? Or go home?"

"No!" He ran a hand over his face and bit down on his lip. "No," he said, more gently. "Look, I need to go out. Patrick. He hit something. Like — a dog, or something. And we need to take care of it."

I wanted him to mean they were taking it to a vet, but he didn't. His voice was so dark-sounding and I'd seen Patrick's face. I clenched my stomach muscles, like I was braced for a punch. I was pretty sure the dog, or something, was dead. "What do you want me to do?"

"Just stay here, till I get back. I won't be long. Can you do that? Please."

I nodded, and Dan turned away.

He was gone for less than an hour. I creeped myself out watching *CSI Miami* and checking my phone. Still nothing from Lynette. Was she going to be mad at me for days this time? It wouldn't be a first. I replayed our argument over and over, and thought about the way she and my dad had been together in the driveway. It made no sense. I was better off thinking about Dan and Patrick.

When they got back, I thought he'd come straight up, but I heard his brother in the room next door and the PlayStation music started up. Still, Dan didn't reappear. It was kind of annoying, and even though initially I'd been impressed at him rushing to help his brother, the longer I was stuck here, the more I wished myself at home. It occurred to me that Dan just wanted me to stay so we could carry on where we'd left off when his brother burst in, but I wasn't in the mood, if I ever even had been. I sat up and put my coat on. It was a crappy evening, and I wanted it to be over.

Glasses clinked as he finally reappeared. For a second I thought he was proving me right, showing up with some drinks to win me over while he fumbled to unhook my bra all over again. His expression said otherwise though.

"Here. You're going to need this." Dan handed me a glass of amber liquid. He sat next to me on the bed, tilting his glass until its contents — scotch or bourbon — swirled and a pungent sweet smell rose up.

"What happened? The dog was dead? He killed it?"

"It wasn't a dog."

His voice was weird. Raw sounding. I saw tears swelling in his eyes and felt a pain in my chest. "What, then?"

"More like, who."

"Jesus." My mind swarmed with a hundred thoughts. A person? If it was a person, what had they been doing for an hour. Where the hell had they been? "You took them to hospital?"

"Drink your drink," he said. "And no. It was too late for that."

"No?" I wanted to grab him and shake the story from him. But I also didn't want to touch him. I wanted to put my hands over my ears and run.

"Take a mouthful. A big one." He turned to look at me, eyes wide and empty.

"It was Lynette. He hit Lynette."

I took a drink. I swallowed. The alcohol ripped like fire down my chest. "Lynette? I don't understand."

"Well, you need to start understanding, Nat. You need to start right now. Patrick's car hit Lynette and she's dead. Get that in your head. But it wasn't his fault, okay? Not his fault."

"Dead?" There was a hissing in my ears. I thought I might throw up.

"Yes. Dead. Want to know where and why?"

I shook my head.

"On the corner of Columbia and Hudson."

"Near my house?"

"Exactly. And who do you think she was with? Who do you think shoved her into the road. Who basically threw her under the wheels of Patrick's truck?"

I don't speak. My hand goes to my mouth.

"Your dad."

* * *

My dad. My dad, who was waiting up for me that night, to tell me oh so gently that I needed to forget having seen him talking to my best friend when she left the house the night before, that people would misinterpret his genuine, fatherly interest in her, that there was no level some people, envious, bitter people, wouldn't sink to these days.

My dad. Who, when I asked him why he needed to say all this to me *right then*, why it was so urgent he had to be sitting there, drinking in the dark in the dining room, *right then*, on that particular night, grabbed me by the arm and pushed me against the wall as if I was someone he'd never seen before, or, no, worse, someone he hated.

My dad. Who, when I asked him why he'd left my friend bleeding in the road on the corner of Hudson, had turned the tables on me, asking how I knew something had happened to Lynette and who I thought *I* was protecting, because he would ruin their life in an instant if he had to. I could trust him on that one.

My dad. Who made me lie to Lynette's mother and aunt and keep on lying, even when her body was found, and we went to her tiny, quiet funeral, and watched Lynette's mother breaking apart in grief while we kept our silence.

My dad.

And so, no. I'm not sorry he's gone.

FIFTY-ONE

Jocelyn
Now

The traffic is light on the way to Patrick's house.

Dan Burrows was definitely lying. I have no doubts on that score. Yes, I heard him out, but I've always observed and known things about people without being told. It's part of being a loner. I've waited so long to fully understand what happened to Lynette. I've made mistakes along the way. Connor Goodman, for one. But lately I've noticed a sharpening in my senses. It's like I'm like a pane of glass, polished to a gleam or a bone picked clean. Dan's story doesn't add up. Natalie's dad, and Dan's brother, just happening to converge? I don't buy it. Natalie looked exhausted. There's nothing more to be learned from her and Dan has said all he is prepared to say. But there is still Patrick. An angry man. Possibly dangerous. But he's not as angry as I am.

Not even close.

As the miles tick by I check through the list of items I stowed in the car days ago, just in case of this eventuality. The taser, of course. Fully charged. A length of nylon rope. A pair of handcuffs. Pepper spray. A knife. I don't dwell on the knife. Blood and I have never gotten on. The drugs. If the knife is plan B, the drugs are plan A. Anyone taking one look at Patrick Burrow's disaster of a home would write him off as an addict in a heartbeat. No one happy lives like that. No one that unhappy doesn't need to spend at least part of their day spaced out or drunk. I have my own little dispensary in a box in the trunk, ready for this moment. It will be my pleasure to share them with Patrick.

It's time to consider the risks. A man like Patrick will own a gun, probably several. They won't be stowed carefully. He lives alone, and like a pig, so I don't see him using a gun safe. This can be a pro or a con for me. If I had to guess, I'd say he has a weapon in his car and one in his bedroom. If there are more, I'd bet on the garage. I don't think he's the kind to sit on his porch and take potshots at the local wildlife, but maybe I'll lead with the taser just in case. I don't want to use it, but like the knife, I haven't brought it without being prepared to use it.

His neighborhood is dark, and I cut my lights as I drive in. It's difficult to see, but I'm lucky it's trash night and the street is lined with clusters of garbage containers. The blue recycling ones are easier to make out through the inky blackness, and I draw up behind Patrick's two cans and kill the engine.

It's warm. Humid. The whine of cicadas fills my ears. There are three trees in Patrick's yard and as I creep beneath them the sound intensifies. I pull in my neck, creeped out by the thought of the hundreds of bugs just feet above me. Patrick will either be vegetating in front of some sports channel or out on his deck drinking beer. I guess the deck and step carefully around the side of the house. It's not difficult. There are no lights on at this side and when I peer in the window, I can see this room is set up as a dining room, although the table and chairs are covered in bags, some stuffed with clothes, others with squared edges, probably paperwork of some kind. If my house was this level of shithole, I'd spend as much time as possible outside, and that's where I find him, sitting on his deck, with nothing more than the moon and the tip of a vape pen lighting up the gloom.

"Who's there?" His voice is thick with alcohol. He shifts in his chair, but his movements are slow and clumsy. I watch him fumble, almost dropping his beer. Looks like he's groping for a gun, but he comes up empty. I have the advantage.

"A friend of Lynette Knox," I say.

"What the fuck?" He leans forward, sets down his beer and switches on a light — one of those bug-zapping lanterns on the small table he'd had his feet on as I approached. I walk up the steps of his wooden deck, counting seven bottles of beer grouped to his left. On his right sits a cool bag. I wonder if he even gets out of his chair to piss? Patrick, meanwhile, is frowning.

"You're the grandma. Nina's grandma." His voice is uncertain, the words coming slow. "You don't know Lynette."

"You going to invite me to sit?"

He rubs a hand over his eyes, and I'm enjoying this. Drunk, Patrick is considerably less intimidating. Not that I'm not on my guard. Drunk/confused can turn to drunk/angry on a dime. I keep my hand on the taser in my pocket while I set down my shoulder bag and sit in the seat he nods toward. What's one hundred percent clear is that Patrick doesn't see me as any kind of threat. He flops back in his chair, a sloppy smile spreading across his slack face. "Make yourself at home." He takes a swig of his beer and wipes his mouth.

"I was her aunt."

Patrick slaps his forehead hard with his palm. "I knew I knew you."

I think back to how he was when Jen and I visited. The scrutiny, the tension. He'd found me familiar. Now I wondered how. I certainly wasn't aware of having seen him before our visit.

"What about Lynette? Did you know her?"

"It was so terrible."

"What happened to her?" He's looking over my shoulder, remembering. I feel a bubble of laughter growing in my chest.

Can it be this easy? This easy after all this time? But then his eyes snap back to my face.

"How can you be Lynette's aunt and Nina's grandma?"

I swallow and run my tongue across my lips. "Your brother's girlfriend is Lynette's sister."

"Genevieve?"

"You know her name?" It comes out as a question but what I really want to ask is, how? How does he know her name? Not that he's listening to me anyway.

"And she's with Dan?"

When I met Patrick Burrows sober, he didn't come across as a great intellectual, to put it mildly. With a drink in him, you'd be forgiven for thinking he'd been lobotomized. It's frustrating, watching the cogs grind, and I don't have time for it.

"We want to know what really happened to Lynette. Nothing more. It's not complicated. What happened to her wasn't an accident. It wasn't suicide. She didn't put herself in that river." His eyes flicker to me. I see pain and confusion. Time to push. "Your brother told us everything. I just need to hear it from you. And then I'll go."

"He didn't."

"He did. I know it all. The truck. Natalie Eason's dad. You were there. He told me you were."

Patrick puts his bottle to his lips and tips it. Nothing happens. He looks at it in dismay before leaning sideways to place it with his other empties. Glass taps glass, two bottles fall and roll away across the decking. He lurches to his feet.

"I need a piss."

Instead of staggering indoors, Patrick steps away from the house to the edge of his deck with the clear plan of pissing right there, right in front of me. The wave of disgust is almost as bad as the sharp whiff of urine that hits me seconds later. This is my opportunity. I take two beers from his cooler and place them on the deck at my feet. There's an opener on the little table. I grab it, pop the caps but keep the bottles on the floor not the table. The sound of peeing stops and I have only a few seconds while he fumbles with his zipper. I slide a vial of fentanyl from my pocket and pour it into one of the bottles. By the time he turns, I'm on my feet with an open beer in each hand.

"Hope you don't mind if I join you," I say, handing him his drink. "I'm amazed you remembered me, by the way. You must have known Lynette well back then."

"She was beautiful." He sits down heavily. I fix my eye on the window behind him. I can't stare while he drinks, and I can't waste time. This is a gamble. It all ends now.

"What happened to her?"

"You said Dan already told you."

"Yeah, but he wasn't there, was he? Not when it happened."

There's a pause. A bug hits the lantern and fries. I jump. He does not. "She was with that old piece of shit again. I don't blame her. She was young. Him, though? Disgusting. Could have been her father."

"Again? That wasn't the first time you saw them?"

"No." His voice hitches and he snorts up snot. Tears are coming. He takes another swig of his beer. "I saw them five, maybe six times before then. I was worried for her. I knew she was mad about Dan seeing Natalie. She was making bad choices. I was trying to keep her safe."

"You were following her."

He nods, abjectly miserable. "I saw them walking up Hudson Street. He put his arm around her. I wanted to be wrong. I thought maybe he was just looking out for her, but she couldn't walk straight. They'd been drinking. I imagined them in the restaurant. Him slipping her drinks. The waitress probably thinking they were father and daughter. It made me sick."

"You were driving?"

He nods. "I drove past them. His arm was too tight around her shoulders. I thought he was going to try something on her. That he'd hurt her."

Now it's me nodding. Not daring to speak. I want to encourage him, though. He's like a boat, heading toward the falls. He mustn't swerve. He must go over.

"I went around the block and came up behind them again. I stopped behind some parked cars and killed my lights. Opened the door and shut it so they'd think I'd gone. They were maybe eight cars away. I wound down my window."

"Could you hear them?"

"Not words. They were arguing, though, I was sure of it. Or nearly sure. I needed to be sure. I was ready to rescue her. All I wanted to do was rescue her." He takes another swig of his beer. His face is wet with tears. His mouth drips with them. "I needed to get nearer. I pulled into the road, my lights still off. They kept walking, though, crossing the intersection between Columbia and Hudson. I was just going to get up alongside them. Just going to hear a bit better before intervening. She'd be mad at me, maybe. But it'd be worth it. I was maybe three cars away when another car swung around behind me." He puts a hand over his eyes. "I was at the intersection. Suddenly there were lights in my mirror. I panicked. Accelerated."

I can see it. These are streets I know. Familiar houses, fences, uneven pavements, narrow roads lined with parked cars. Limited lighting. "He didn't push her? Your brother said he pushed her."

"He might have. I don't know."

"Then what?"

He drinks again. I imagine the opioids spreading from his stomach into his bloodstream. Will it be painful or peaceful? I won't be here to find out.

"I drove away. It was pitch black again. The car behind me had turned up to the right at the stop sign. I turned left. Switched my lights on. Circled back round, expecting to see — him or her, I didn't know which one I'd hit — calling for help.

"But he'd gone. The bastard. She was lying between two cars. Her head was all blood. One leg bent the wrong way."

"Why not take her to hospital?"

"I wanted to. I just needed Dan to go with me. To help me explain. But she was dead already."

I say nothing. There is nothing to say. The rest of it, I'm sure, will be as Dan Burrows told us earlier. The way Eason abandoned her makes me thankful I was able to visit with him earlier, whether he pushed her or he didn't, if I could have my time in that room back again, it would only be to make his ending more painful than I suspect it was. I almost feel a little sorry for Patrick. But I can't take back what I've done to him this evening, any more than he can change Lynette's story. He also can't change the two months of torture Sal went through before Lynette was found. Or the months after, until she decided not to take any of it anymore. I get to my feet.

"You're going?" Patrick sounds almost bereft. But he's probably no longer himself. Everything I have read has said it won't take long.

"You told me what I wanted to know. All I've ever wanted, was to know."

He nods into his chest, the flesh under his chin spreading across the neck of his Eagles hoodie. "You deserved the truth." His voice fades. His eyes close.

"It was an accident," I say.

I can't explain the swell of emotion as I stand there, watching him dying. It's unexpected. Perhaps because he's given me peace, I want him to have some also? Hard to say. Time to get my shit together.

I pick up my bag, grab two small bottles and press his fingers around them, one after the other. His flesh is heavy and soft. I settle his hand back on his lap and walk past him into his house. He doesn't remark on this or try to follow me. He may even be unconscious already. Let's be honest. He won't leave that chair again, not under his own steam anyway. My last act in Patrick's house is to stash two bottles of pills. Both opioids, bought months ago online. Not traceable to Jocelyn Silver, but to Marcie, a woman who used to live in Havre de

Grace, but no one's seen for a year. A neighbor, if they get that far, will likely tell the cops that Marcie moved in with a new man she'd met, and although someone else was there for a while, they haven't been around lately either. They'll have to dream up an explanation for Marcie's pain meds showing up in Patrick's bathroom cabinet, with his fingerprints on them, of course. Good luck with that.

Naturally, I wear rubber gloves. I put them on while Patrick was weeping. The bottle of beer I drank is in my bag. I let myself out and cross the grass again. The cicadas seem quieter. Or maybe that's just me. Within a minute, I'm on the road again.

I have one last thing to deal with. Jen.

FIFTY-TWO

Jen
Now

We miss her by minutes. There's no sign of her car and no answer when we ring Patrick's doorbell. Dan races round the back, and then he's hollering for me to call 911. I don't even make it up the three steps to Patrick's deck. I can't bear to look.

The next few hours are a blur. Ambulance. Police. Neighbors coming over to see what the problem is. Dan, ashen, but dry-eyed, telling the cops how we'd driven up to see Patrick and found him out on the deck, sprawled out, unresponsive. Other people take over. They walk in and out with little baggies on their shoes and spinning blue and red lights from emergency vehicles keep catching my eyes, making my head ache.

Jocelyn.

Patrick.

Natalie's father.

It's hard to imagine she has killed these two men.

Difficult to believe she has not.

I wait for Dan to say her name to the police. I wait for him to say that we were following her up here, using my

269

phone to track her. Can they make me hand it over? Force me to let them access it? I'm guessing they can. I know any moment I'll be handing it over and the hunt for her will start. Still, Dan says nothing. Maybe he's waiting for some moment when I'm not there? But we're stuck together in Patrick's living room, where the police led us and asked us to wait. A policewoman leans against the doorframe. No one speaks. It's a strange room. Very formal. I get the feeling Patrick hasn't sat in here for years. There's none of the clutter and mess in the kitchen and dining room. There's no TV, no plants, no books, and only one photograph on the mantelpiece, a photograph of Patrick and Dan. It looks like a first day of school pic, taken on the front steps of their house, and they're both shouldering backpacks. Their hair is long and they're grinning. It's a happy photograph.

"I'm so sorry," I say, but Dan doesn't answer. He won't meet my eyes, even though we're sitting opposite each other in two snug armchairs.

A little later a policeman in plain clothes comes in and sits on the couch. He's about our age and looks fit, like a runner or a swimmer. His knees are wide apart, and he leans forward onto his elbows.

"There's no easy way to say this," he says, looking at Dan. "It looks like an overdose. Painkillers. Bad ones. We see it all too often. Did you know he was self-medicating? Had he had any illnesses lately? We'll speak to his doctor, of course, but there's plenty of evidence."

"He has a long-standing back injury." Dan closes his mouth into a flat line and maintains eye contact with the cop for a few seconds. I wait for the but . . . but it never comes. Instead, Dan puts his face in his hands.

"It's a lot to take in," the cop says. "But all too common these days. Do you know who his doctor is?"

Dan gives him chapter and verse. The two men get into a lengthy conversation about Patrick's doctor, his medical history, and Dan's own medical background. The cop reacts well to him, he's respectful, nodding in a way that makes my teeth grind. Dan is so smooth. I want to scream that his brother has just died, and if it wasn't for Jocelyn, I'd do it, I swear.

Jocelyn.

I need to check my phone. I also need to check on Nina. I wait until the policeman has finished discussing the opioid crisis with Dan — they are practically best buddies by this point — and he leaves us to go and "check on things." My text to Booker is straightforward. I ask how Nina is and say I'll call in the morning. For the first time, I'm thankful he's mad at me. He'll be in no rush to put Nina on FaceTime to say goodnight and I've no desire to let him know where I am right now. At least he's not so mad that he doesn't reply right away. Nina is brushing her teeth and they are all good. Good.

"Nina's fine," I tell Dan, more out of habit than anything else. He simply nods. With a glance at the woman officer at the door I open up Find My iPhone. No Location Found. Jocelyn has turned off location sharing. I swipe to WhatsApp. No new messages. And there's only one new text in the neighborhood group chat — Daisy, asking if there's an estimate for the power coming back on. That was half an hour ago and no one has responded. What I can't get my head around is Dan. He knows Jocelyn was just here. Why say nothing? Is it possible she found Patrick in that state and simply left again? I can see her doing that. Finding him. Not calling for help. Is that what Dan thinks has happened? But can I believe that's really what happened? Given Natalie's dad? Suddenly, I'm glad of the policewoman standing there. I have a lot to think about, and only one real priority. Nina.

After maybe an hour, the ambulance departs carrying Patrick's body. We watch them roll him out on a gurney and even while I know it's him in the body bag, I feel detached from reality and a little lightheaded. Food would be good, but the thought of opening Patrick's fridge or pantry seems almost scandalous. There are a few neighbors out watching. No one comes over. I imagine Patrick kept to himself, and a wave of sadness hits me. Dan seems very in control of his emotions, but he has lost his brother. There will be a hole in his life. I know how that feels. But as my mind circles toward Lynette and everything I've learned tonight about what happened to her, I'm brought back to Jocelyn, to Patrick, and Natalie's dad, and just how fucked up the woman I've told Nina is her grandmother really is. I've wanted a normal life for me and Nina. But nothing about this has been normal. I am a terrible mother. I can't stop thinking it. I'm a terrible, terrible mother and Nina, my beautiful girl, deserves so much better.

* * *

The rest of the evening feels surreal. The police leave. Dan and I lock up the house. We don't say much — normal functioning is a struggle — but we do what needs to be done and get in the car. About halfway back "home", Dan pulls off the highway and into a McDonald's Drive Thru. He orders for us both — coffee and Quarter Pounders. I could have eaten two. It ought to taste like nothing, but the pickle, ketchup, and fat are frankly delicious. The ride is silent. I can't talk, and Dan doesn't seem to want to either. When we pull into the neighborhood every light in our house is on. The power is back on.

"We'll talk in the morning," Dan says as we park the car and walk through the kitchen and up the stairs. There's no discussion. I grab what I need and head for the spare room. I brush my teeth and plug in my phone. Still no location for Jocelyn. Still no message. I feel relieved, confused, and angry all at the same time. For a long time, I just lie in the dark, staring at the ceiling. I have never felt my life was better without my mother. But would Nina's be better without me?

FIFTY-THREE

Booker
Now

Staying in a hotel with Nina is surprisingly fun, despite the circumstances. We do pizza and a movie — a blur of color, some brainless Disney nonsense — but I don't mind because Nina, smart though she is, is only ten years old. When she finally falls asleep in the queen bed next to mine, I sip on a beer and gaze at her. So beautiful. So innocent. Jen has done a good job with her — no, a great job. Angry as I am, I can still see that.

Once I'm sure Nina is asleep, I open my laptop. I'm a journalist, this is what I'm trained for, and it doesn't take me long to find everything there is to find about Jen's sister's death. There isn't much. A few weeks' worth of newspaper reports in the *Ithaca Journal*. Much the same content in the *Times*. I note the names of the detectives involved and text a few contacts.

Mom arrives at 9 a.m. She's gotten the first flight down and knocks on our door with a smile on her face and not a hair out of place. She brings coffee for me, orange juice for Nina, and a bag of orange and cranberry muffins, literally the only thing she's been able to tempt Nina with for breakfast, a fact I know just drives her crazy. She can be a little intimidating, my mom. I can see why Jen found her so, at least. Right now, though, with the bear hug she gives me? She's the tonic I needed. If this kid of mine feels the same way about me when she's grown, I'll be a happy man.

My interview goes well. I walk out of the *Inquirer* offices confident there will be a job offer coming and that I'll take it. I knew I wanted to be nearer to Nina, but Jen's recent actions have shown me I need to be here. I'm trying, really trying, to understand how she could have got so involved with Dan Burrows, and under false pretenses, but it's tough. How could she have done it? I just can't fathom it.

My phone buzzes as I head to the park where I've agreed to meet Mom and Nina. One of the folks I texted last night has come through with a number for the woman on the cop team that looked into Lynette Knox's disappearance. She's been out of the job for ten years. The area code says she's still in Ithaca, though. I'm not sure what I think she'll tell me, but I call the number and hope she'll pick up. She does.

"Detective Prentice? Thanks for taking my call. My name is Booker Tomlin and I'm a reporter with the *Philly Inquirer*." I hope I'm not jinxing myself. By the end of the week, it should be true.

"Okay." She sounds cautious, as you'd expect.

"Is this a good time to talk?"

She gives a little snort, quiet, but I hear it. I already know she's retired and hasn't worked since she left the force. Ex-detective Prentice has no kids, lives alone, and has plenty of time on her hands. "I can give you a few minutes," she says. "What's it about?"

"Well, ma'am, I'm working on a project about missing teenagers. You probably know true crime is pretty big these days. There are podcasts. Netflix shows . . ."

"I know."

I try and keep the smile out of my voice. Maybe not every ex-cop is waiting for their docudrama debut, but plenty of them are. Her interest is piqued for sure. "So, the case I wanted to ask you about is from a while back. Lynette Knox. Do you remember it?"

"Do I remember it?" She sighs low and heavy. "Absolutely I remember it. What a shitshow. But hey — what's your angle here? If you're just in it to bash the blue, then I can't be talking to you. I'm prepared to say mistakes were made, but not for some hit piece."

"Oh no, no, nothing like that." I look around, spotting a café with some outdoor seating. I need to sit and concentrate. If she doesn't talk now, I fear she won't pick up if I try and call another time. "Let me lay it out for you. We've been looking at missing teens from a societal perspective. You know — why they run, how they survive, what, if anything, the police can do when a teen runs, and what the long-term outcomes for these kids are. Lynette Knox was presumed a runaway, right? And then was found — what, two months later? Yeah so, we are wanting to include her story for balance. Showing how hard it is when a teen disappears. I mean, she was believed to be a runaway pretty much from the get-go, right?"

"Right." There's a pause. I try and imagine this woman, sitting in her house somewhere. There's probably some daytime show on her TV, but it's muted while she takes my call. This is likely the most interesting thing that's happened to her in months. She's wary, but also tempted. I don't try and talk. People hate silence. They long to fill it. "Okay," she says. "I'll tell you what I remember. You can see if it's useful for you."

"Perfect. Thank you. Okay. Let's start when she first disappeared, then. You and Detective Markham got the call?"

"We did. It was Sunday morning. John — that's Detective Markham — was in no rush. The mother had called it in the night before but Saturday night in a small town there's always something more urgent going on than a missing teen. She was told to make some calls and sit tight. We showed up there around 3 p.m.

"John took the lead but to be fair to him, there wasn't anything out of the ordinary, not really. She hadn't come home. Her room was a mess but only usual teenage girl mess, no sign of a struggle. The mom loved her, but she was a drinker: known to us, well, to John, at least. I was new in town at that point, but in fact the whole family was kind of well-known."

"Why?" There's a waiter trying to take my order, but I wave him off and listen closely.

"The house had belonged to the mother's parents. They were some brand of crackpots, John said. Religious. They'd be on the Commons every weekend holding signs, trying to talk to people about Jesus, that kind of thing. No one liked them. I asked around after John told me all this, and his picture of them was pretty accurate. Anyhow, one day he'd been called to the house. The sister called it in, not the mom."

"The sister? Jocelyn Silver?"

"Correct. The mom and Lynette were in the house too, though, and I think the sister was living there. This was before the younger girl was born. When Lynette was three or four years old."

"And?"

"They'd shot themselves. Lynette's grandparents. In the kitchen. A suicide pact. There were notes. They were going to be with God blah, blah, blah. They were crazy, no doubt."

"Wow."

"Right. What a family. Lynette was young, but she was right there. John said she probably grew up planning to get the hell out of Ithaca as soon as she could. It made a lot of sense."

"Any other thoughts on the family?"

"I thought the mother was unbalanced. Her sister gave me the creeps. So intense. Always staring. Clearly the boss of her sister and very angry with us, with the girl's friends, with the world, most likely. I remember feeling sorry for the younger daughter. Seemed to me like she hid out in her room most of the time, reading books. Who could blame her? The mother was either drunk or borderline hysterical. The aunt was clearly controlling, even though she didn't live there anymore."

"How did you feel when Lynette Knox's body was found?"

"Terrible. We'd clearly got it wrong."

"What about Detective Markham?"

"Not so much. I think he even used the phrase 'win some, lose some.' He told me to 'chalk it up to experience.' Those were his exact words. He wasn't the biggest thinker, John. As soon as the body turned up, he went to the next most likely option, at least in his mind. He believed it was suicide."

"And you? What did you think?" She falls silent and I wonder how she feels, recalling past events. Perhaps past mistakes.

"Look, the autopsy was inconclusive, okay? There was alcohol in her blood, but the body was pretty banged up. She was in water for two months. You don't even want to imagine what that looks like. We knew she'd fallen out with her friend. Maybe stormed off. She was known as a sassy kid, I remember that. We didn't see her as the kind of girl to get in a stranger's car. We did wonder if she'd had a fight or something like that. Kids and booze, you know? Bad things happen. I'm not going to say I felt good about it. But we interviewed all her friends and got nothing. There were no leads. It could have been an accident. But the family history was there. On balance, suicide seemed most likely." She falls silent for a moment. "Although maybe saying it was an accident would have been easier on the family. They took it hard. Real hard."

"I heard the mom killed herself."

"Yup." She says this slowly, regretfully. I picture her nodding. "A year or so later. I wasn't on duty that day, but we all knew about it. That poor young girl. Finding her like that."

I'm afraid to ask. I have to ask. "The younger sister found her mom's body?"

"They said she didn't speak a word for months afterwards."

"Right." I'm trying to digest what she's telling me about Jen. It isn't easy. "So, there was just the girl left, then? And her aunt? Ever wonder what happened to them?"

"Probably nothing good. I mean, the aunt was clearly a wacko. That little girl lost her sister and her mom. Hate to say it, but I can't see someone coming out of that experience unscathed. Can you?"

* * *

I end the call not long after, with some vague promises of future consultation. She seems like an unhappy woman who'd had an unfulfilling career in the police service. What she had to say weighs on me, changes things. I hadn't planned to talk to Mom about any of this, but when I meet her soon afterwards, and we're watching Nina flying up on some swings in the park, I spill it all — Jen, her sister, her mother, and the whole crazy move to the neighborhood. Mom surprises me.

"Poor Jen."

"Really? *Poor Jen*? That's all you got to say? Mom, she took Nina to live with that guy. Even thought about marrying him. When the whole thing was about her sister. I mean, who does that? It's insane."

"Nina didn't come to harm."

"Mom!"

She holds a hand up. This is her way. When the hand goes up, she speaks, you listen. "I'm not saying I approve, Booker, I'm not saying that at all. It's ill-judged at best. Foolish too. You were right to bring Nina out of there. But think about it. Jen's childhood was traumatic. The loss of her sister and then her mother. No father figure even rating a mention. Brought up by her aunt, a woman whose parents and sister have all committed suicide. There's nothing normal about any of it. And yet look at Nina."

I follow my mom's gaze toward my daughter. She's gotten off the swings now and sits on the edge of the play area with another girl who looks about the same age. The other girl is showing her something, it looks like a caterpillar, and as Nina holds out her hand the girl lets it crawl from her hand to Nina's and they smile at each other.

"You need to talk to Jen," Mom says quietly. "She hurt you when she left, I saw how much. But what you're learning, changes everything. See if she'll talk to you. And if she does, make sure you listen."

FIFTY-FOUR

Jen
Now

I don't text Booker in the morning. He has his interview and must have made some arrangement for Nina. I don't feel in a position to ask what it might be. I do know, though, that I won't abandon my daughter like my mom abandoned me. I need to trust Booker with our daughter while I decide how to handle Jocelyn. Even while I think this, I know the answer already. Jocelyn and I are done. For Nina's sake, for my own sake, we are done. I send her a WhatsApp message telling her I never want to see or hear from her again.

The sound of the microwave bleeping downstairs reminds me I have other immediate issues to address. Dan. This house. The conversation we're about to have. Confident he's downstairs making something to eat, I slip into our bedroom to grab some clothes. Pajamas don't seem appropriate. Downstairs, Dan's perched at the end of the island eating oatmeal. His hair looks damp from the shower, and he's dressed in a tee-shirt and shorts, so if he had a shift at the hospital, he must have moved it.

"Coffee's in the pot," he says, looking up. His face is expressionless, and I don't know why I'd expected anything different, but I had. He has lost his brother. And we are finished. But any anxiety or distress he might be feeling on the inside isn't showing outside in the least.

"Why didn't you tell them about Jocelyn?"

"You have to ask?"

"Yes!"

He straightens up and folds his arms across his chest. "Nina."

I close my eyes, as relief floods my chest. "Thank you."

"Don't thank me." His voice is cool, detached. "What happened to Lynette has hurt enough people."

"I'm so sorry about your brother."

He nods slowly, picks up a spoonful of oatmeal, looks at it, and puts it down again. "I'm sorry about your sister. And your mom." He looks on the verge of saying more, but his gaze falls to his bowl, and I realize I'm just standing there watching him.

"I'm leaving," I offer. "I mean, I'll have to come back and pack stuff up, but I won't stay over again."

He shrugs, as if it's of little interest to him. "You should cut ties with Jocelyn," he says.

I have a mug of coffee at my lips. I hold it there as we lock eyes across the room. "I already did."

I wait, thinking there is more to say, more he must want to know or say about me, about Jocelyn, about the deception, about Lynette and Ithaca, but he says nothing. I'm struck by how self-contained he is, how unemotional, how he fits in this sterile white kitchen, whereas suddenly I can see that I, just as Booker said, really, really do not. I wonder if Dan will stay here or move again but don't care enough to ask.

"Okay, then," I say. "I'd better get on."

* * *

Two hours later, I've packed the car with our most essential belongings. The rest — winter clothes, books, my desk and chair, her bed and nightstand — will have to wait a few days while I try to repopulate our apartment and organize a van, maybe even hire someone to help me move. The neighborhood's quiet as I pull out of the garage. I've a strange feeling of guilt, as if I'm sneaking out, or acting furtively. It crosses my mind to leave a note for Natalie, who has lost her father, and I'm sure must be grieving, notwithstanding his involvement with my sister all those years ago. She's a connection to Lynette, and I don't want to lose that. I have her cell number. That's enough for now. My phone buzzes as I pause at the stop sign, reminding me I should text Booker and let him know I'm on my way into the city. My mouth goes dry when I see I have a message from Jocelyn. Even though I swore I'd delete any message unread, I find myself swiping it open.

Just do one last thing for me, it reads. *Rescue the cat.*

* * *

On the drive down to Havre de Grace, I finally feel able to think about what I've learned about Lynette. She didn't kill herself. That's the first thing. And, in fact, as I drive along and the houses fall away and all I see is the long stretch of Route 1, lined with lush trees under a sweeping blue sky, it comes to me that this is enough. She didn't kill herself. She was hit by a car, and it killed her. Am I grasping for straws, feeling thankful it was quick? There were no pounding moments of fear, no adrenaline spike, no last gasps, prayers, or desperation. I wish our mother could have known this. I wish . . . I wish . . . But no. Tears prick my eyes. For years I have practiced not thinking this way. Thoughts of Sal remain off-limits. There was only that short period, after I had Nina, when I opened a door in my mind and remembered the mother who deserted me. But look where it got me? Back to Rochester, back to Jocelyn. Here. So this is where I need to change. For myself, and for Nina. I will get help with this. I have to. For Nina. For myself.

But not for Jocelyn. In the cold light of day, my suspicions about her seem less real. I have no proof, after all, that she even went to Natalie's home. Am I mad to even think such a thing, simply on the strength of one sentence from Natalie Preston, a woman I barely know? The police were very confident that Patrick's death was an overdose, and Dan didn't have a problem believing his brother was self-medicating. Do I really believe my aunt is actually a killer? A woman who just begged me to look after her cat? I so — *so* — want to be wrong about Jocelyn. Even if we never see her again, I can't help hoping to be wrong.

And, of course, I am thinking of Nina. Nina who knows nothing of this family she comes from and of how I made her move from her home, her friends, and her school to satisfy my own, and Jocelyn's, obsession with the past. Guilt heats my neck and face. She's my priority and I'm angry with myself, with Dan, with Jocelyn, with my mother, all of it. I should be on my way to Philly to be with my daughter.

Fuck Jocelyn, I think. *Fuck this cat. What the fuck am I doing?*

But I don't turn the car around. I go and get the damned cat.

FIFTY-FIVE

Dan
Now

I watch Jen drive away and feel nothing. Nothing but liberated. The moment I saw Patrick slumped on his deck, the relief was like a blast of air to my lungs, or the bolt of a drop of acid on my tongue. Life-changing. Our parents are upset, of course. But I call them and trot out some bullshit about Patrick being a victim of the opioid crisis, and they listen and believe me like they always do. Like most people do. The police at Patrick's house obviously did. And there was no point in dragging Jocelyn's name into it all. The last thing I need is Jocelyn talking to the police about Lynette Knox, and me and my brother. I hope she got a good fright when she drove up there and found him dead like that. Jocelyn Silver is no innocent in all this. If Lynette's family hadn't been so effed-up, she might never have wound up on that street corner with someone old enough to be her father. Nobody comes out of this story well. Nobody.

My next task is to open up my laptop and fire off an email breaking the lease on this stupid house. There's a new block of apartments recently opened much closer to the hospital with a gym and a pool. I'll like it there. The idea of a family — of this suburban lifestyle — was appealing, but it isn't as great as folks made it out to be. Do I resent Jen and her deception? Yes, but saying goodbye to her, and to Patrick, means saying goodbye to Lynette. It's the opportunity to forget, finally and fully about Ithaca, and the worst thing I've ever done. The true story, the real story of that night remains mine alone. No one has ever known the whole of it, but me.

Fucking Patrick.

His truck was a blue Mazda. He'd bought it a year before and lavished attention on it, vacuuming the inside, handwashing the outside, polishing the trim, constantly topping up the oil and water. He had a whole special set of car-cleaning cloths on a shelf in the garage and woe betide anyone who moved them so much as an inch. Mom and Dad teased him, but they were happy about it. Patrick had struggled through school and although he was working shifts now at Home Depot, he didn't make much and showed no sign of leaving home. He'd never had a girlfriend and his friends from school no longer came around. He was a loner who loved his car. And then came the night he barged in on me and Nat.

I followed Patrick out to his truck, cursing him under my breath and shivering as the cold November air hit me. I didn't even have shoes on, and my mind was still half upstairs with Natalie. It was dark in the driveway, but Patrick handed me a flashlight. He hung back from the car, inside the garage, with his arms wrapped around his stomach. His voice was thick with snot and tears. "On the backseat," he said.

I didn't want to shine the light too widely. Before switching it on, I turned a full three-sixty, looking at the neighboring houses. There were lights on. I could see a glow through the hedge that separated us from next door, but their upstairs was in darkness. The house directly across from us was fully dark. Good. The Patersons were friendly with my parents. They'd often hang out over there, out on their back patio where they had a firepit we used to love to burn marshmallows on when we were younger. I sniffed. No smoke. It looked like they were out too. Good. I opened the back passenger door of the car and turned on the flashlight.

It wasn't a dog, but I already knew that. I knew the moment I saw my brother's face that he'd hit someone. And my anger had already shifted to calm. I was here to assess the damage. Her feet were nearest me. She wore black Keds and had small feet. That told me she was young. She wore jeans and a black cropped jacket. I couldn't see her face. I flicked off the light, closed the car door and went around to the other side. I wasn't expecting to know her. I was looking to see how beat up she was, and confirm she was dead. I brought no emotion to it. My mind was on next steps. Decisions needed to be made, and Patrick losing his shit in the garage only made me more determined.

Her head was covered in blood. I didn't have time for gloves, so I pulled my hand in my sleeve and used that to shift her long hair from her neck so I could check for a pulse. That's when I saw her face. When everything got even more compli-cated. I turned the flashlight on again, just for a moment, just to be sure, and closed the door. A car went past the end of the road, its lights sweeping our way, casting light into shadows and out again, but not turning in, thank God. I went back in the garage and told Patrick to pull himself together while I spoke to Natalie. Two minutes later, Patrick was in the car, and I was driving.

"What did you tell her? Will she call the police?" He had stopped crying, but he was whispering, and it annoyed the hell out of me.

"I told her you hit a dog."

"Did she believe you?"

"No idea. But she's not going anywhere. I'll deal with her when we get back."

"Where are we going?"

I hated him then, his quivering voice, his neediness. And at the same time, his weakness made me feel stronger. He thought I was doing this for him. But I knew our parents. Our brother's illness and death had consumed them. This mess of Patrick's would consume them too — emotionally, financially. My expensive plans for college would mean nothing. From the moment he crashed into my room, I knew whatever came next, it was my future I was protecting. "To the river."

* * *

I'd given some thought to our geography. Wherever we went it had to be out of the way of any route that might connect Patrick to Lynette. The bridge on Giles Street came to mind out of nowhere. I killed the lights on the truck as we crossed the bridge and turned down into the lot across the road from the old water pump building. A plan was forming, but I needed to take a few moments to think it through and make sure Patrick could keep his nerve long enough for us to do the necessary.

We sat in darkness and silence. I didn't think about her lying there behind me. But I did need to know what happened.

"Where were you? Did anyone see it?"

Patrick sniffled and didn't answer.

"Just fucking tell me," I said.

"You know who it is, right?"

"Yes."

"It was up on Hudson."

"What were you even doing there. It's nowhere near your work." An uncomfortable suspicion rose up. "Tell me you weren't following her."

"Not really."

Not really. Which meant yes. "How often have you done that?"

"A bit."

"What the heck, Patrick! Did she know you were doing this?"

"No! She'd no idea. And it was only a couple of times. I just wanted to see her. I liked her."

287

"You liked her." I felt myself nodding, and my teeth pushing against each other. "So, what happened tonight?"

"She was arguing with a man."

"A man? What like a young man? Someone our age?"

"Older."

"They were standing next to a car when I drove by."

"Wait what? You drove by and saw them? And then went back?"

"They were arguing. In the road. I was worried about her. I went round the block. I thought maybe they'd be gone when I went back. They were about six houses away from hers. I thought he'd be gone, and I'd maybe see her walking to her house. Make sure she was safe. I turned off my lights. But they were still there, pushing and shoving. A car came up behind me. It spooked me. I sped up. And then it happened."

I wanted to smack him in the face. "What did you do then?"

"I panicked. I drove away. I think. Yes. I pulled over and threw up. I was just around the corner. I thought there'd be sirens. But there was nothing. And so I drove back round again."

"And where was this guy she was with?"

"Gone! He'd disappeared. Left her in the road. Can you believe that?" He sounded genuinely shocked.

"And so you put her there?" I gestured with my head. Neither of us had looked in the back since we'd left home. "And no one saw you."

"I don't think so. I'm sorry, Dan. It felt wrong to leave her."

I'd no words for that. "This man. Did he see you? Do you think he could ID the truck?"

"I don't know." Patrick rubbed his arms like he was freezing cold. There was a tremor in his voice. I couldn't have him going into shock on me, not right now.

"Okay. Here's what we're going to do. We're going to carry her up there." I pointed to the road. This side of the bridge the river was slow and shallow. But I knew from walks when we were kids that across the road a waterfall moved with real force, although there were also rocks with deep still black pools where we could hide her, at least for now. Patrick didn't even question it.

"Now?" he asked.

"Yes. Right now."

We dragged her out from my side. I made Patrick take her shoulders and hooked my arms under her knees as he slid her out. His clothes were already bloody. I'd put on his old fishing jacket when we left the house and it somehow made me feel better, knowing her mess would be all over his shit, not mine, because none of this was my fault. We shuffled up to the road with her slung between us like a sack of laundry. Laundry. I would have to think of a way to run the laundry without my mother seeing. I had a whole to-do list forming as a consequence of Patrick's fucking stupid behavior. This was just step one.

The road was quiet, thank God. It was pitch dark and although the road bent away around high banks at both ends, it was narrow enough and we were quick enough to cross in total darkness. We struggled down the rocks on the other side. Only one car passed, and we crouched, letting her body bump on the stones.

"Shit," Patrick said, his voice breaking.

"Forget it. She's already banged up. I've thought about this. Let's just get rid of her."

But at the water's edge he started shaking.

"We shouldn't do this." We were under the bridge now and it was dark, but my eyes were accustomed to the light. I could see his teeth. See his mouth working. Lynette lay between us on the ground.

"Go back to the car."

"I—"

"Just do as I goddam say." I wanted to grab him, shake him. I did neither. I sucked in a breath and stayed calm. "Go and wait in the car, Patrick. It's been a lot. You've done great.

Just go and wait in the car. I can do the rest. We've come too far now. And you know it."

He looked down and I heard him breathing heavily. His shoulders shifted up and down. He'd never won an argument with me. We both knew that wasn't going to change. "Go," I said. "Go now."

Another car passed over the bridge above us as he turned away. I saw his face then, and how crushed he was, like a punctured football, or a piece of shriveled fruit. But I wasn't going to be crushed by this. Not by stupid Lynette fucking Knox, arguing with some piece-of-shit boyfriend I didn't know she had. Anger flared in my chest as Patrick crept back to the bank and scrambled to the road. I looked up. Imagined Lynette jumping, falling, being pushed from the bridge above. Impact injuries. Might they be consistent with being hit by a car? I'd like to hope so. I knew next to nothing about dead bodies and post-mortems, but the longer the body was hidden, surely the more it would decay and the harder it would be to work out what had happened. We might even be really lucky. She might never be found.

That's when I heard her moan.

It wasn't much. A quiet groan, rolling from her throat, so quiet I thought I'd imagined it. But it shook me into action. I knelt and felt again for a pulse. I'd been sure at the car there was none, but I'd also been realizing just who Patrick had hit and in the heat of the moment — yes, I'd missed it. There it was, a slight, but unmistakable pulse. Well, it was too damn late for that. I saw a future with Lynette Knox still in it and it was like watching my life topple like a line of dominoes. I knew this girl. She was loud and she was angry, and she'd never keep her mouth shut about this, never understand why we brought her here, or that it was all an accident.

I put one hand on her shoulder and another on her hip and rolled her into the water. Then I held her down and counted to one hundred.

* * *

290

When I got back to the car I was shivering and could hardly feel my fingers. We drove back in silence. I was too busy thinking of next moves to bother about Patrick, sniveling pathetically in the passenger seat. Our clothes and the car. What was the best way to deal with them? And then there was Natalie. Shit. I should have made her leave. I'd have to tell her something.

"I should have said it was a deer. Shit." I slammed my palms against the wheel. "Or you should have called me down. Why did you have to come in my room, man?"

"She's gonna find out anyway." Patrick's voice was thick, like he was drowning in his own snot and tears. I pushed away the memory of my hand on the back of Lynette's head in the water. "He's probably called the police already. They'll be there when she gets home."

"What the fuck are you talking about? When who gets home?"

"Natalie Eason." He dragged his sleeve across his face.

"But who's 'he'? Who's probably called the police."

We were at a set of lights. Bathed in red. I turned to him. "Patrick?"

"Mr. Eason. David Eason's dad. I used to see him at the football field all the time when we were in high school. That's who Lynette was with."

"Natalie and David Eason's *dad* was arguing in the street with Lynette Knox?" I couldn't get my head around it, but I saw Patrick's face. He was sure of it. The light changed to green. I pressed my foot on the accelerator, looked straight ahead.

"And they were arguing?"

"Yes."

I drew in a long breath. I needed to say this just right. We were brothers. We both knew who led and who followed. "And that's when he pushed her. Right into the path of your car."

Patrick said nothing. Took another swipe of his sleeve across his face. We were minutes from home.

"Yes," he said. "That's what happened."

"Which means it wasn't your fault, Patrick." I kept my eyes on the road but reached across and squeezed his shoulder. "With any luck, no one will ever ask you a thing about it, but I want you to remember that one thing. It was an accident. It wasn't your fault."

FIFTY-SIX

Jen
Now

The apartment complex overlooks the harbor. I've only been here a couple of times — Jocelyn always seemed a bit weird about having me and Nina visit — but I know my way around and she's sent me the codes to access the building. The key is under the mat. The last time I was here I tried to tell her to leave it with a neighbor, but she waved off my concerns and now I'm sure, wherever she is, she's saying a silent *I told you so*. It's strange to think I'll never hear her voice for real again. That she will stay in my head, I don't doubt. So long as she's not in Nina's life, I'll take it.

The cat is thrilled to see me, yowling, and purring and wrapping its orange furry self around my legs. I pet him for a minute, while my eyes scope out Jocelyn's living space. There is literally nothing of her here. It's someone else's apartment. A woman who moved in with some new guy but pays Jocelyn to house- and cat-sit for her. When Nina and I were here last year there were a couple of framed photographs of Nina on display, a stack of library books, Jocelyn's computer chair at the dining table by the window, and a pile of notebooks she always keeps together with a thick rubber band. Now that's all gone. I check the kitchen. The fridge has been cleaned out apart from one can of cat food. Seinfeld set up crying again the moment I walked into the kitchen, and so I feed him, thinking about the empty fridge, the missing chair and vanished computer. Had she planned to leave? Everything yesterday was so chaotic but now I'm not so sure. She must have driven back here from Patrick's house last night and cleaned the place out . . . but then why not take the cat? I leave Seinfeld tucking into his meal and check out the bedroom. The closets are empty. The bed is made. On her nightstand, there is a single notebook.

I don't believe for a minute she's forgotten it.

The cat's the lure.

The notebook is the reason Jocelyn wants me here.

I pick it and open it. It's blank. But two items fall from it, and I sit on the bed and unfold them on my lap. One is a newspaper article, from the *Binghamton Press and Sun*. "Local man found dead," is the headline. There's a photo of an apartment building, and a smaller inset photograph of a man in his twenties. I don't recognize him. I take a quick glance at the other item. It's a bus ticket. From Rochester to Binghamton, about a three-hour trip, maybe a little less. Frowning, I go back to the paper. That's when I see the name of the dead man. Connor Goodman. I check the date of the article with the bus ticket. The ticket bears the same date. The last day Connor Goodman was alive.

In a hot minute I'm back in Rochester with Jocelyn. It's several years after I took Nina and went back to live with her. She was showing me around her investigation, and I was into it, not involved, but encouraging her, like the complete fool that I am. I hear her telling me: "Connor Goodman died, by the way. Accidental drug overdose. Very sad."

Very sad?

The two items in my hands tell a different story. Connor Goodman hanged himself. With the hook for a Christmas tree

294

wreath and one of his own neckties. Just like my mom, except Connor Goodman wasn't found for a week.

It's a while before I'm in a fit state to drive.

* * *

The journey from Havre de Grace to Philadelphia takes just under two hours. The damned cat cries the whole way while I wrestle with what to do about the ticket and the article. They sit on the passenger seat next to me and draw my eyes from the road. I need to get this straightened out in my head before I see Nina and Booker. Nina can never know this truth about Jocelyn. It's the one thought I have that feels like firm ground. Why has Jocelyn left these things for me to find? She doesn't know Dan and I followed her to Patrick's home last night. She doesn't know I suspect her of sneaking into Natalie Preston's home while I was upstairs. Why leave this evidence for me? Why tell me she has murdered Connor Goodman, leaving his body to be found exactly as I found my mom years earlier? Why? And what am I supposed to do about it?

* * *

I'm just past the exit for Philadelphia airport when I press the window button. Air and engine noises rush at me. It's the work of a moment to let the paper and ticket fly from my fingers. Gone.

* * *

I think about how I've just thrown the evidence she left me out the window. They were paper, probably caught now in some bush or hedgerow. Neither will survive the elements long. I've already acted to protect Jocelyn, even though the person I truly want to protect is not her, but Nina. Jocelyn knows me. She knows I'd do anything to protect my family.

My mind slides to thoughts of Dan and Natalie. Protecting family. Isn't that what they thought they were doing, back in Ithaca, all those years ago?

That's when the tears come. Because as well as Jocelyn knows me, I know Jocelyn. Jocelyn, who didn't protect her family. Who lost her niece and her sister and struggled to understand why or how it all began. As hard as it was for me to imagine this morning that Jocelyn had taken someone's life, it is all undeniable now. By telling me what she did to Connor Goodman — Connor Goodman who had nothing to do with Lynette's disappearance and death — she's making sure I will never let her near Nina again. I have to believe she's also killed both Natalie's father and Patrick. Everything about the way she left the condo tells me she did so with intention and design. She may have acted in the moment, but Jocelyn was prepared. And yet I'll keep her secrets to keep my girl safe. Jocelyn can be nowhere near Nina. And we both know it. Neither of us can risk it. Jocelyn is so many things.

Mad.

Vengeful.

Obsessive.

Loyal.

Wounded.

Smart.

Dangerous.

She's also the past. And I'm leaving her there.

FIFTY-SEVEN

Jocelyn
Philadelphia
One year later

They are moving again, but not far. I've checked online. Nina won't need to change school, and people do say having two parents in the home is better than one. That was hardly my and Sal's experience, but Nina is living a very different life than we did, thank God.

I watch them from a distance. They have a couple of friends helping them load a van. Booker is hands-on, laughing, as he lugs out Jen's desk, pretending to stagger under its weight. That prompts smiles from Jen, Nina, and a tall Black woman I assume is Booker's mom. She's holding Nina's hand. At her feet, I spot a cat box.

Jen takes off first, probably wanting to be at the new place before Booker and the van. His mom and Nina turn and walk my way. I'm in a car, new to me so they won't recognize it, and with handily tinted windows. I used to think those things were just for drug dealers but turns out they're legal in Pennsylvania and pretty useful if you need to keep an eye on your family without them knowing. I won't risk being seen, but the temptation to hear Nina's voice is strong and my rear passenger windows are both open.

"Does this animal never stop crying, Nina?" the woman asks as they draw level. Seinfeld is yowling. He's a terrible cat.

"Ida B., Grandma. That's his name now."

"*His* name? You're calling a boy cat, Ida?" Her voice is light with amusement. I strain to catch Nina's reply.

"Why not! Cats don't care about gender identity!"

And then they are gone, and I find I'm smiling.

* * *

Nina is doing fine. Jen and Booker are together. I have witnessed their happiness this morning, and countless other times, and know I am not missed. Does it hurt a little? Maybe. But you can't come back from the things I've done and expect to go on as before. Their lives are normal. And I'm anything but.

Jen goes to therapy now. Once a week, on a Tuesday afternoon at 2 p.m. I've watched her come and go, and seen how it lifts her spirits, how she leaves each session a little straighter, how quick she is to jump in her car and head off to pick up Nina from school. Sometimes, when she's in there, I've imagined myself lying on some shrink's black couch, staring up at a high ceiling, and recounting my many misdemeanors.

Not that I'm remorseful. Natalie Eason's father got what he deserved, and he was only two steps from night-night when I intervened. It was only fair that I was there to see him leave. Natalie doesn't miss him, not so far as I can see. There was quite the flurry of activity on Facebook Marketplace in the weeks after he died. Seemed to me she couldn't get rid of his belongings quickly enough. I don't blame her. Patrick Burrows wasn't much mourned either. The online obituary was less than a paragraph and only his brother and parents showed up for his funeral, I know, because I was there, marking the moment, and wondering if that was how he'd recognized me:

if Patrick had been lurking back then, at Lynette's funeral, just as I was lurking in the shadows at his. Who's to know?

But then there is Connor Goodman, and what I did to him. I don't really need a therapist to unpack it. It was retribution, pure and simple. And I could labor on feeling bad about tracking him down, but then it was Connor, in his last moments, that put me on to Dan.

Dan Burrows, he had said. *Dan Burrows was the one who acted like he never so much as said hi to Lynette Knox when she went missing. Dan Burrows was who Lynette and Natalie had been fighting over. It was Dan Burrows I should be hunting down and hurting, not him.*

* * *

The van has gone now. They will be at their new place soon, Jen, Booker, and Nina, unloading boxes, filling new kitchen cupboards, hanging clothes in new spaces, laying out furniture in different rooms. I was planning to follow and watch for a while, but I think I'll let them be for now. Dan Burrows, I would tell my imaginary therapist. Dan Burrows. Hasn't he come out of all this a little too well? Yes, he lost his brother, but I can't believe he ever cared for Patrick. Not like I cared for Sal.

And so, I have a little plan for Dan I've been working on, and it all takes place from the comfort of my own home. Internet trolling, I believe they call it. I do a fine line in anonymous complaints from patients. His rating on Vitals on has really nosedived lately. There's also Healthgrades, ZooDoc, and RateMDs.com. Oh, and then there's the fake profile I have spreading gossip about him in a neighbor group in his new apartment complex. As well as delivery of unwanted packages and food orders. There's a lot of options, if you're creative and ready to put in the time.

It can also be a lot of fun.

THE END

ACKNOWLEDGMENTS

In 2010, my husband, my three kids, and I moved into a neighborhood of eighteen houses, near Kennett Square, Pennsylvania. Despite our strange British accents, we were warmly welcomed. It was a great choice for our family. While living there inspired me in writing *The People Next Door,* none of the crazy things in this story happened to us, and all the characters are entirely made up . . . apart from one. Emma Hill makes a cameo appearance when the neighborhood women are talking about swim lessons. Emma (December 30, 2005–February 19, 2022) was one of those kids you are always happy to see your own kid be friends with: smart, funny, honest, chatty, full of life. You don't forget people like that. Emma is very much missed by her loving family and many friends.

After writing four historical novels, this book was a different, and fun, writing experience. I've needed my early readers even more than usual, and so big thanks go to Chris Braithwaite, Jean Taylor, Shannon Albert, Jen Blab, Zoe Bell, Kathy Smith, and Maren Albans. Any stray Briticisms left in this book are entirely their responsibility (not really!). At Joffe/Lume, I'd particularly like to thank the editorial team for helping lick this thing into shape, including Becky Slorach, Kate Ballard, Alice Latchford and Jon Appleton.

Readers, thank you for picking up this book. If you enjoyed it, please tell your friends!

THE LUME & JOFFE BOOKS STORY

Lume Books was founded by Matthew Lynn, one of the true pioneers of independent publishing. In 2023 Lume Books was acquired by Joffe Books and now its story continues as part of the Joffe Books family of companies.

Joffe Books began in 2014 when Jasper agreed to publish his mum's much-rejected romance novel and it became a bestseller.

Since then we've grown into the largest independent publisher in the UK. We're extremely proud to publish some of the very best writers in the world, including Joy Ellis, Faith Martin, Caro Ramsay, Helen Forrester, Simon Brett and Robert Goddard. Everyone at Joffe Books loves reading and we never forget that it all begins with the magic of an author telling a story.

We are proud to publish talented first-time authors, as well as established writers whose books we love introducing to a new generation of readers.

We won Trade Publisher of the Year at the Independent Publishing Awards in 2023 and Best Publisher Award in 2024 at the People's Book Prize. We have been shortlisted for Independent Publisher of the Year at the British Book Awards for the last five years, and were shortlisted for the Diversity and Inclusivity Award at the 2022 Independent Publishing Awards. In 2023 we were shortlisted for Publisher of the Year at the RNA Industry Awards, and in 2024 we were shortlisted at the CWA Daggers for the Best Crime and Mystery Publisher.

We built this company with your help, and we love to hear from you, so please email us about absolutely anything bookish at feedback@joffebooks.com.

If you want to receive free books every Friday and hear about all our new releases, join our mailing list here: www.joffebooks.com/freebooks.

And when you tell your friends about us, just remember: it's pronounced Joffe as in coffee or toffee!

www.ingramcontent.com/pod-product-compliance
Ingram Content Group UK Ltd.
Pitfield, Milton Keynes, MK11 3LW, UK
UKHW020734280325
456826UK00004B/189

9 781839 015991